BOO

THE WORLD'S CUTEST DOG™

A WALK IN THE PARK

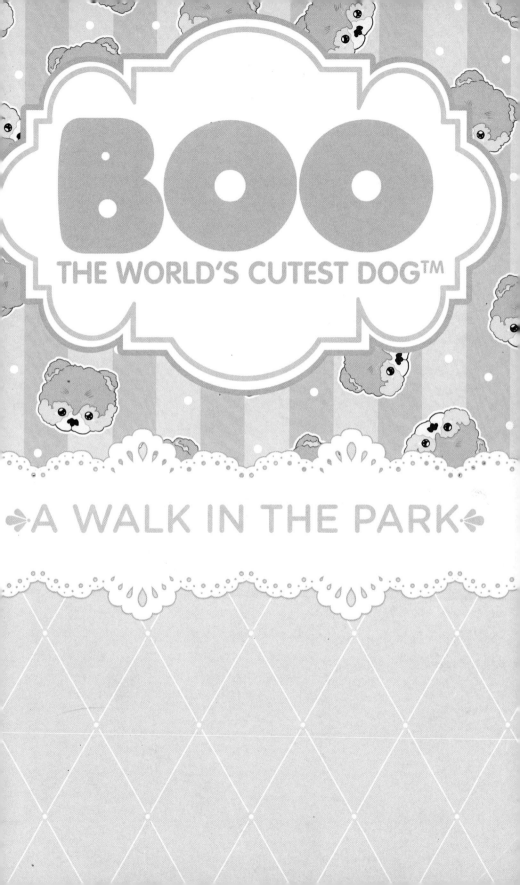

Boo And The Birthday Bash

Written by Kristen Deacon
& Audrey Elizabeth
Art & Color by Tony Fleecs
Lettered by Tom Napolitano

One Boo Over The Cuckoo's Nest

Story & Art by Fernando Ruiz
Colors by Ma. Victoria Robado
Lettered by Tom Napolitano

Boovie Star

Written by Joelle Sellner
Art & Color by Rob Robbins
Lettered by Tom Napolitano

Photoshoot

Written by Adara Sanchez
& Ricardo Sanchez
Art & Color by Steve Uy
Lettered by Tom Napolitano

Cloak & Dog-ger

Written by Sholly Fisch
Art by Agnes Garbowska
Lettered by Tom Napolitano

Walk In The Park

Written by Jeff Dyer

Art by Ma. Victoria Robado

Lettered by Tom Napolitano

Boo-Squatch

Story and Art by Agnes Garbowska

Letters by Tom Napolitano

Crazy Sunday

Story by Eric M. Esquivel

Art by Rob Robbins

Letters by Tom Napolitano

Boo's Doggy Diary

Story and Art by Fernando Ruiz

Design and Letters by Tom Napolitano

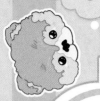

Special Thanks To

Jodi Gottlieb and Ken Wong

Edits By

Anthony Marques and Joe Rybandt

Collection Design By

Alexis Persson

Nick Barrucci, CEO / Publisher
Juan Collado, President / COO

Joe Rybandt, Executive Editor
Matt Idelson, Senior Editor
Anthony Marques, Associate Editor
Kevin Ketner, Editorial Assistant

Jason Ullmeyer, Art Director
Geoff Harkins, Senior Graphic Designer
Cathleen Heard, Graphic Designer
Alexis Persson, Production Artist

Chris Caniano, Digital Associate
Rachel Kilbury, Digital Assistant

Brandon Dante Primavera, V.P. of IT and Operations
Rich Young, Director of Business Development

Alan Payne, V.P. of Sales and Marketing
Keith Davidsen, Marketing Director
Pat O'Connell, Sales Manager

HC ISBN13: 978-1-5241-0233-3

SC ISBN13: 978-1-5241-0234-0

Frist Printing

1 2 3 4 5 6 7 8 9 10

Online at www.DYNAMITE.com
On Facebook /Dynamitecomics
On Instagram @Dynamitecomics
On Tumblr dynamitecomics.tumblr.com
On Twitter @dynamitecomics
On YouTube /Dynamitecomics

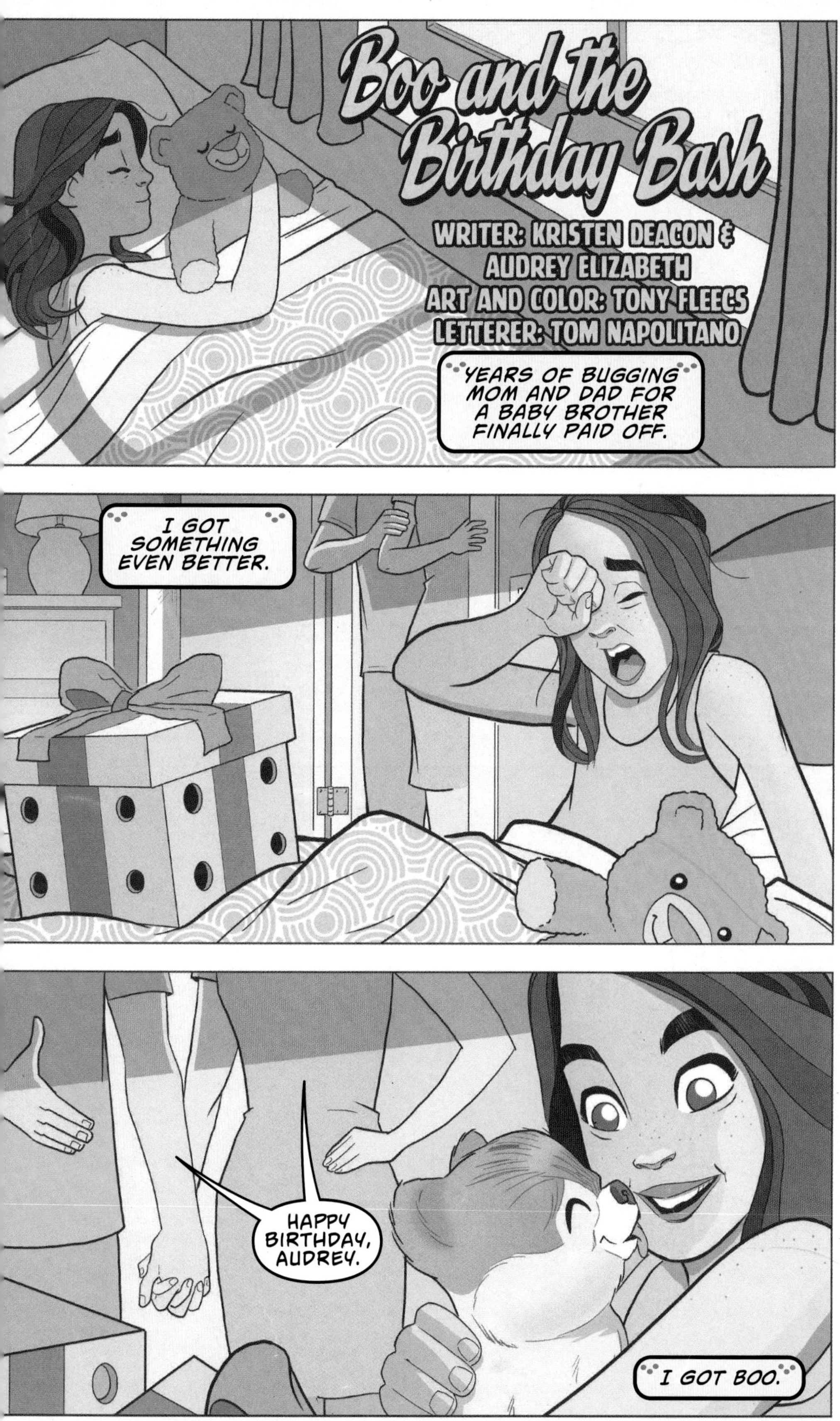
Boo and the Birthday Bash
WRITER: KRISTEN DEACON & AUDREY ELIZABETH
ART AND COLOR: TONY FLEECS
LETTERER: TOM NAPOLITANO
YEARS OF BUGGING MOM AND DAD FOR A BABY BROTHER FINALLY PAID OFF.
I GOT SOMETHING EVEN BETTER.
HAPPY BIRTHDAY, AUDREY.
I GOT BOO.

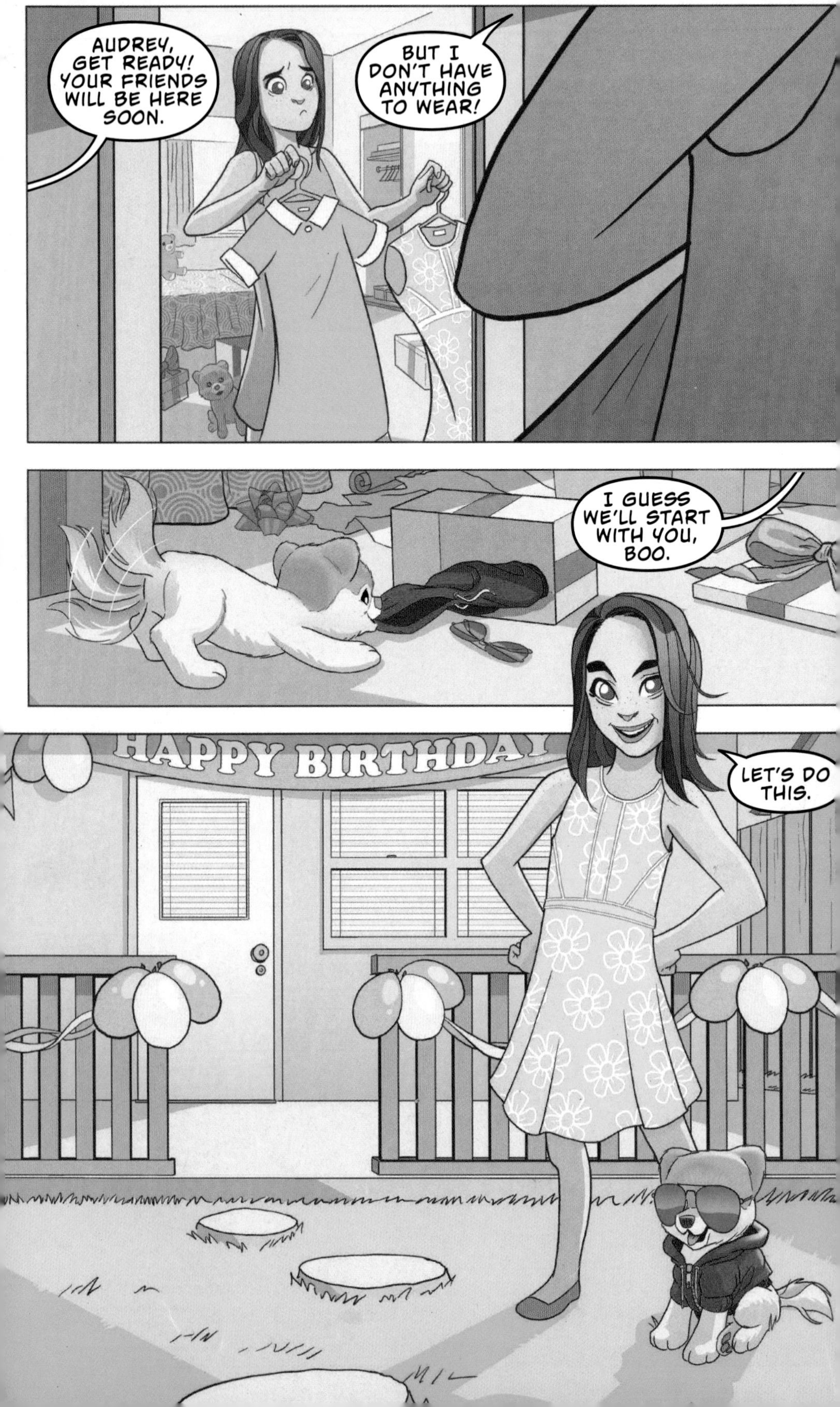
AUDREY, GET READY! YOUR FRIENDS WILL BE HERE SOON.
BUT I DON'T HAVE ANYTHING TO WEAR!
I GUESS WE'LL START WITH YOU, BOO.
HAPPY BIRTHDA
LET'S DO THIS.

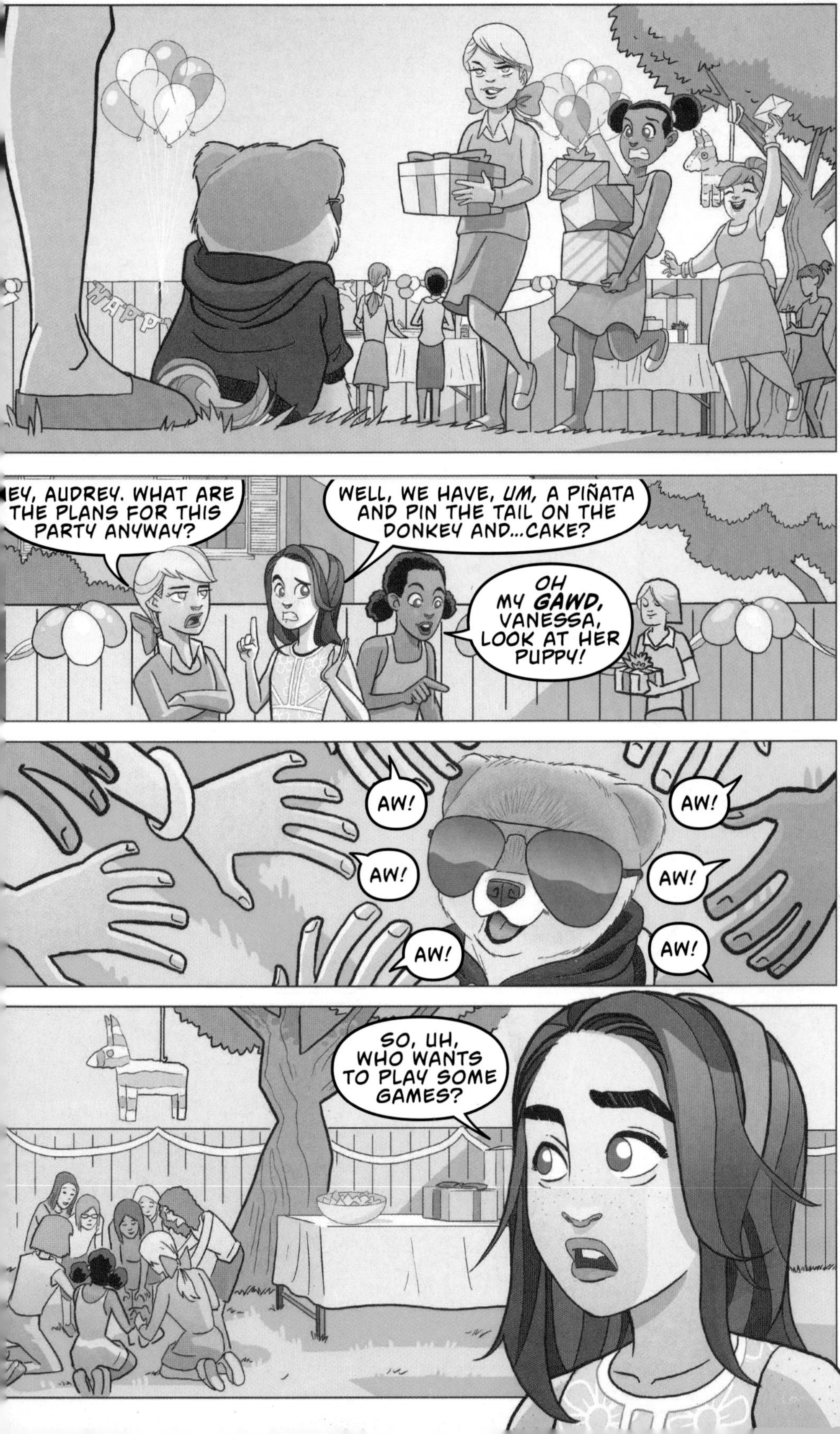
EY, AUDREY. WHAT ARE THE PLANS FOR THIS PARTY ANYWAY?
WELL, WE HAVE, UM, A PIÑATA AND PIN THE TAIL ON THE DONKEY AND...CAKE?
OH MY GAWD, VANESSA, LOOK AT HER PUPPY!
AW!
AW!
AW!
AW!
AW!
AW!
SO, UH, WHO WANTS TO PLAY SOME GAMES?

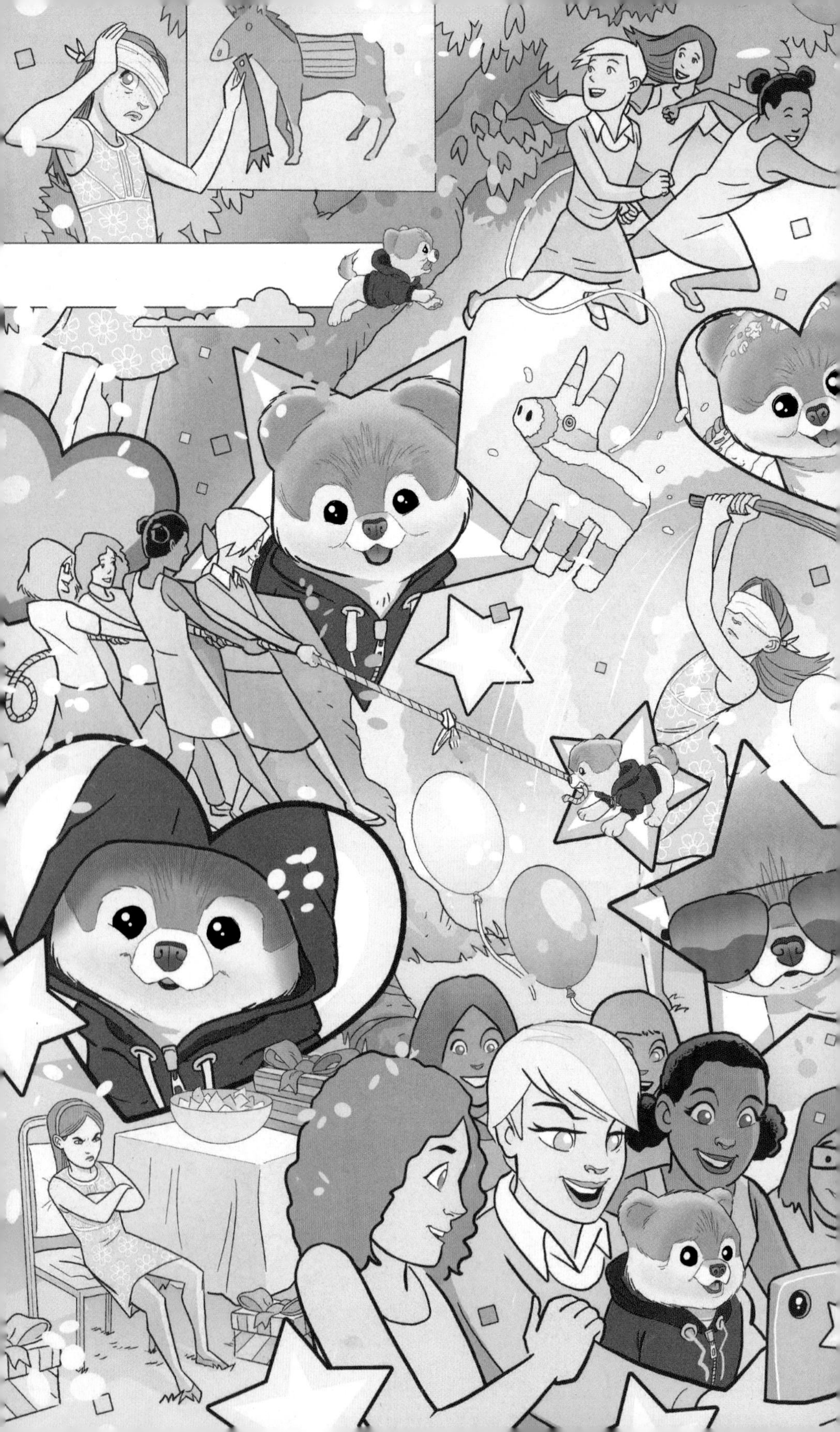

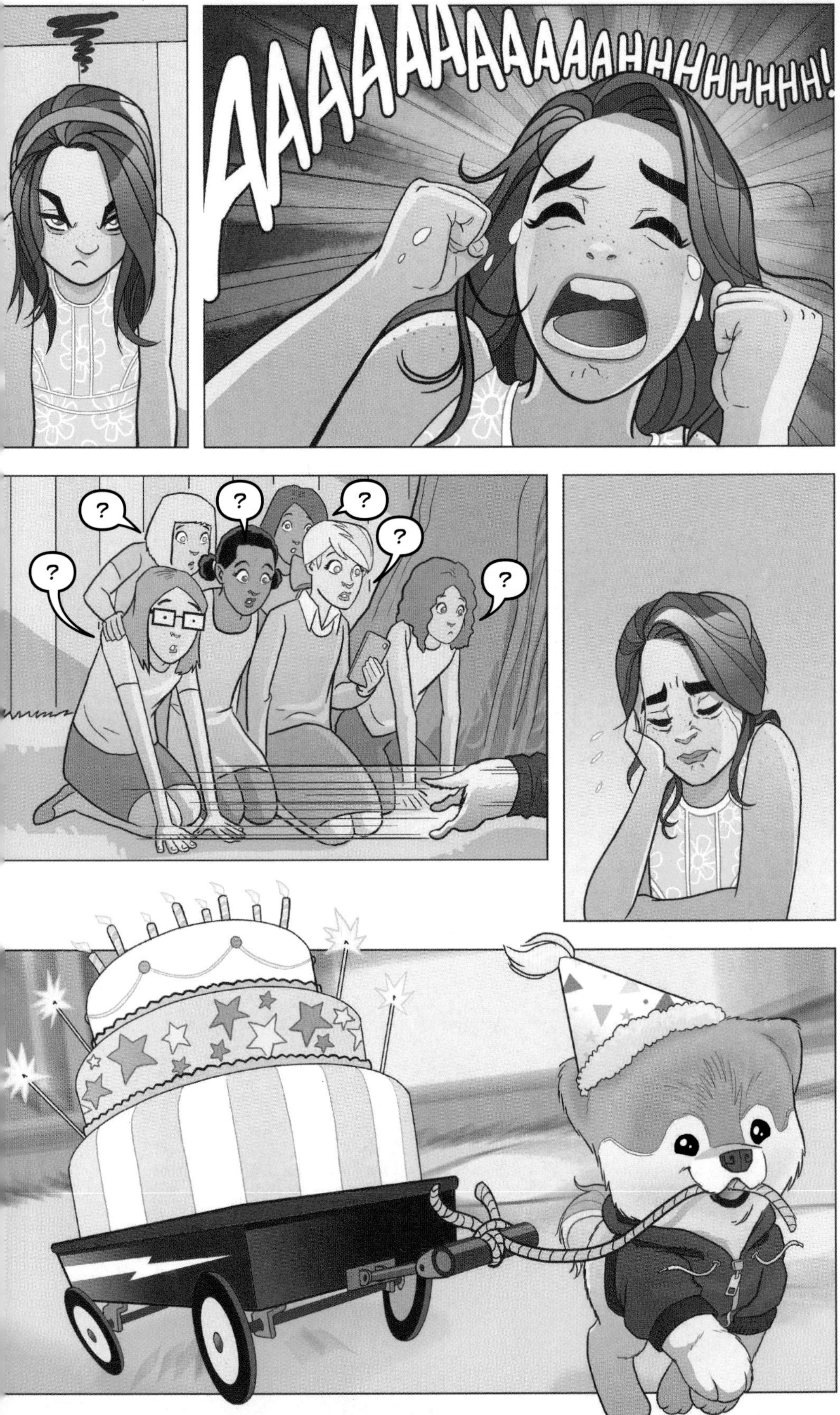
AAAAAAAAAAAHHHHHHHHH!
?
?
?
?
?
?

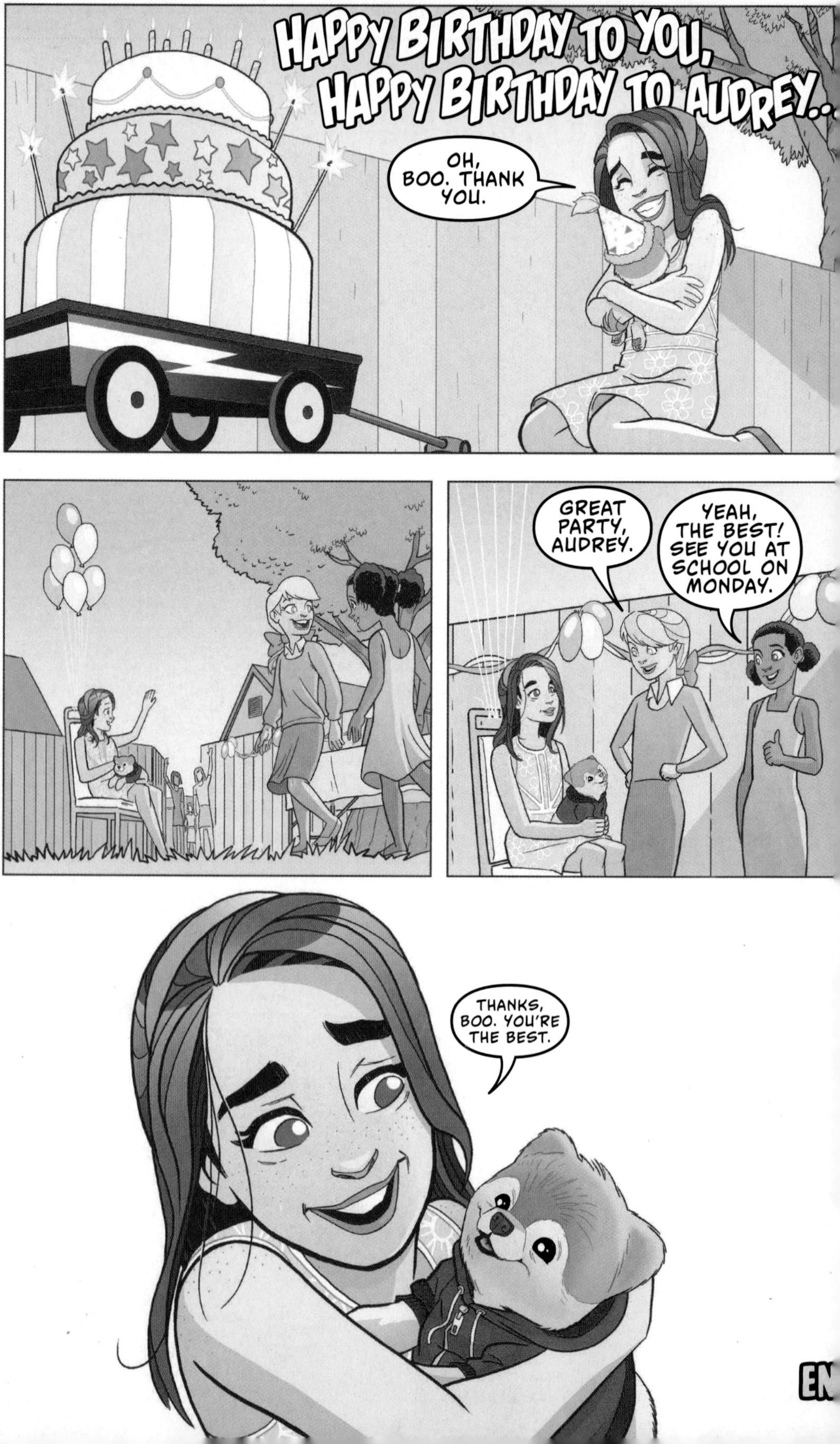
HAPPY BIRTHDAY TO YOU,
HAPPY BIRTHDAY TO AUDREY...
OH, BOO. THANK YOU.
GREAT PARTY, AUDREY.
YEAH, THE BEST! SEE YOU AT SCHOOL ON MONDAY.
THANKS, BOO. YOU'RE THE BEST.

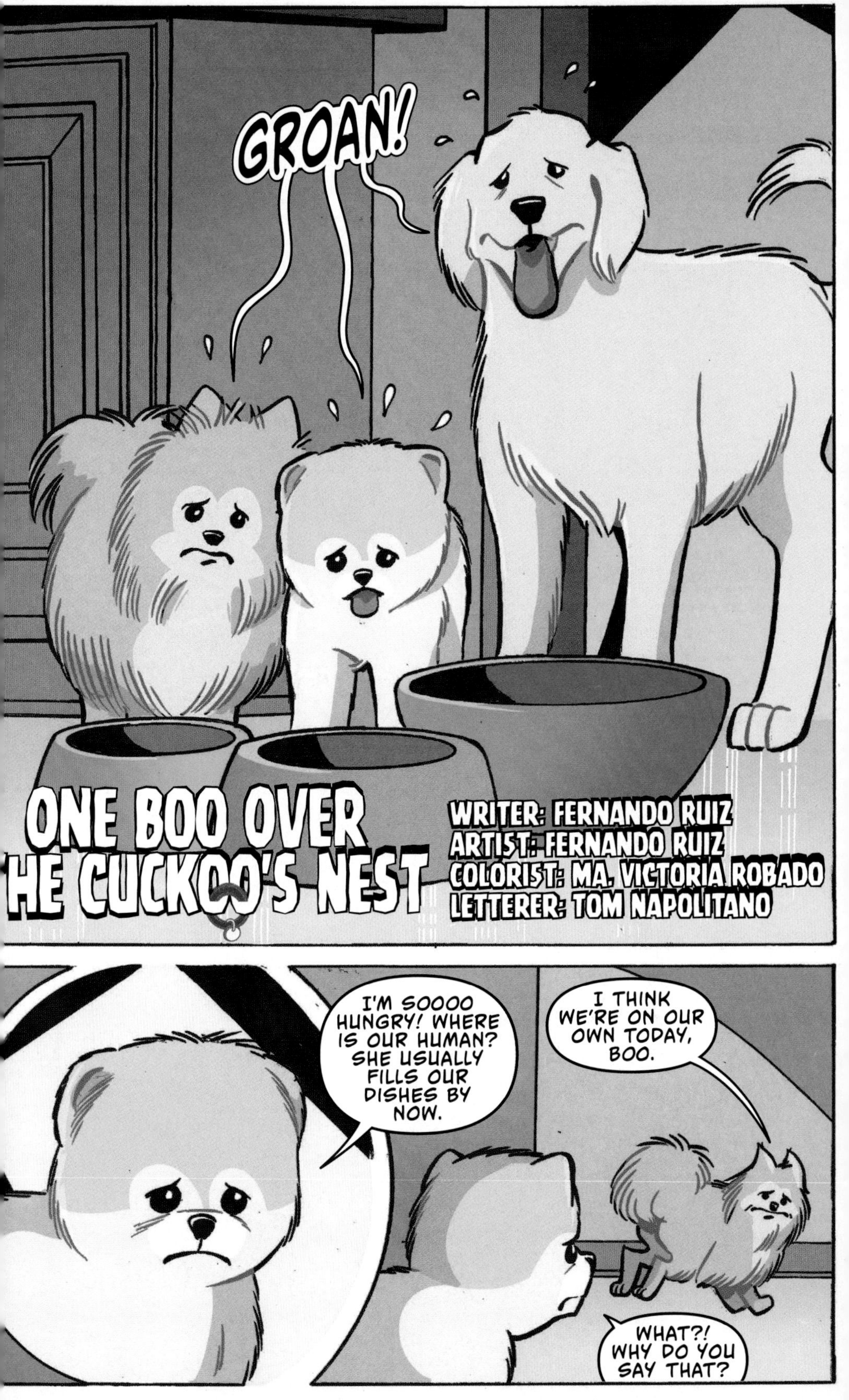
GROAN!
ONE BOO OVER
HE CUCKOO'S NEST
WRITER: FERNANDO RUIZ
ARTIST: FERNANDO RUIZ
COLORIST: MA. VICTORIA ROBADO
LETTERER: TOM NAPOLITANO
I'M SOOOO HUNGRY! WHERE IS OUR HUMAN? SHE USUALLY FILLS OUR DISHES BY NOW.
I THINK WE'RE ON OUR OWN TODAY, BOO.
WHAT?! WHY DO YOU SAY THAT?

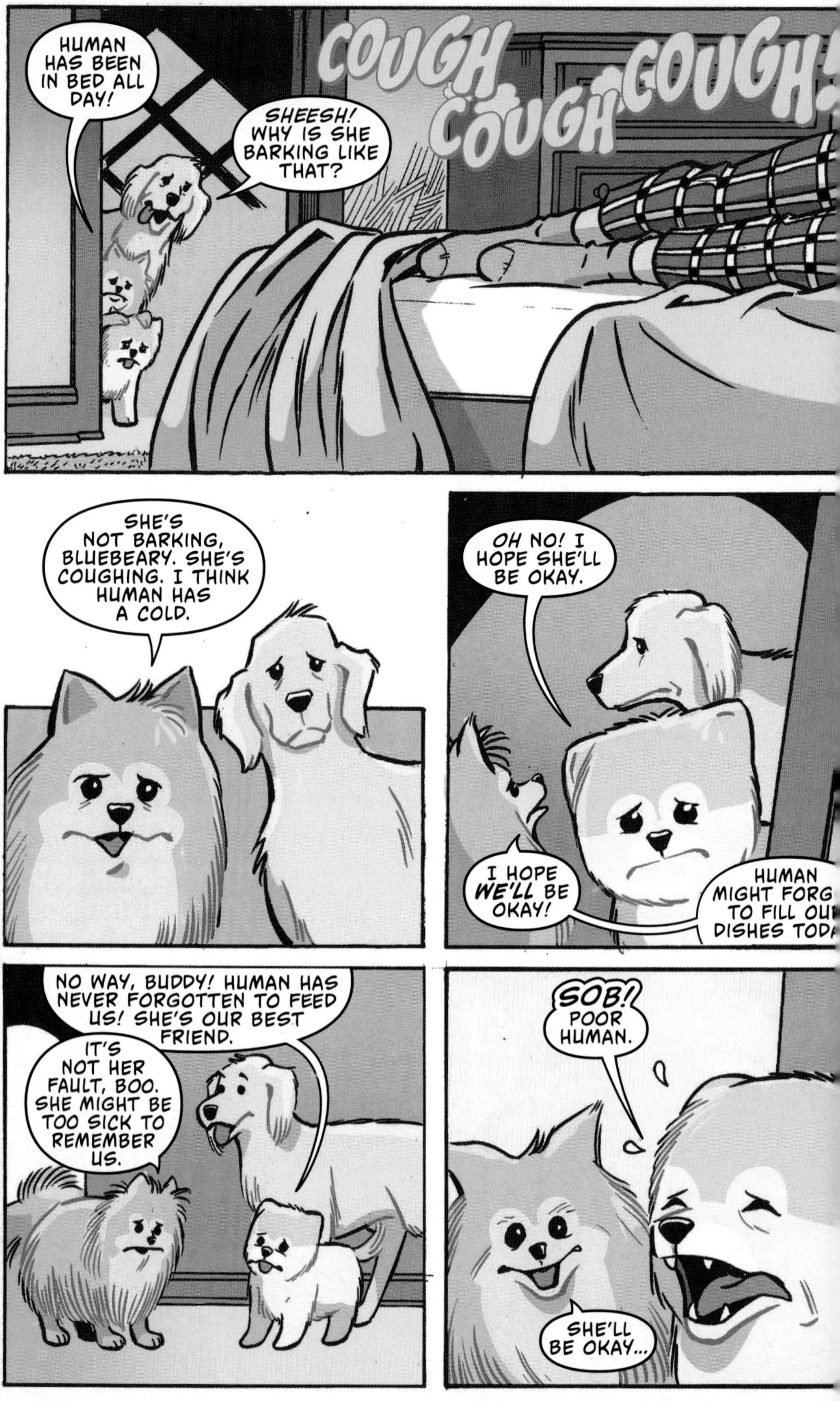
HUMAN HAS BEEN IN BED ALL DAY!
COUGH COUGH COUGH!
SHEESH! WHY IS SHE BARKING LIKE THAT?
SHE'S NOT BARKING, BLUEBEARY. SHE'S COUGHING. I THINK HUMAN HAS A COLD.
OH NO! I HOPE SHE'LL BE OKAY.
I HOPE WE'LL BE OKAY!
HUMAN MIGHT FORG TO FILL OU DISHES TOD
NO WAY, BUDDY! HUMAN HAS NEVER FORGOTTEN TO FEED US! SHE'S OUR BEST FRIEND.
IT'S NOT HER FAULT, BOO. SHE MIGHT BE TOO SICK TO REMEMBER US.
SOB! POOR HUMAN.
SHE'LL BE OKAY...

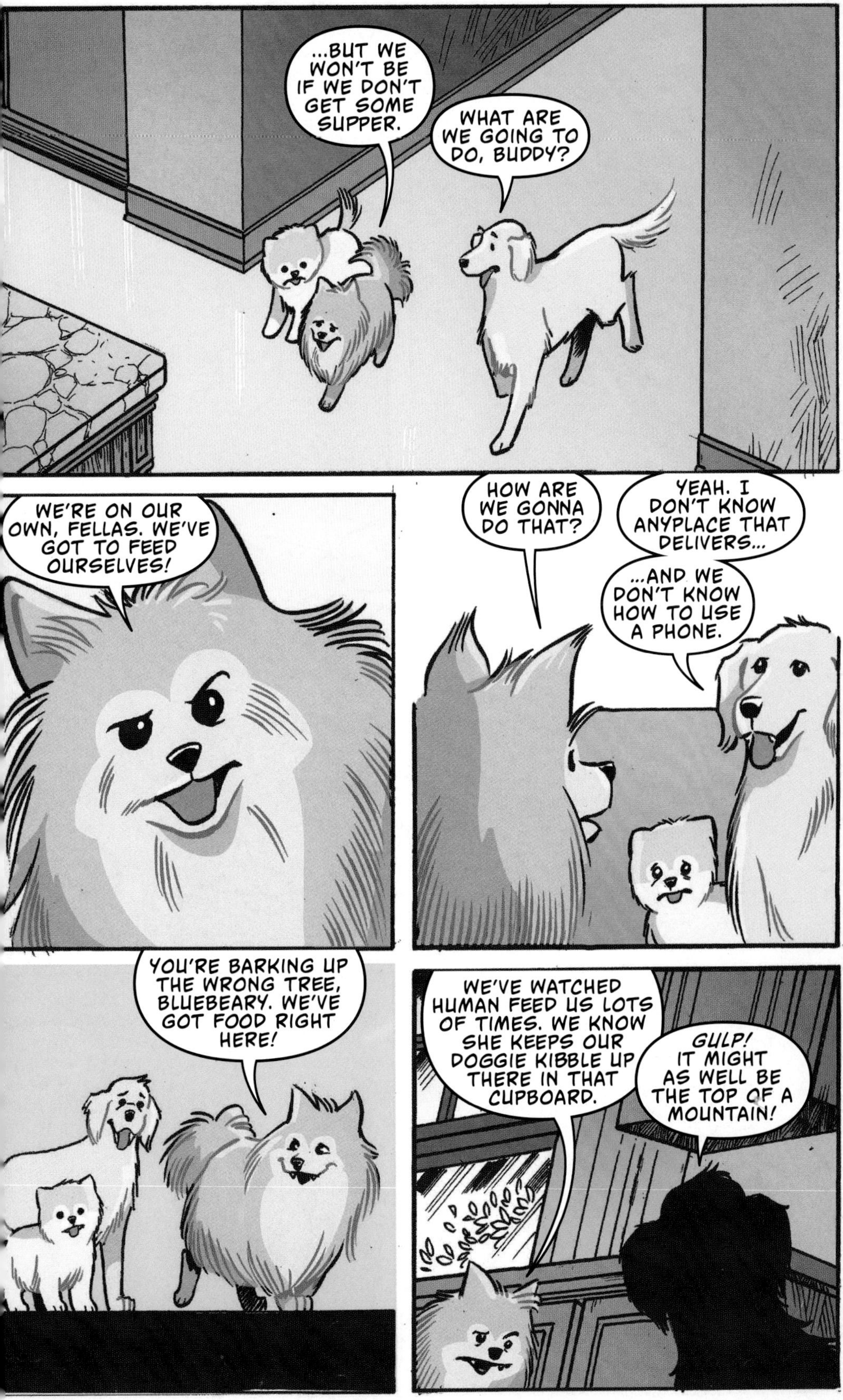
...BUT WE WON'T BE IF WE DON'T GET SOME SUPPER.
WHAT ARE WE GOING TO DO, BUDDY?
WE'RE ON OUR OWN, FELLAS. WE'VE GOT TO FEED OURSELVES!
HOW ARE WE GONNA DO THAT?
YEAH. I DON'T KNOW ANYPLACE THAT DELIVERS...
...AND WE DON'T KNOW HOW TO USE A PHONE.
YOU'RE BARKING UP THE WRONG TREE, BLUEBEARY. WE'VE GOT FOOD RIGHT HERE!
WE'VE WATCHED HUMAN FEED US LOTS OF TIMES. WE KNOW SHE KEEPS OUR DOGGIE KIBBLE UP THERE IN THAT CUPBOARD.
GULP! IT MIGHT AS WELL BE THE TOP OF A MOUNTAIN!

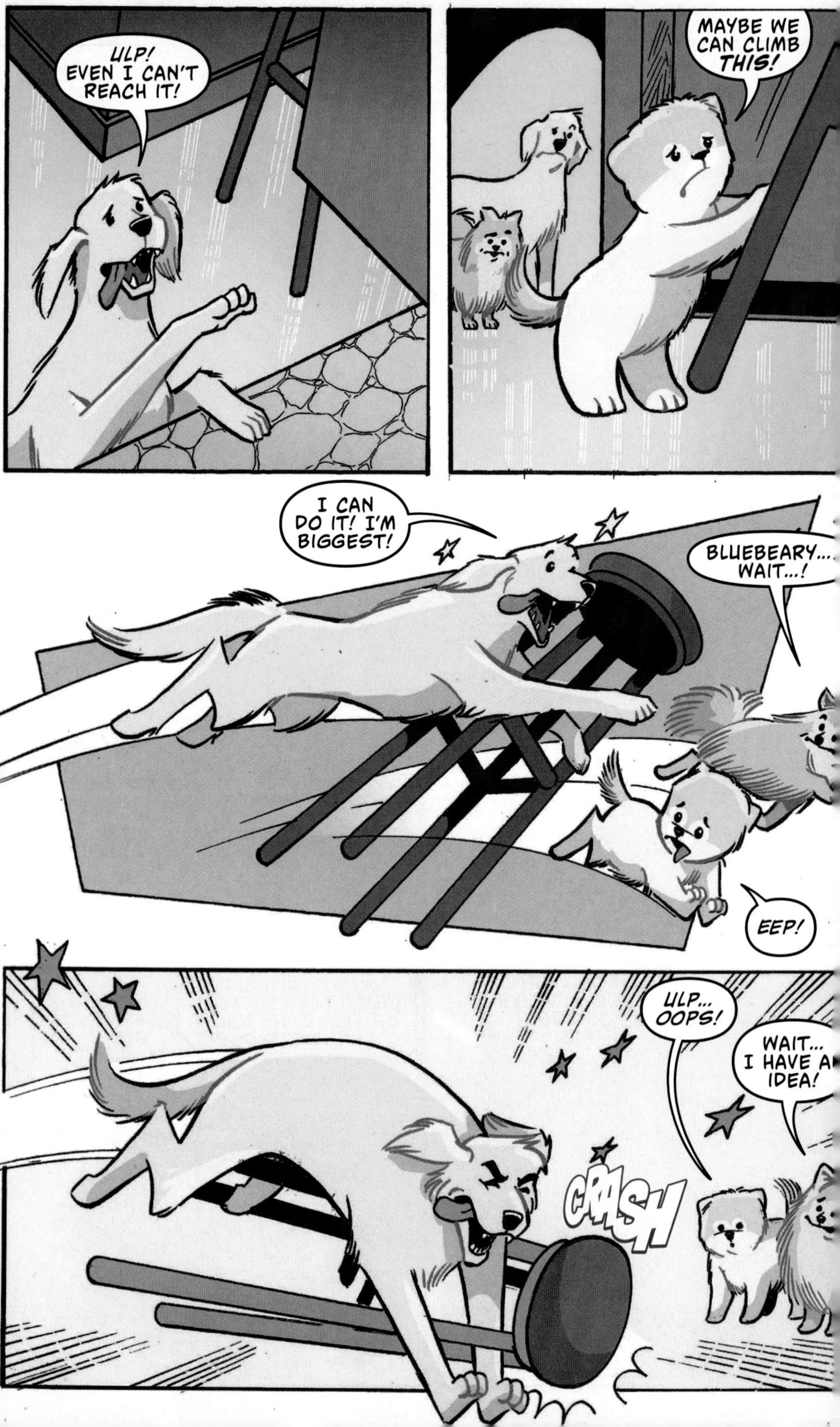
ULP!
EVEN I CAN'T
REACH IT!
MAYBE WE
CAN CLIMB
THIS!
I CAN
DO IT! I'M
BIGGEST!
BLUEBEARY...
WAIT...!
EEP!
ULP...
OOPS!
WAIT...
I HAVE A
IDEA!
CRASH

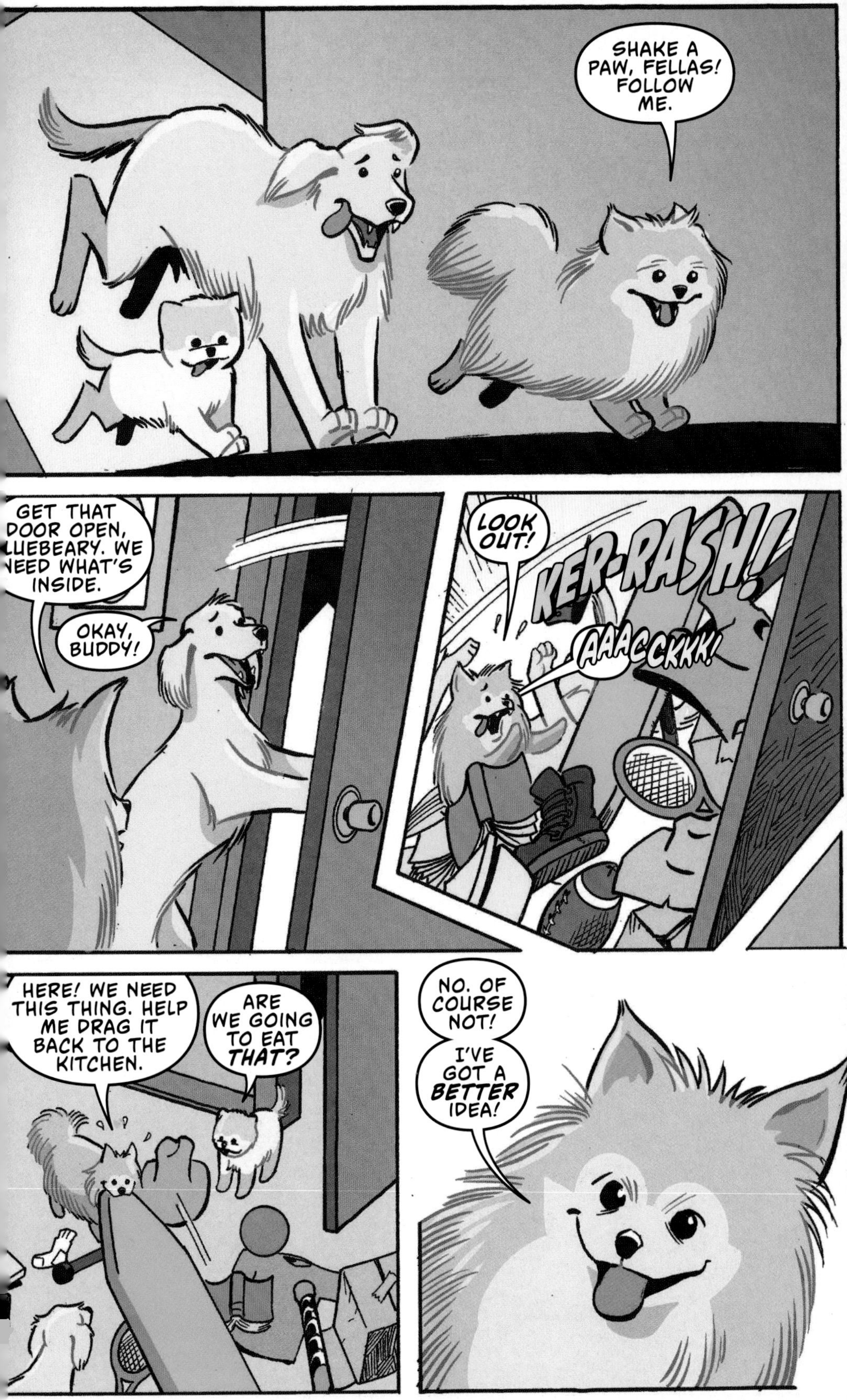
SHAKE A PAW, FELLAS! FOLLOW ME.
GET THAT DOOR OPEN, LUEBEARY. WE NEED WHAT'S INSIDE.
OKAY, BUDDY!
LOOK OUT!
KER-RASH!!
AAACCKKK!
HERE! WE NEED THIS THING. HELP ME DRAG IT BACK TO THE KITCHEN.
ARE WE GOING TO EAT *THAT?*
NO. OF COURSE NOT!
I'VE GOT A *BETTER* IDEA!

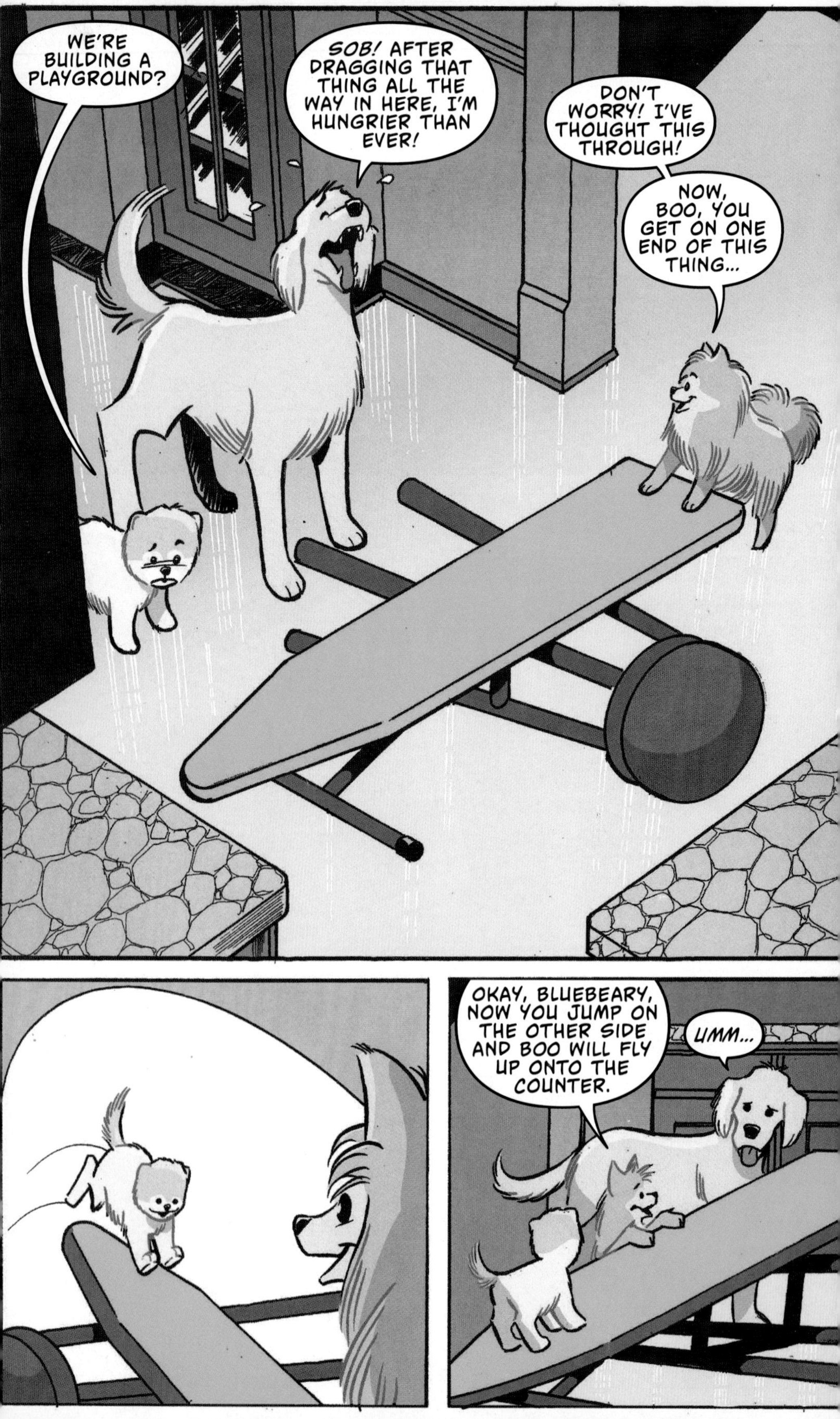
WE'RE BUILDING A PLAYGROUND?
SOB! AFTER DRAGGING THAT THING ALL THE WAY IN HERE, I'M HUNGRIER THAN EVER!
DON'T WORRY! I'VE THOUGHT THIS THROUGH!
NOW, BOO, YOU GET ON ONE END OF THIS THING...
OKAY, BLUEBEARY, NOW YOU JUMP ON THE OTHER SIDE AND BOO WILL FLY UP ONTO THE COUNTER.
UMM...

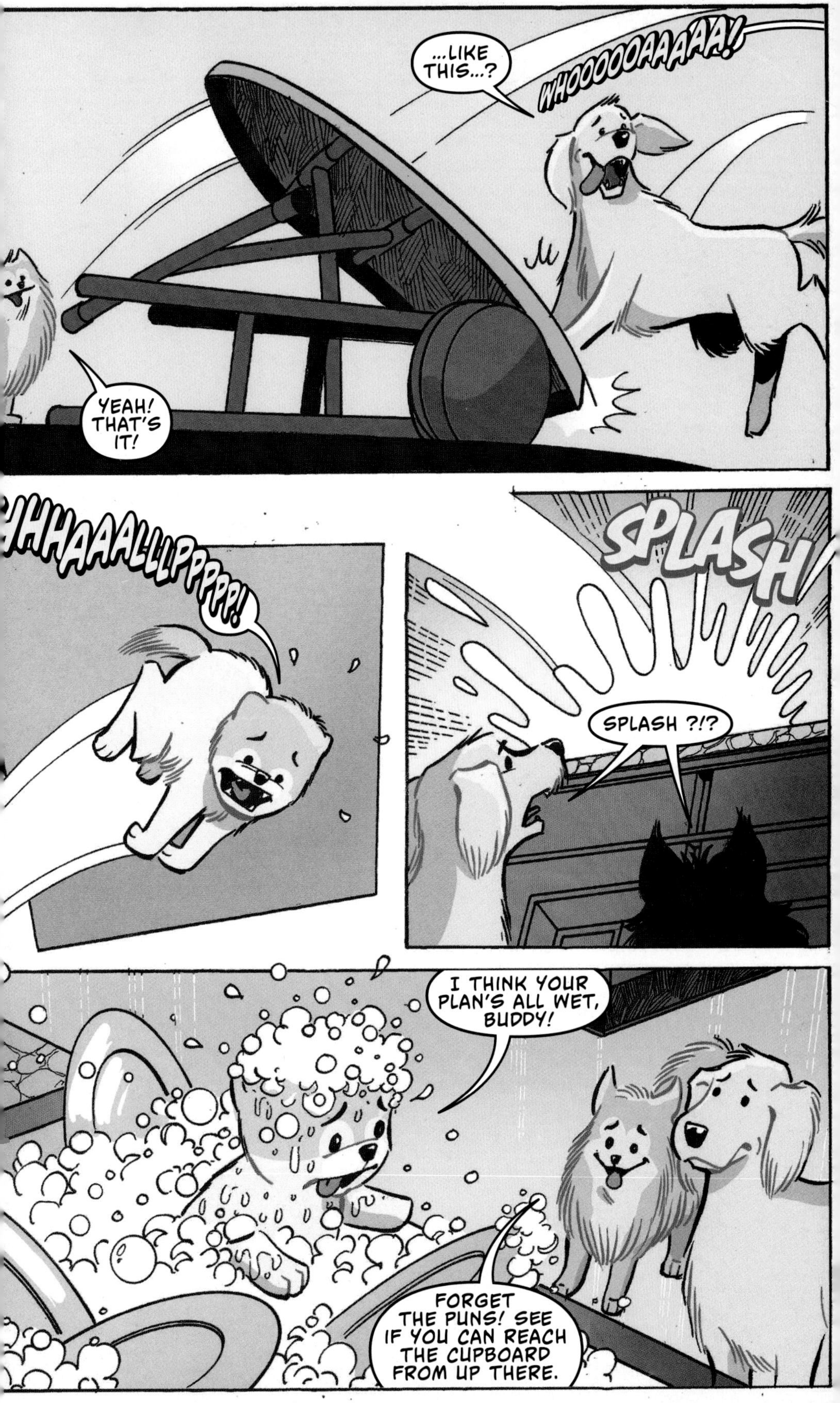
...LIKE THIS...?
WHOOOOOOAAAAA!
YEAH! THAT'S IT!
HHAAALLLPPPPP!
SPLASH
SPLASH ?!?
I THINK YOUR PLAN'S ALL WET, BUDDY!
FORGET THE PUNS! SEE IF YOU CAN REACH THE CUPBOARD FROM UP THERE.

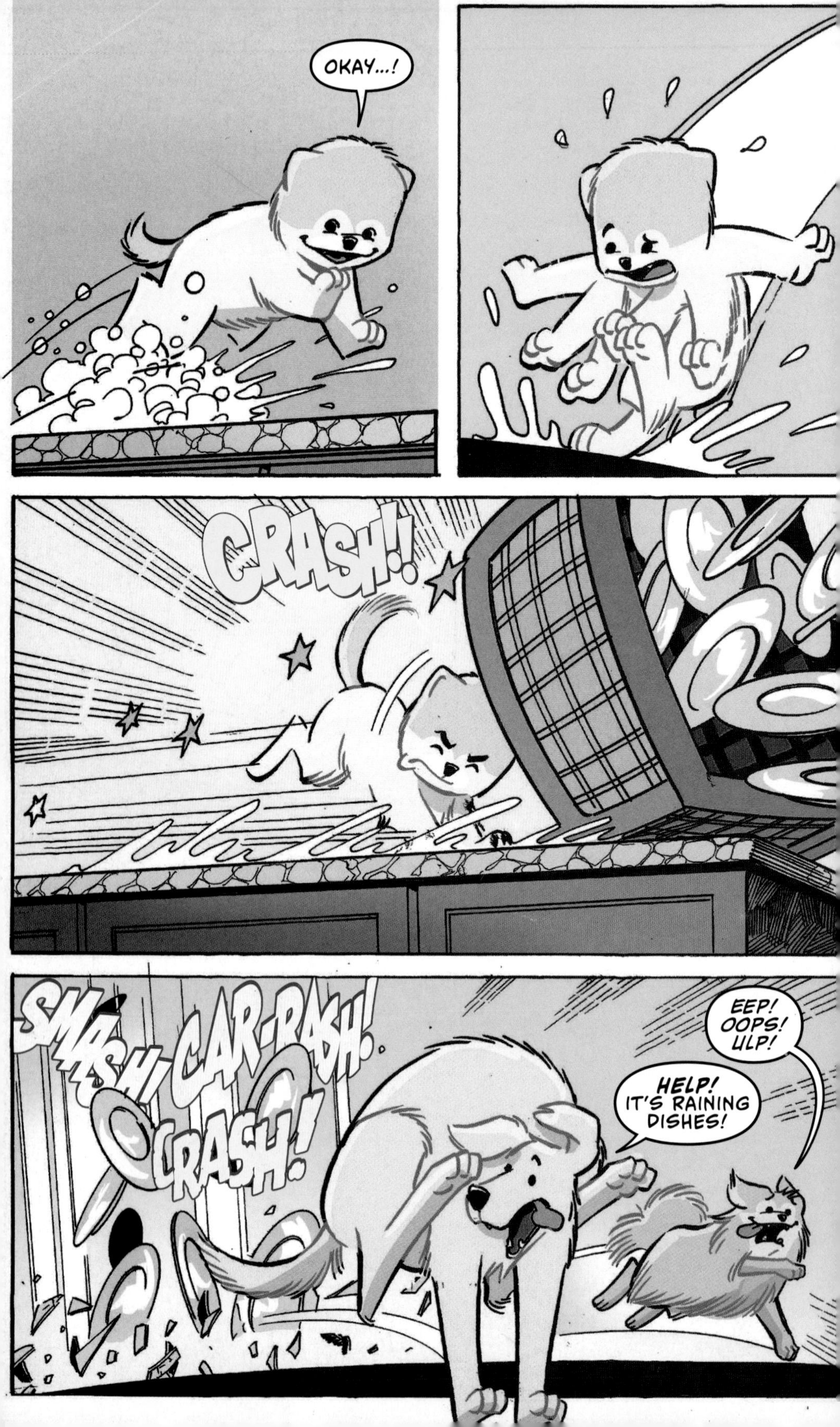
OKAY...!
CRASH!!
SMASH! CAR-RASH!
CRASH!
EEP! OOPS! ULP!
HELP! IT'S RAINING DISHES!

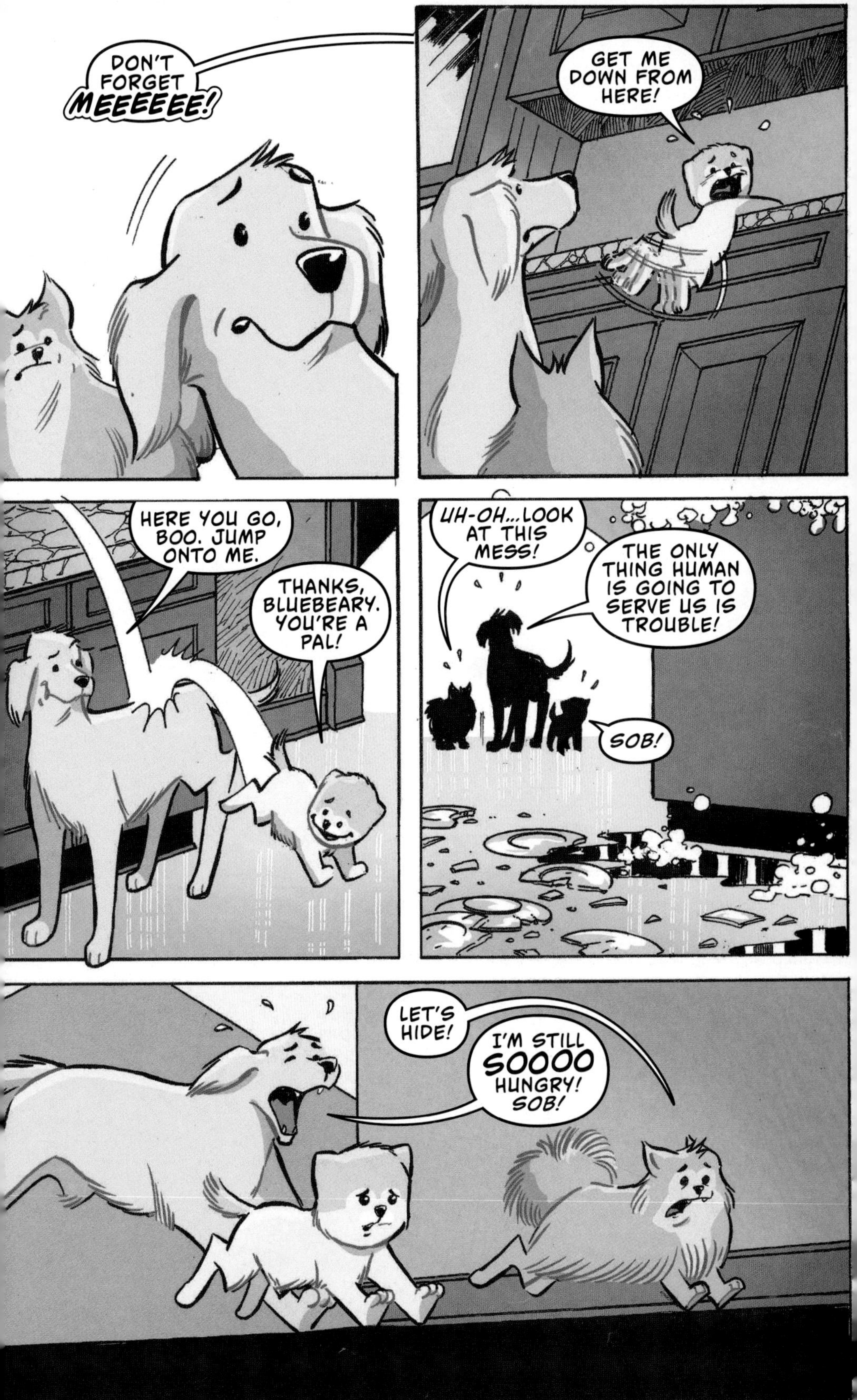

DON'T FORGET MEEEEEEE!
GET ME DOWN FROM HERE!
HERE YOU GO, BOO. JUMP ONTO ME.
THANKS, BLUEBEARY. YOU'RE A PAL!
UH-OH...LOOK AT THIS MESS!
THE ONLY THING HUMAN IS GOING TO SERVE US IS TROUBLE!
SOB!
LET'S HIDE!
I'M STILL SOOOO HUNGRY! SOB!

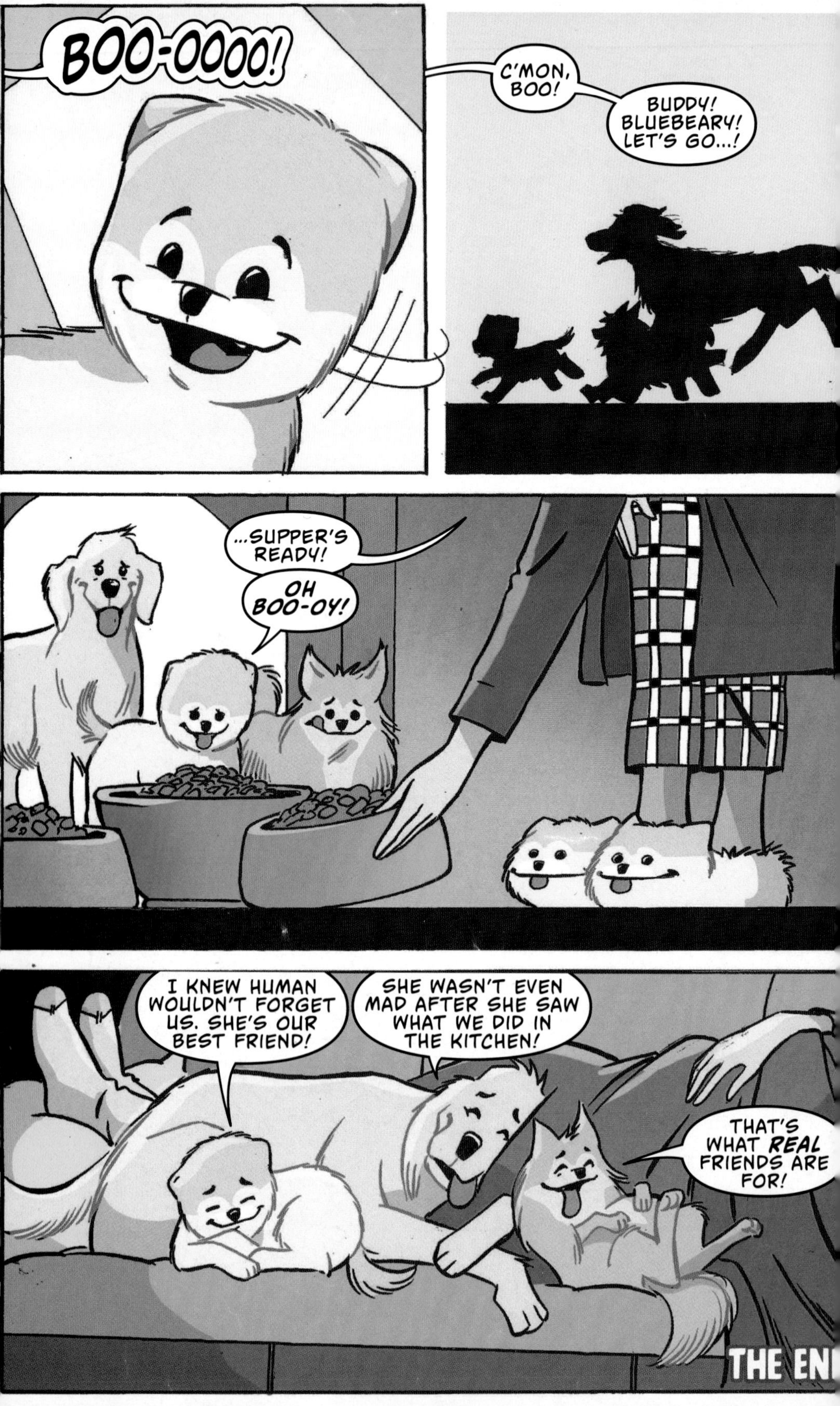
BOO-OOOO!
C'MON, BOO!
BUDDY! BLUEBEARY! LET'S GO...!
...SUPPER'S READY!
OH BOO-OY!
I KNEW HUMAN WOULDN'T FORGET US. SHE'S OUR BEST FRIEND!
SHE WASN'T EVEN MAD AFTER SHE SAW WHAT WE DID IN THE KITCHEN!
THAT'S WHAT *REAL* FRIENDS ARE FOR!
THE END

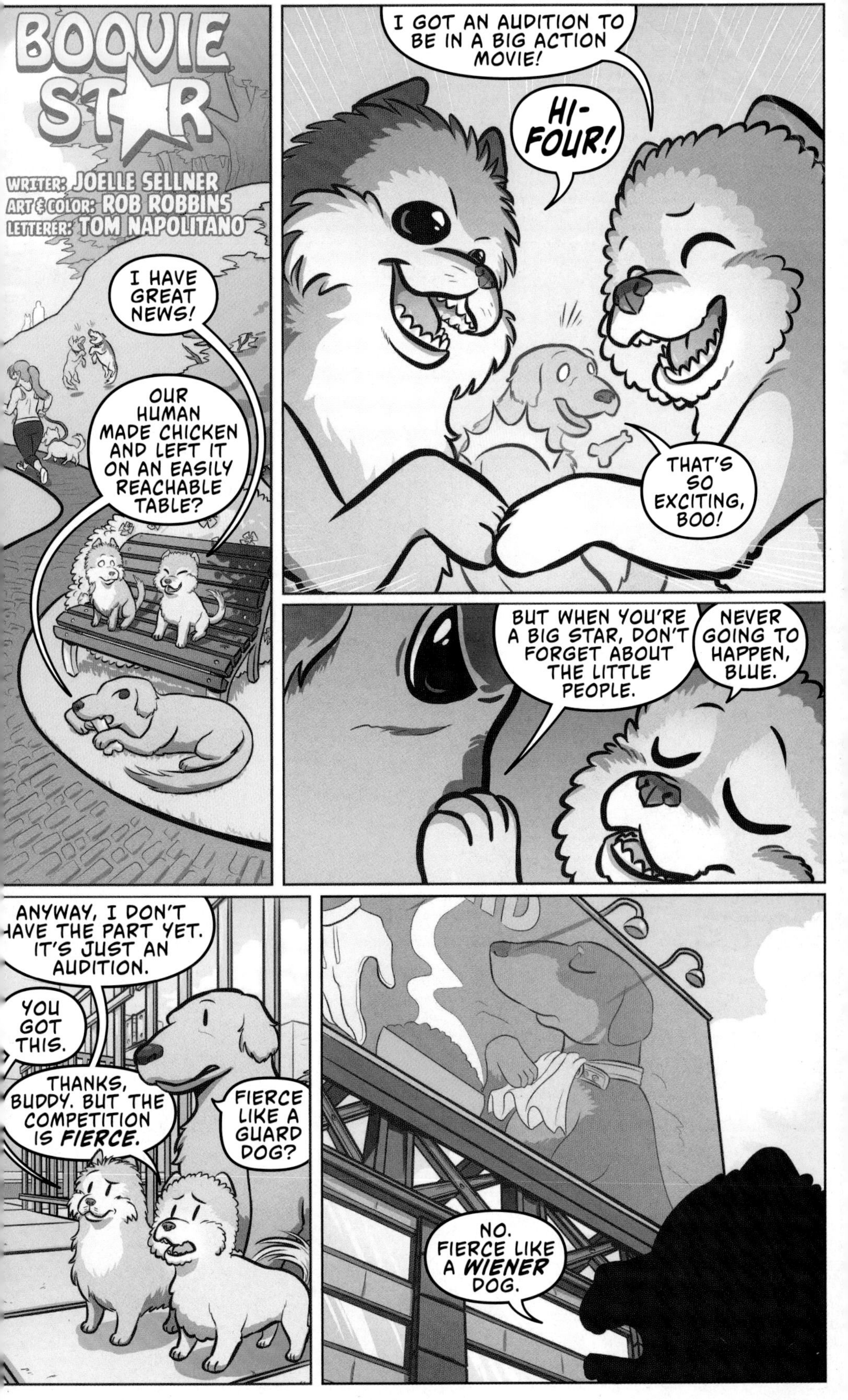
BOOVIE STAR
WRITER: JOELLE SELLNER
ART & COLOR: ROB ROBBINS
LETTERER: TOM NAPOLITANO
I HAVE GREAT NEWS!
OUR HUMAN MADE CHICKEN AND LEFT IT ON AN EASILY REACHABLE TABLE?
I GOT AN AUDITION TO BE IN A BIG ACTION MOVIE!
HI-FOUR!
THAT'S SO EXCITING, BOO!
BUT WHEN YOU'RE A BIG STAR, DON'T FORGET ABOUT THE LITTLE PEOPLE.
NEVER GOING TO HAPPEN, BLUE.
ANYWAY, I DON'T HAVE THE PART YET. IT'S JUST AN AUDITION.
YOU GOT THIS.
THANKS, BUDDY. BUT THE COMPETITION IS FIERCE.
FIERCE LIKE A GUARD DOG?
NO. FIERCE LIKE A WIENER DOG.

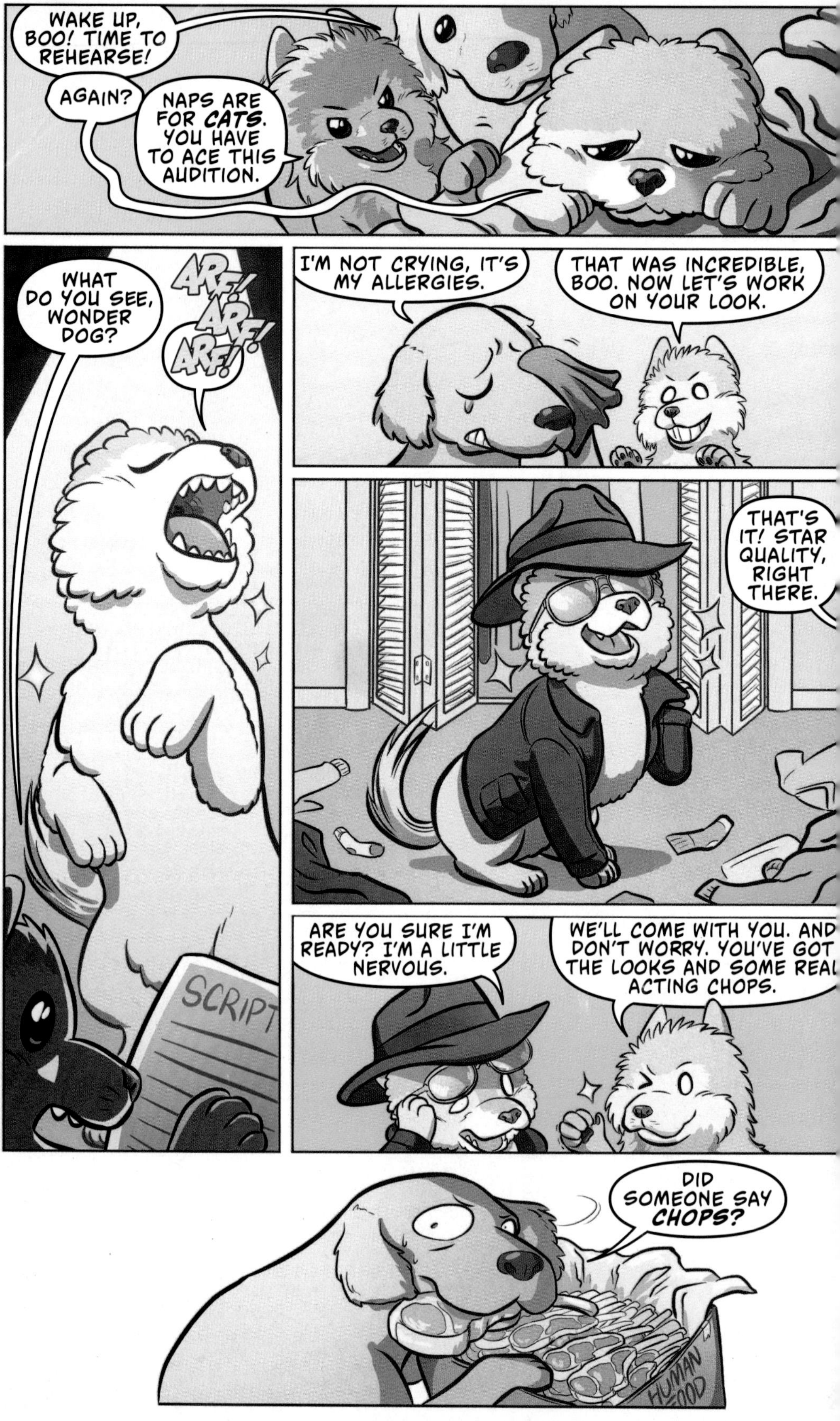
WAKE UP, BOO! TIME TO REHEARSE!
AGAIN?
NAPS ARE FOR **CATS**. YOU HAVE TO ACE THIS AUDITION.
WHAT DO YOU SEE, WONDER DOG?
ARF! ARF! ARF!
SCRIPT
I'M NOT CRYING, IT'S MY ALLERGIES.
THAT WAS INCREDIBLE, BOO. NOW LET'S WORK ON YOUR LOOK.
THAT'S IT! STAR QUALITY, RIGHT THERE.
ARE YOU SURE I'M READY? I'M A LITTLE NERVOUS.
WE'LL COME WITH YOU. AND DON'T WORRY. YOU'VE GOT THE LOOKS AND SOME REAL ACTING CHOPS.
DID SOMEONE SAY **CHOPS?**
HUMAN FOOD

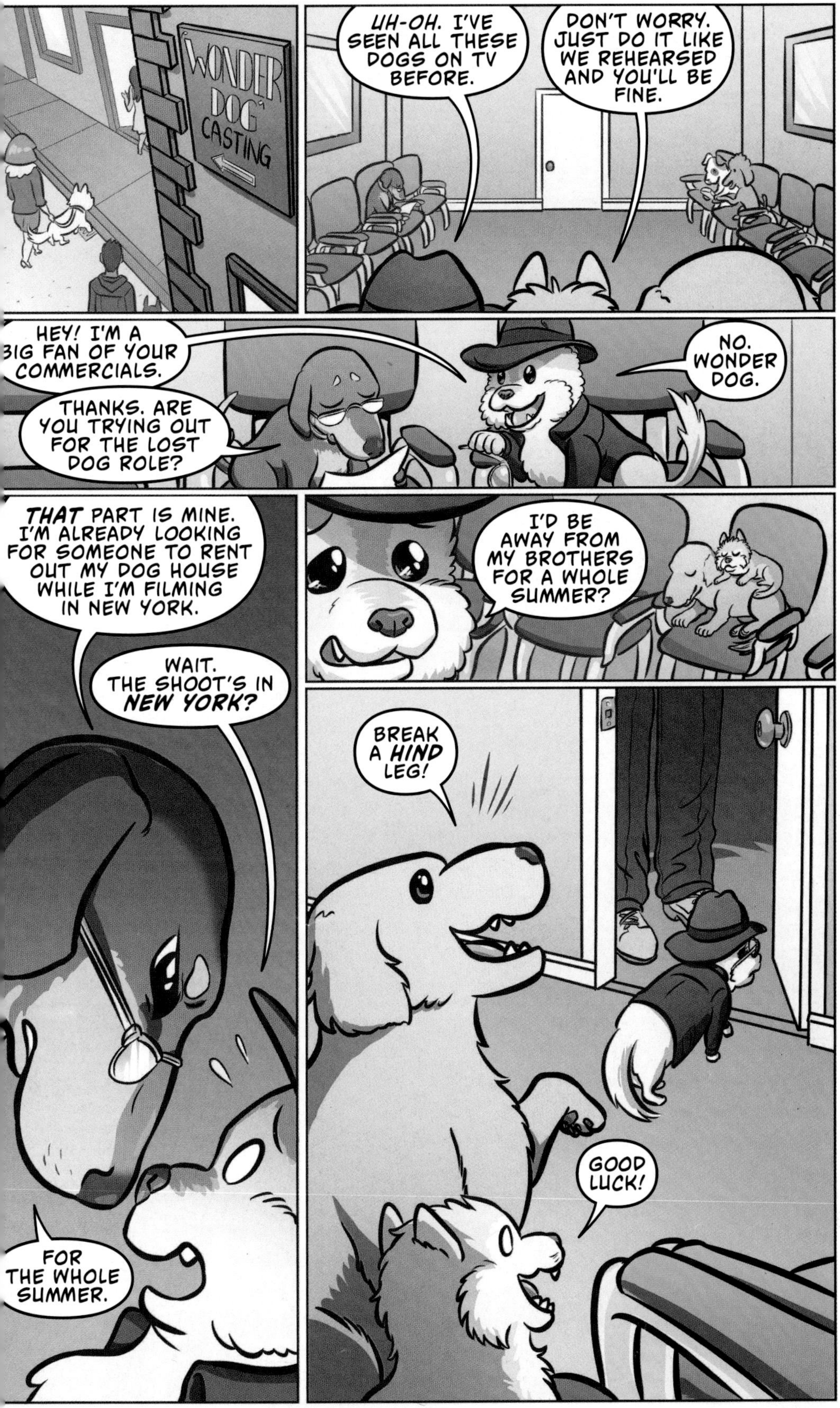
WONDER DOG CASTING
UH-OH. I'VE SEEN ALL THESE DOGS ON TV BEFORE.
DON'T WORRY. JUST DO IT LIKE WE REHEARSED AND YOU'LL BE FINE.
HEY! I'M A BIG FAN OF YOUR COMMERCIALS.
THANKS. ARE YOU TRYING OUT FOR THE LOST DOG ROLE?
NO. WONDER DOG.
THAT PART IS MINE. I'M ALREADY LOOKING FOR SOMEONE TO RENT OUT MY DOG HOUSE WHILE I'M FILMING IN NEW YORK.
WAIT. THE SHOOT'S IN NEW YORK?
FOR THE WHOLE SUMMER.
I'D BE AWAY FROM MY BROTHERS FOR A WHOLE SUMMER?
BREAK A HIND LEG!
GOOD LUCK!

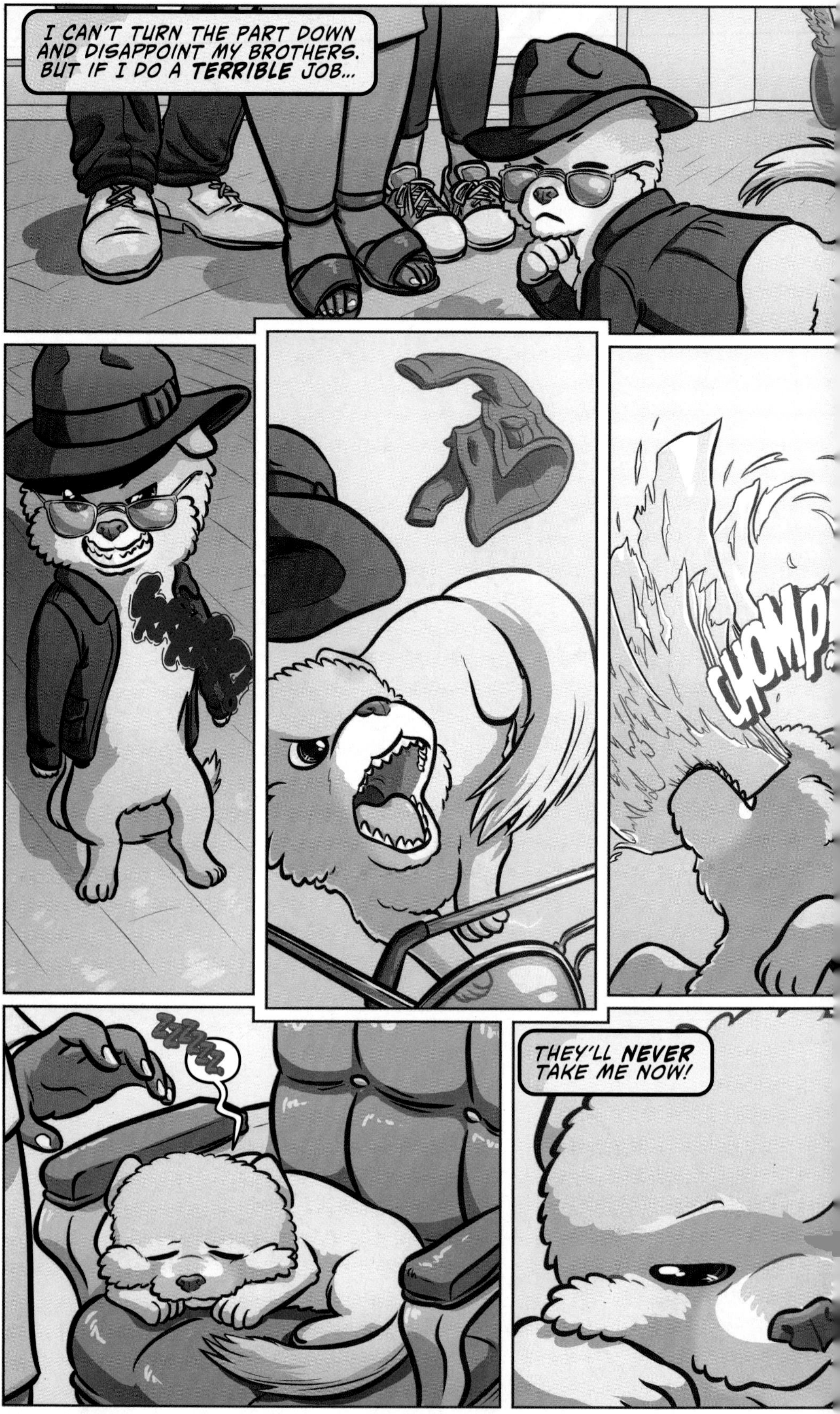
I CAN'T TURN THE PART DOWN AND DISAPPOINT MY BROTHERS. BUT IF I DO A **TERRIBLE** JOB...
CHOMP!
ZZZZZZ
THEY'LL **NEVER** TAKE ME NOW!

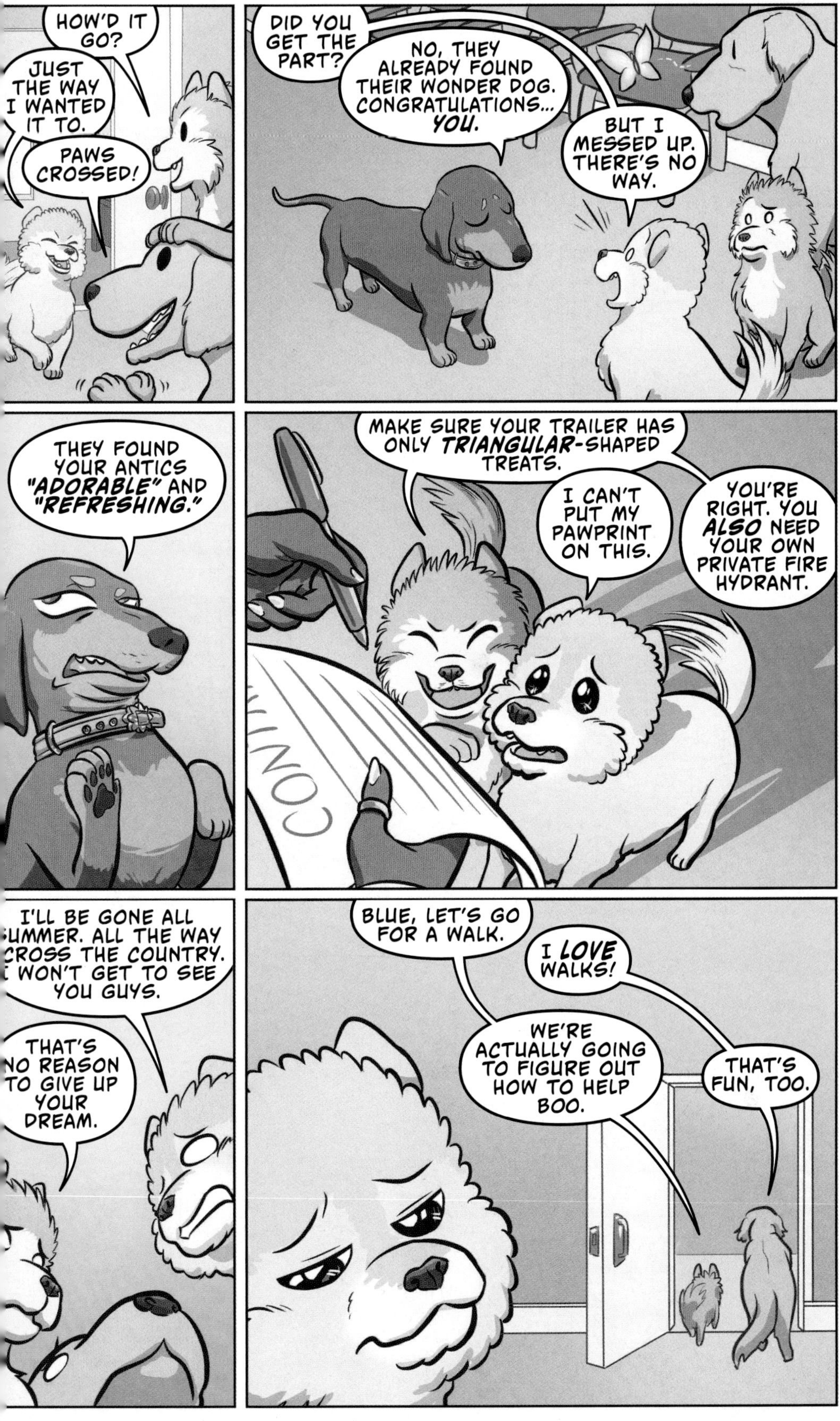
HOW'D IT GO?
JUST THE WAY I WANTED IT TO.
PAWS CROSSED!
DID YOU GET THE PART?
NO, THEY ALREADY FOUND THEIR WONDER DOG. CONGRATULATIONS... *YOU.*
BUT I MESSED UP. THERE'S NO WAY.
THEY FOUND YOUR ANTICS *"ADORABLE"* AND *"REFRESHING."*
MAKE SURE YOUR TRAILER HAS ONLY *TRIANGULAR*-SHAPED TREATS.
I CAN'T PUT MY PAWPRINT ON THIS.
YOU'RE RIGHT. YOU *ALSO* NEED YOUR OWN PRIVATE FIRE HYDRANT.
CONT
I'LL BE GONE ALL SUMMER. ALL THE WAY CROSS THE COUNTRY. I WON'T GET TO SEE YOU GUYS.
THAT'S NO REASON TO GIVE UP YOUR DREAM.
BLUE, LET'S GO FOR A WALK.
I *LOVE* WALKS!
WE'RE ACTUALLY GOING TO FIGURE OUT HOW TO HELP BOO.
THAT'S FUN, TOO.

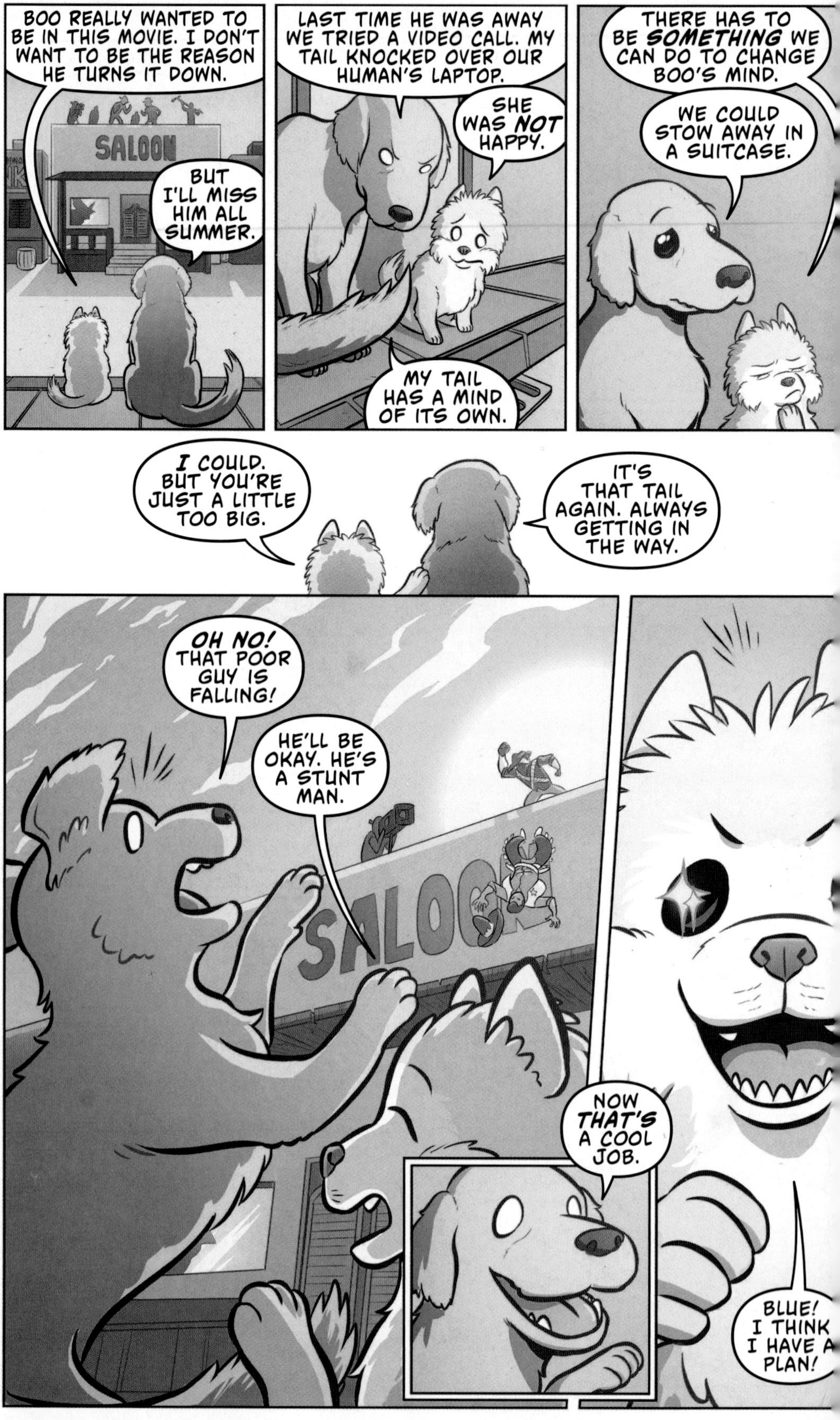
BOO REALLY WANTED TO BE IN THIS MOVIE. I DON'T WANT TO BE THE REASON HE TURNS IT DOWN.
SALOON
BUT I'LL MISS HIM ALL SUMMER.
LAST TIME HE WAS AWAY WE TRIED A VIDEO CALL. MY TAIL KNOCKED OVER OUR HUMAN'S LAPTOP.
SHE WAS NOT HAPPY.
MY TAIL HAS A MIND OF ITS OWN.
THERE HAS TO BE SOMETHING WE CAN DO TO CHANGE BOO'S MIND.
WE COULD STOW AWAY IN A SUITCASE.
I COULD. BUT YOU'RE JUST A LITTLE TOO BIG.
IT'S THAT TAIL AGAIN. ALWAYS GETTING IN THE WAY.
OH NO! THAT POOR GUY IS FALLING!
HE'LL BE OKAY. HE'S A STUNT MAN.
SALOON
NOW THAT'S A COOL JOB.
BLUE! I THINK I HAVE A PLAN!

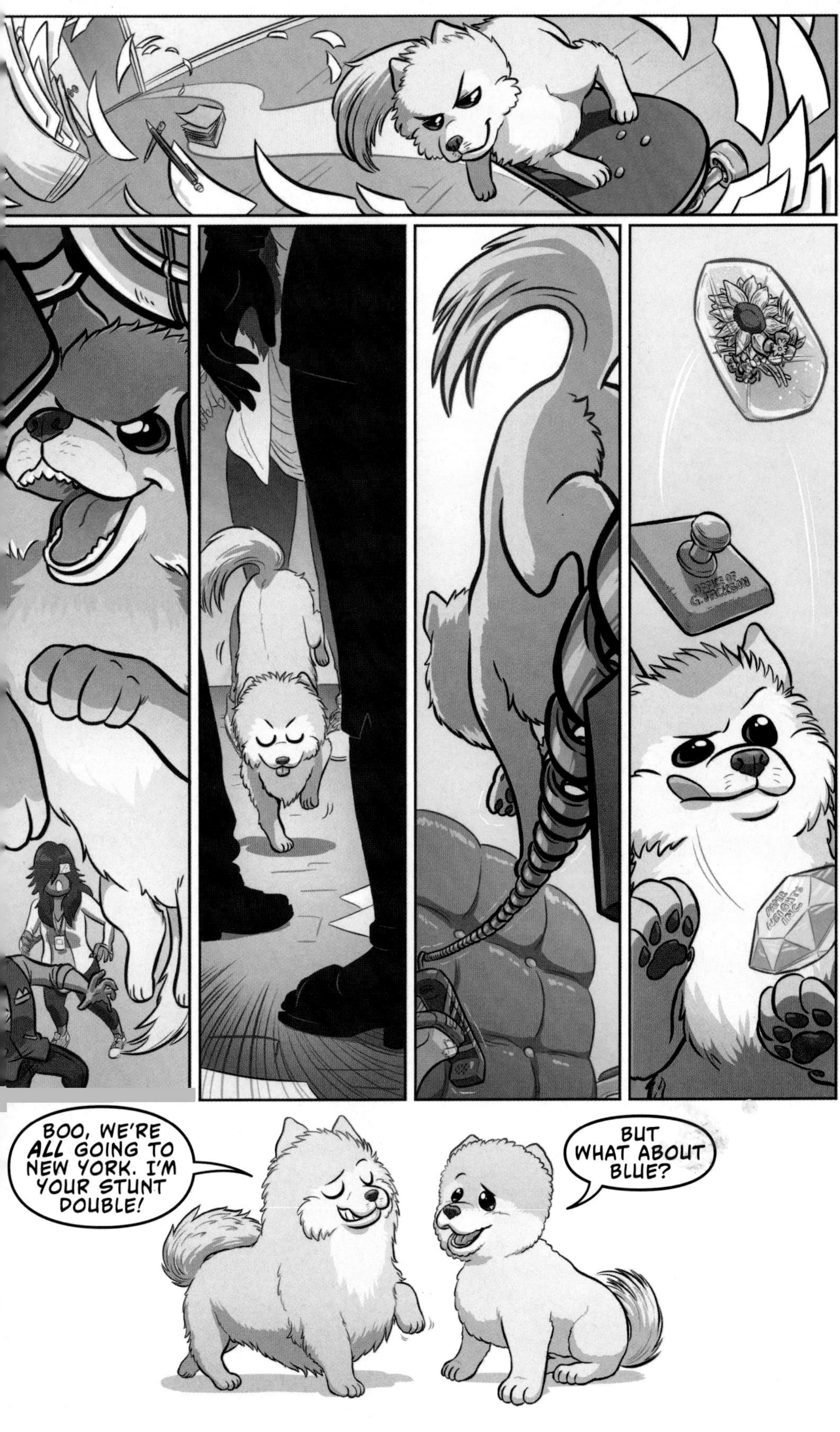
BOO, WE'RE ALL GOING TO NEW YORK. I'M YOUR STUNT DOUBLE!
BUT WHAT ABOUT BLUE?

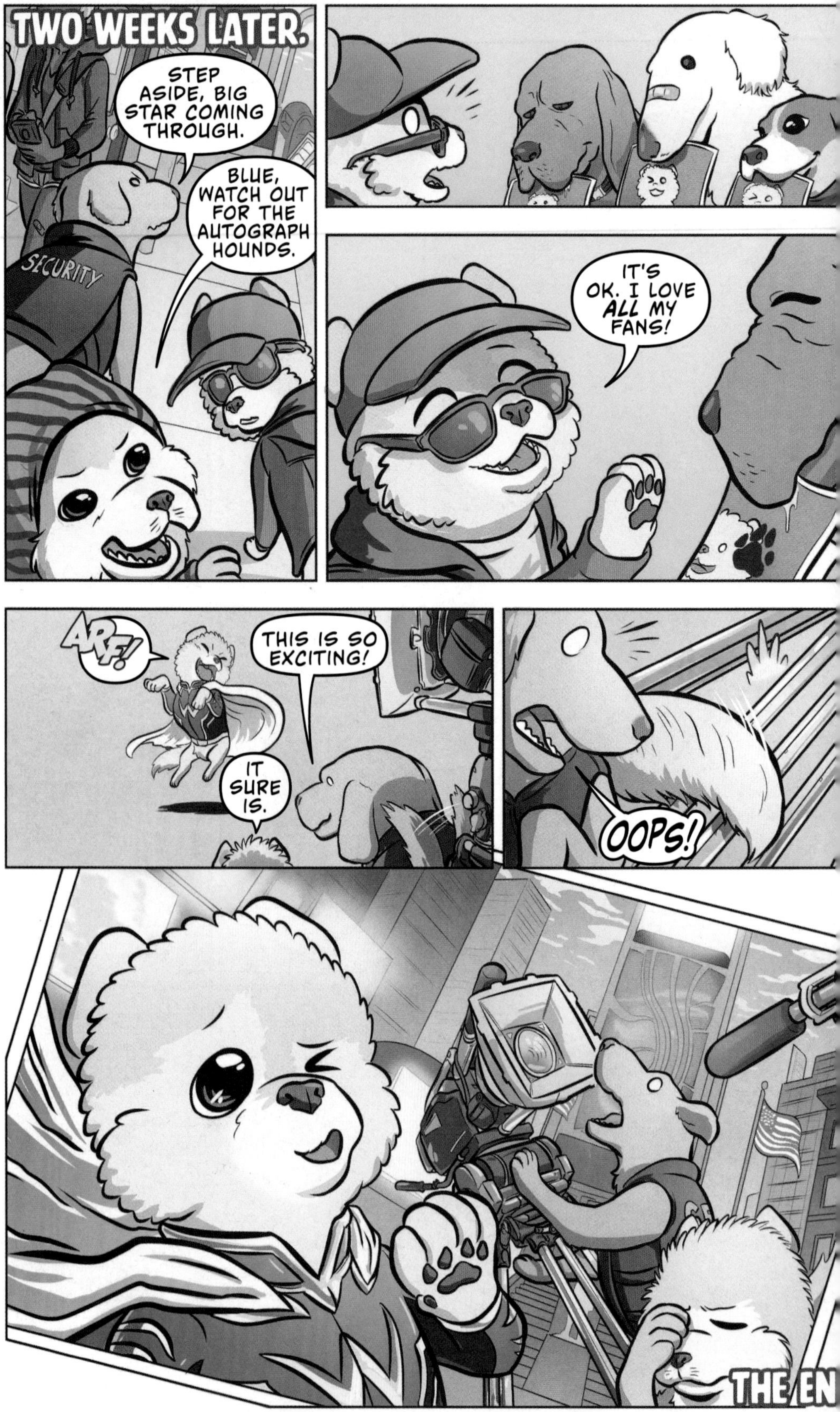
TWO WEEKS LATER.
STEP ASIDE, BIG STAR COMING THROUGH.
BLUE, WATCH OUT FOR THE AUTOGRAPH HOUNDS.
SECURITY
IT'S OK. I LOVE ALL MY FANS!
ARF!
THIS IS SO EXCITING!
IT SURE IS.
OOPS!
THE EN

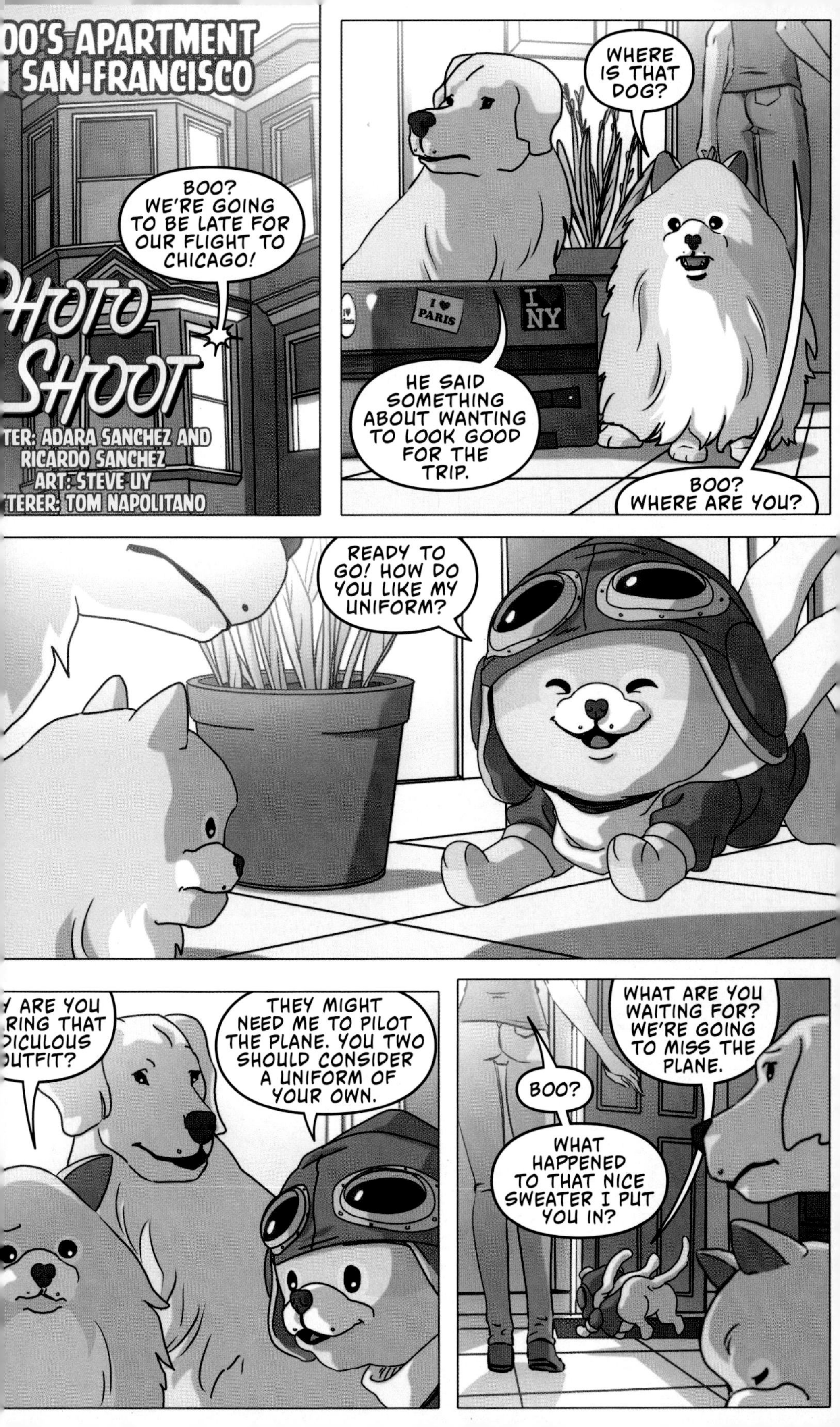
OO'S APARTMENT
SAN-FRANCISCO
BOO? WE'RE GOING TO BE LATE FOR OUR FLIGHT TO CHICAGO!
HOTO SHOOT
TER: ADARA SANCHEZ AND RICARDO SANCHEZ
ART: STEVE UY
TERER: TOM NAPOLITANO
WHERE IS THAT DOG?
I ♥ PARIS
I ♥ NY
HE SAID SOMETHING ABOUT WANTING TO LOOK GOOD FOR THE TRIP.
BOO? WHERE ARE YOU?
READY TO GO! HOW DO YOU LIKE MY UNIFORM?
Y ARE YOU RING THAT DICULOUS UTFIT?
THEY MIGHT NEED ME TO PILOT THE PLANE. YOU TWO SHOULD CONSIDER A UNIFORM OF YOUR OWN.
WHAT ARE YOU WAITING FOR? WE'RE GOING TO MISS THE PLANE.
BOO?
WHAT HAPPENED TO THAT NICE SWEATER I PUT YOU IN?

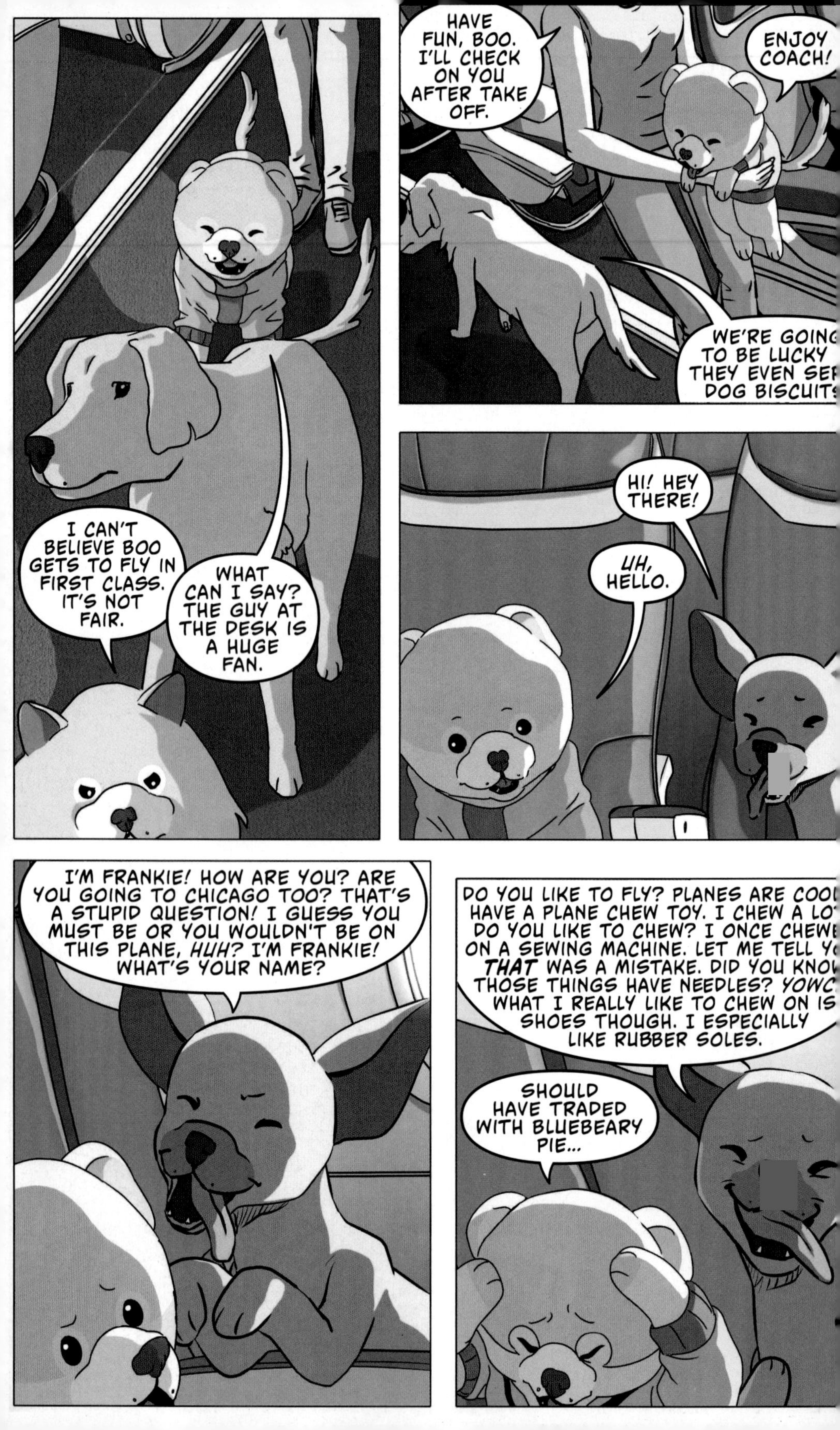
HAVE FUN, BOO. I'LL CHECK ON YOU AFTER TAKE OFF.
ENJOY COACH!
WE'RE GOING TO BE LUCKY THEY EVEN SER DOG BISCUITS
I CAN'T BELIEVE BOO GETS TO FLY IN FIRST CLASS. IT'S NOT FAIR.
WHAT CAN I SAY? THE GUY AT THE DESK IS A HUGE FAN.
HI! HEY THERE!
UH, HELLO.
I'M FRANKIE! HOW ARE YOU? ARE YOU GOING TO CHICAGO TOO? THAT'S A STUPID QUESTION! I GUESS YOU MUST BE OR YOU WOULDN'T BE ON THIS PLANE, HUH? I'M FRANKIE! WHAT'S YOUR NAME?
DO YOU LIKE TO FLY? PLANES ARE COO HAVE A PLANE CHEW TOY. I CHEW A LO DO YOU LIKE TO CHEW? I ONCE CHEW ON A SEWING MACHINE. LET ME TELL Y THAT WAS A MISTAKE. DID YOU KNO THOSE THINGS HAVE NEEDLES? YOWC WHAT I REALLY LIKE TO CHEW ON IS SHOES THOUGH. I ESPECIALLY LIKE RUBBER SOLES.
SHOULD HAVE TRADED WITH BLUEBEARY PIE...

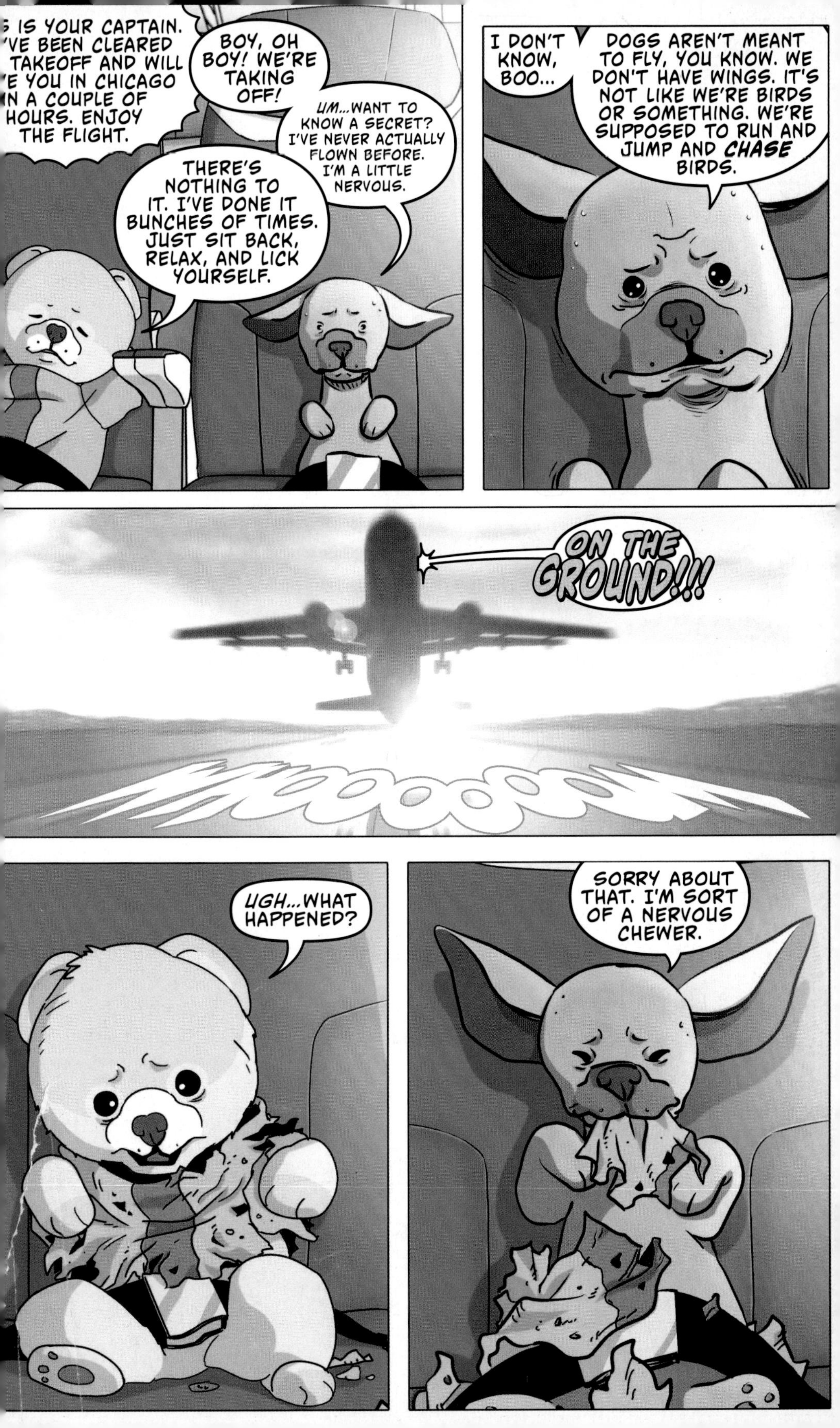

S IS YOUR CAPTAIN. 'VE BEEN CLEARED TAKEOFF AND WILL E YOU IN CHICAGO N A COUPLE OF HOURS. ENJOY THE FLIGHT.
BOY, OH BOY! WE'RE TAKING OFF!
UM...WANT TO KNOW A SECRET? I'VE NEVER ACTUALLY FLOWN BEFORE. I'M A LITTLE NERVOUS.
THERE'S NOTHING TO IT. I'VE DONE IT BUNCHES OF TIMES. JUST SIT BACK, RELAX, AND LICK YOURSELF.
I DON'T KNOW, BOO...
DOGS AREN'T MEANT TO FLY, YOU KNOW. WE DON'T HAVE WINGS. IT'S NOT LIKE WE'RE BIRDS OR SOMETHING. WE'RE SUPPOSED TO RUN AND JUMP AND *CHASE* BIRDS.
ON THE GROUND!!!
UGH...WHAT HAPPENED?
SORRY ABOUT THAT. I'M SORT OF A NERVOUS CHEWER.

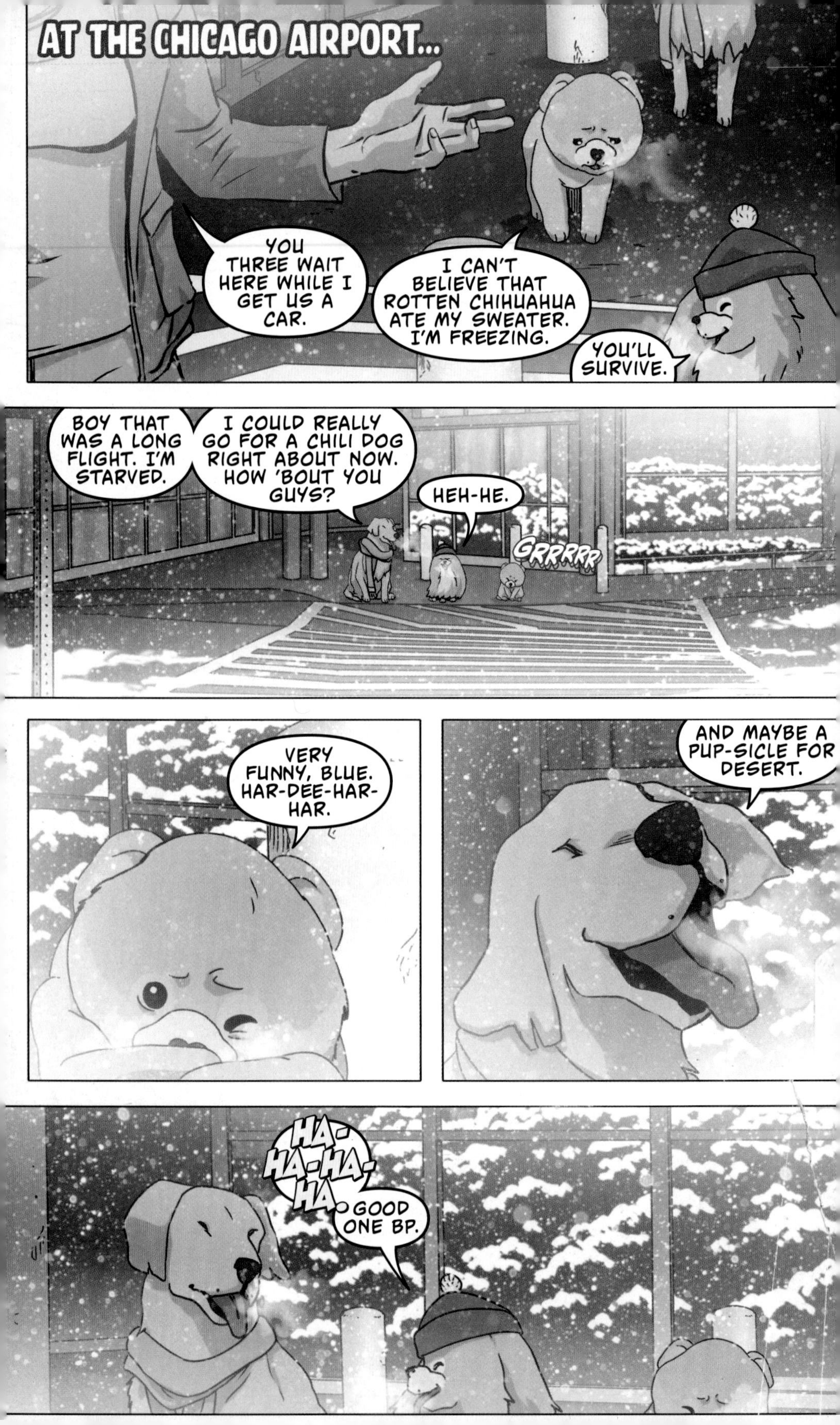
AT THE CHICAGO AIRPORT...
YOU THREE WAIT HERE WHILE I GET US A CAR.
I CAN'T BELIEVE THAT ROTTEN CHIHUAHUA ATE MY SWEATER. I'M FREEZING.
YOU'LL SURVIVE.
BOY THAT WAS A LONG FLIGHT. I'M STARVED.
I COULD REALLY GO FOR A CHILI DOG RIGHT ABOUT NOW. HOW 'BOUT YOU GUYS?
HEH-HE.
GRRRRR
VERY FUNNY, BLUE. HAR-DEE-HAR-HAR.
AND MAYBE A PUP-SICLE FOR DESERT.
HA-HA-HA-HA
GOOD ONE BP.

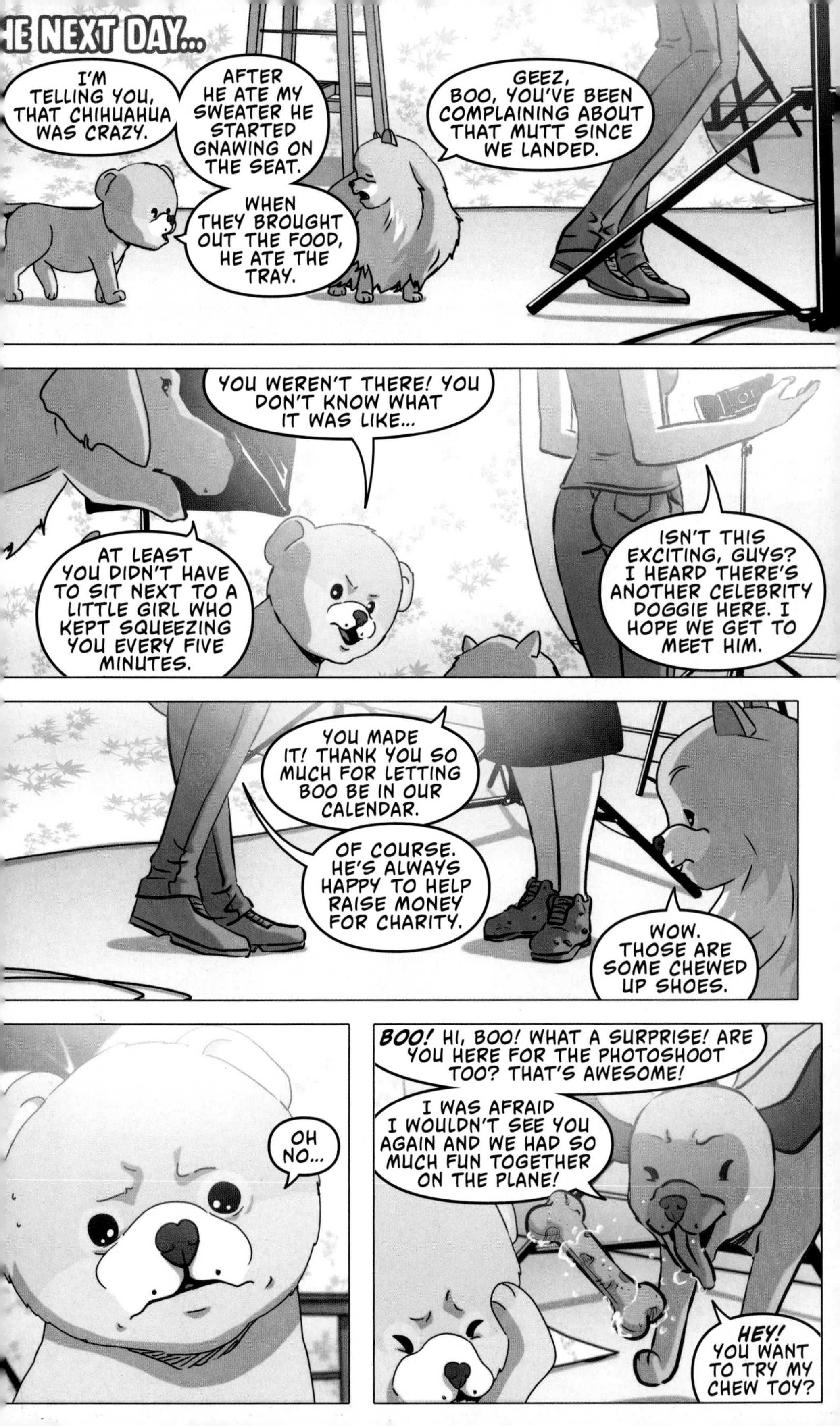

E NEXT DAY...
I'M TELLING YOU, THAT CHIHUAHUA WAS CRAZY.
AFTER HE ATE MY SWEATER HE STARTED GNAWING ON THE SEAT.
WHEN THEY BROUGHT OUT THE FOOD, HE ATE THE TRAY.
GEEZ, BOO, YOU'VE BEEN COMPLAINING ABOUT THAT MUTT SINCE WE LANDED.
YOU WEREN'T THERE! YOU DON'T KNOW WHAT IT WAS LIKE...
AT LEAST YOU DIDN'T HAVE TO SIT NEXT TO A LITTLE GIRL WHO KEPT SQUEEZING YOU EVERY FIVE MINUTES.
ISN'T THIS EXCITING, GUYS? I HEARD THERE'S ANOTHER CELEBRITY DOGGIE HERE. I HOPE WE GET TO MEET HIM.
YOU MADE IT! THANK YOU SO MUCH FOR LETTING BOO BE IN OUR CALENDAR.
OF COURSE. HE'S ALWAYS HAPPY TO HELP RAISE MONEY FOR CHARITY.
WOW. THOSE ARE SOME CHEWED UP SHOES.
OH NO...
BOO! HI, BOO! WHAT A SURPRISE! ARE YOU HERE FOR THE PHOTOSHOOT TOO? THAT'S AWESOME!
I WAS AFRAID I WOULDN'T SEE YOU AGAIN AND WE HAD SO MUCH FUN TOGETHER ON THE PLANE!
HEY! YOU WANT TO TRY MY CHEW TOY?

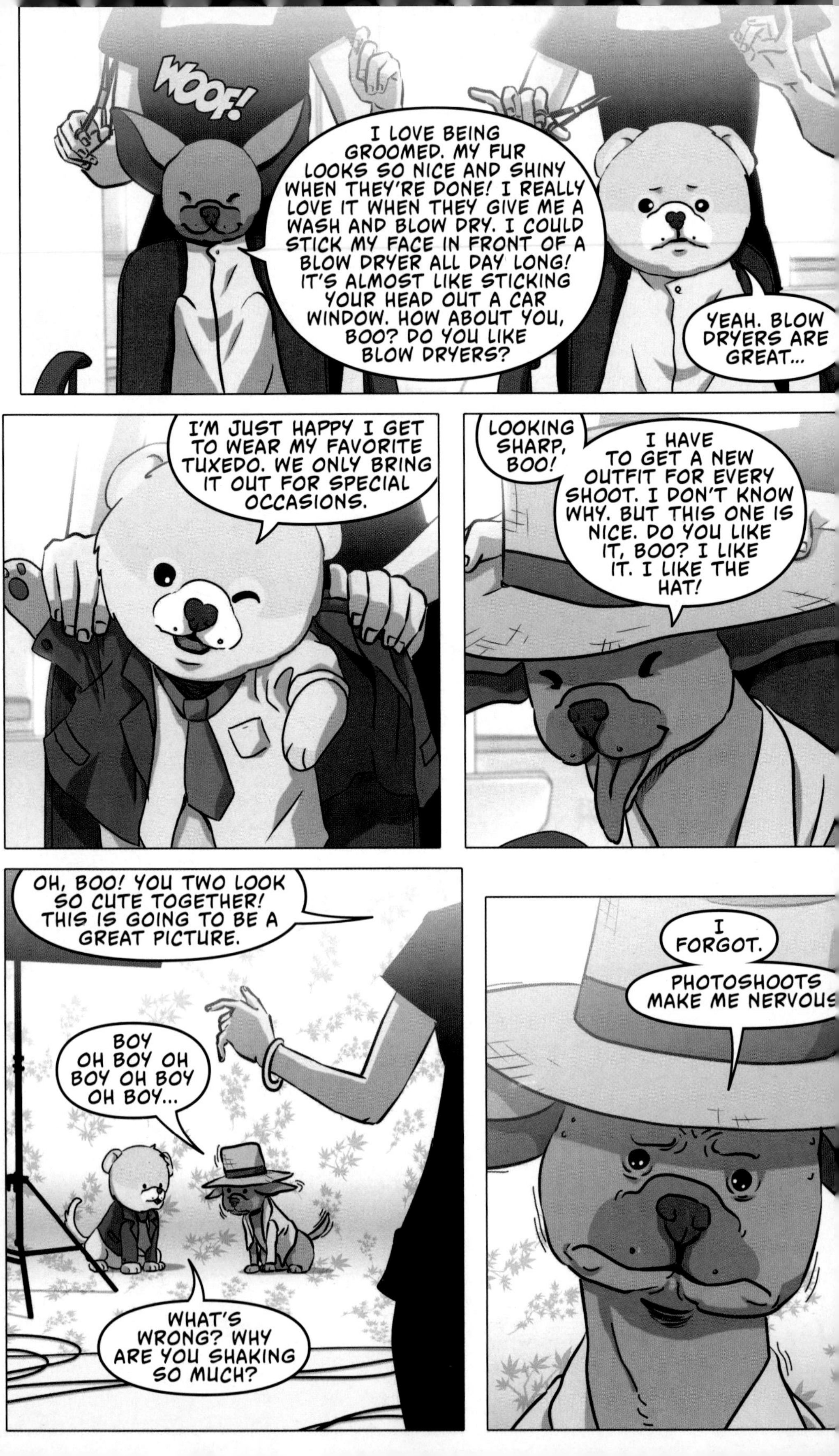
WOOF!
I LOVE BEING GROOMED. MY FUR LOOKS SO NICE AND SHINY WHEN THEY'RE DONE! I REALLY LOVE IT WHEN THEY GIVE ME A WASH AND BLOW DRY. I COULD STICK MY FACE IN FRONT OF A BLOW DRYER ALL DAY LONG! IT'S ALMOST LIKE STICKING YOUR HEAD OUT A CAR WINDOW. HOW ABOUT YOU, BOO? DO YOU LIKE BLOW DRYERS?
YEAH. BLOW DRYERS ARE GREAT...
I'M JUST HAPPY I GET TO WEAR MY FAVORITE TUXEDO. WE ONLY BRING IT OUT FOR SPECIAL OCCASIONS.
LOOKING SHARP, BOO!
I HAVE TO GET A NEW OUTFIT FOR EVERY SHOOT. I DON'T KNOW WHY. BUT THIS ONE IS NICE. DO YOU LIKE IT, BOO? I LIKE IT. I LIKE THE HAT!
OH, BOO! YOU TWO LOOK SO CUTE TOGETHER! THIS IS GOING TO BE A GREAT PICTURE.
BOY OH BOY OH BOY OH BOY OH BOY...
WHAT'S WRONG? WHY ARE YOU SHAKING SO MUCH?
I FORGOT.
PHOTOSHOOTS MAKE ME NERVOUS

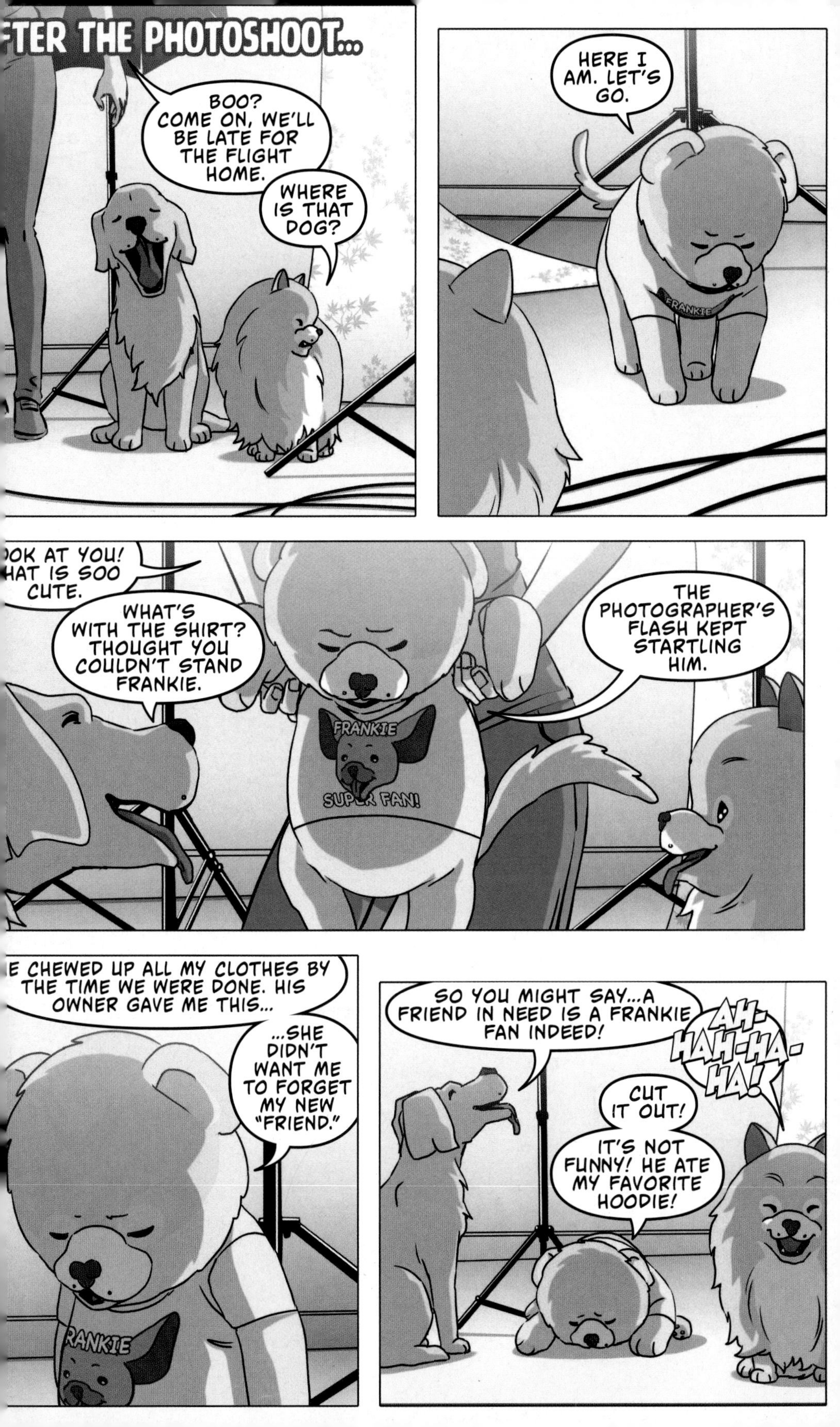

TER THE PHOTOSHOOT...
BOO? COME ON, WE'LL BE LATE FOR THE FLIGHT HOME.
WHERE IS THAT DOG?
HERE I AM. LET'S GO.
FRANKIE
OK AT YOU! HAT IS SOO CUTE.
WHAT'S WITH THE SHIRT? THOUGHT YOU COULDN'T STAND FRANKIE.
THE PHOTOGRAPHER'S FLASH KEPT STARTLING HIM.
FRANKIE
SUPER FAN!
E CHEWED UP ALL MY CLOTHES BY THE TIME WE WERE DONE. HIS OWNER GAVE ME THIS...
...SHE DIDN'T WANT ME TO FORGET MY NEW "FRIEND."
RANKIE
SO YOU MIGHT SAY...A FRIEND IN NEED IS A FRANKIE FAN INDEED!
AH-HAH-HA-HA!
CUT IT OUT!
IT'S NOT FUNNY! HE ATE MY FAVORITE HOODIE!

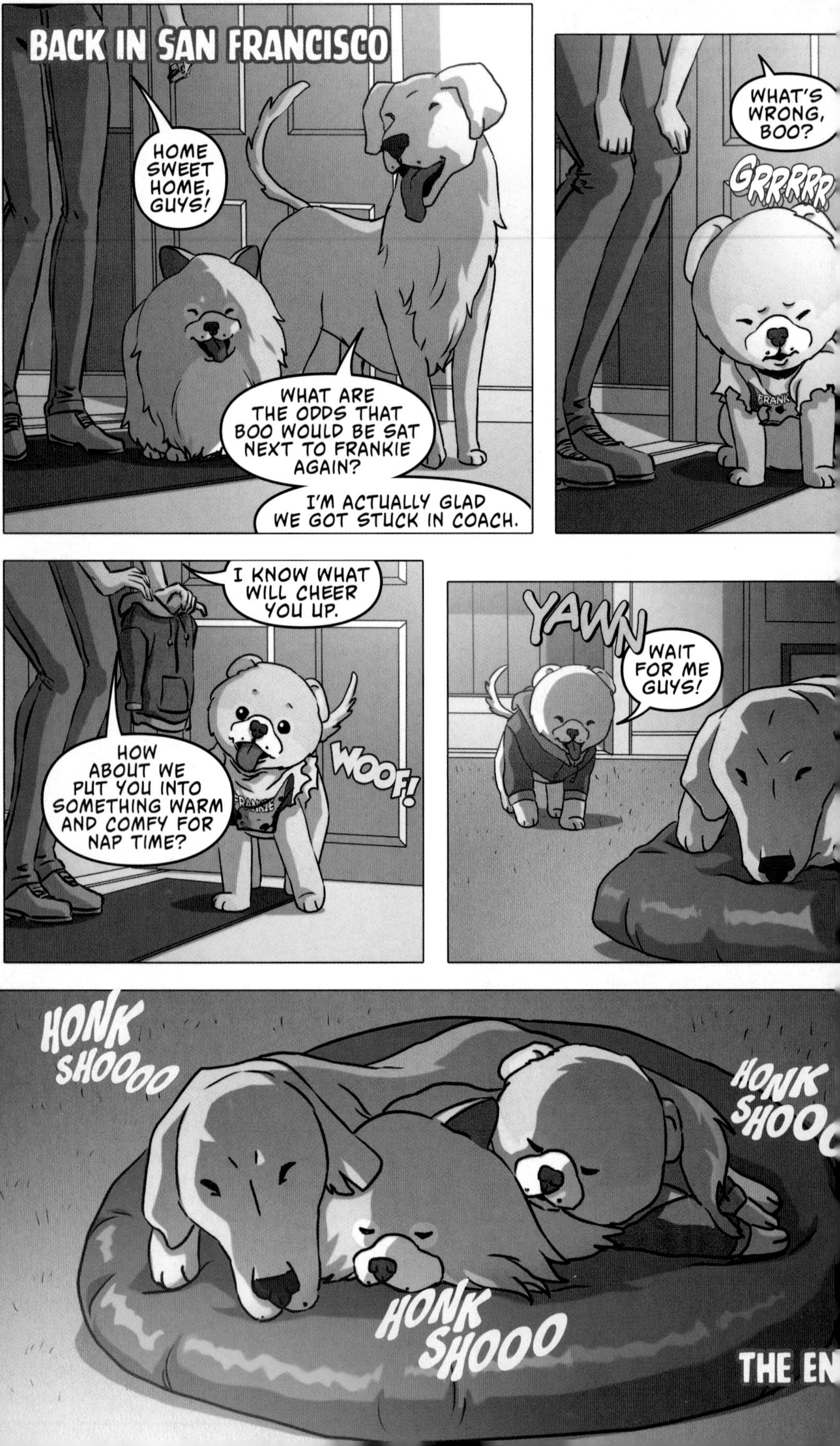
BACK IN SAN FRANCISCO
HOME SWEET HOME, GUYS!
WHAT ARE THE ODDS THAT BOO WOULD BE SAT NEXT TO FRANKIE AGAIN?
I'M ACTUALLY GLAD WE GOT STUCK IN COACH.
WHAT'S WRONG, BOO?
GRRRRR
FRANKIE
I KNOW WHAT WILL CHEER YOU UP.
HOW ABOUT WE PUT YOU INTO SOMETHING WARM AND COMFY FOR NAP TIME?
FRANKIE
WOOF!
YAWN
WAIT FOR ME GUYS!
HONK SHOOOO
HONK SHOOO
HONK SHOOO
THE EN

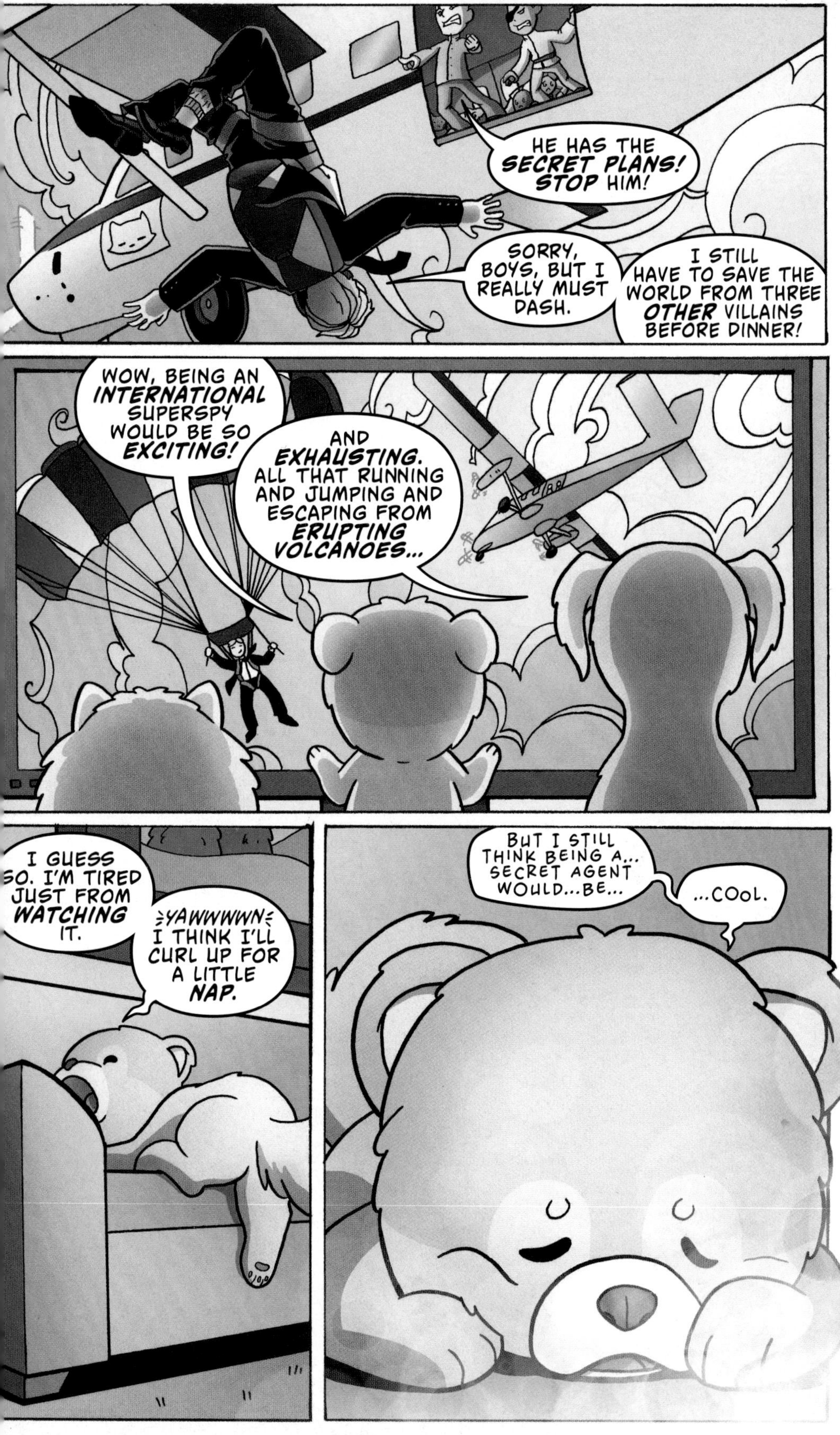
HE HAS THE SECRET PLANS! STOP HIM!
SORRY, BOYS, BUT I REALLY MUST DASH.
I STILL HAVE TO SAVE THE WORLD FROM THREE OTHER VILLAINS BEFORE DINNER!
WOW, BEING AN INTERNATIONAL SUPERSPY WOULD BE SO EXCITING!
AND EXHAUSTING. ALL THAT RUNNING AND JUMPING AND ESCAPING FROM ERUPTING VOLCANOES...
I GUESS SO. I'M TIRED JUST FROM WATCHING IT.
YAWWWWN I THINK I'LL CURL UP FOR A LITTLE NAP.
BUT I STILL THINK BEING A... SECRET AGENT WOULD...BE...
...COOL.

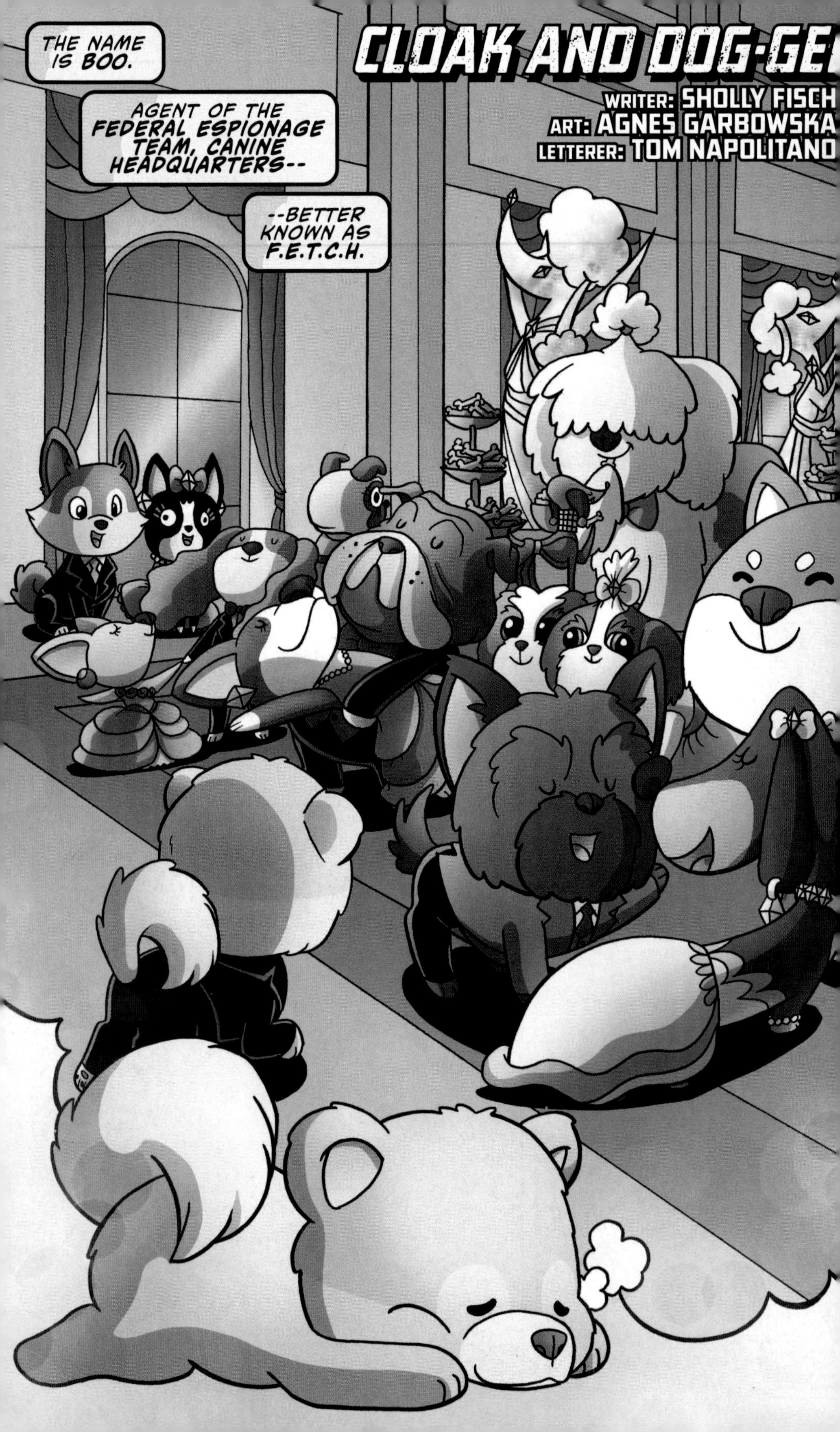
THE NAME IS BOO.
AGENT OF THE FEDERAL ESPIONAGE TEAM, CANINE HEADQUARTERS--
--BETTER KNOWN AS F.E.T.C.H.
CLOAK AND DOG-GE
WRITER: SHOLLY FISCH
ART: AGNES GARBOWSKA
LETTERER: TOM NAPOLITANO

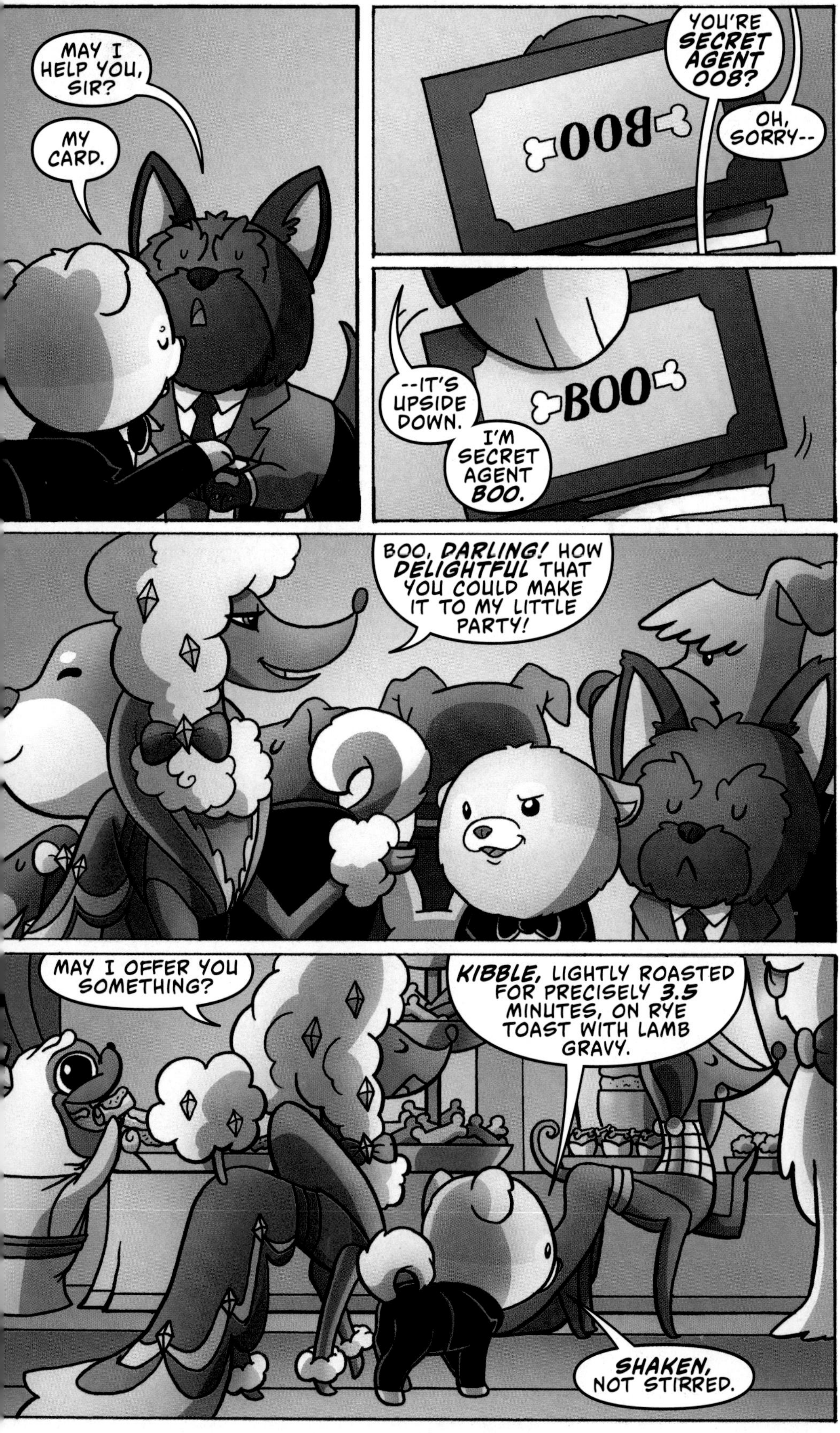

MAY I HELP YOU, SIR?
MY CARD.
YOU'RE SECRET AGENT 008?
BOO
OH, SORRY--
BOO
--IT'S UPSIDE DOWN.
I'M SECRET AGENT BOO.
BOO, DARLING! HOW DELIGHTFUL THAT YOU COULD MAKE IT TO MY LITTLE PARTY!
MAY I OFFER YOU SOMETHING?
KIBBLE, LIGHTLY ROASTED FOR PRECISELY 3.5 MINUTES, ON RYE TOAST WITH LAMB GRAVY.
SHAKEN, NOT STIRRED.

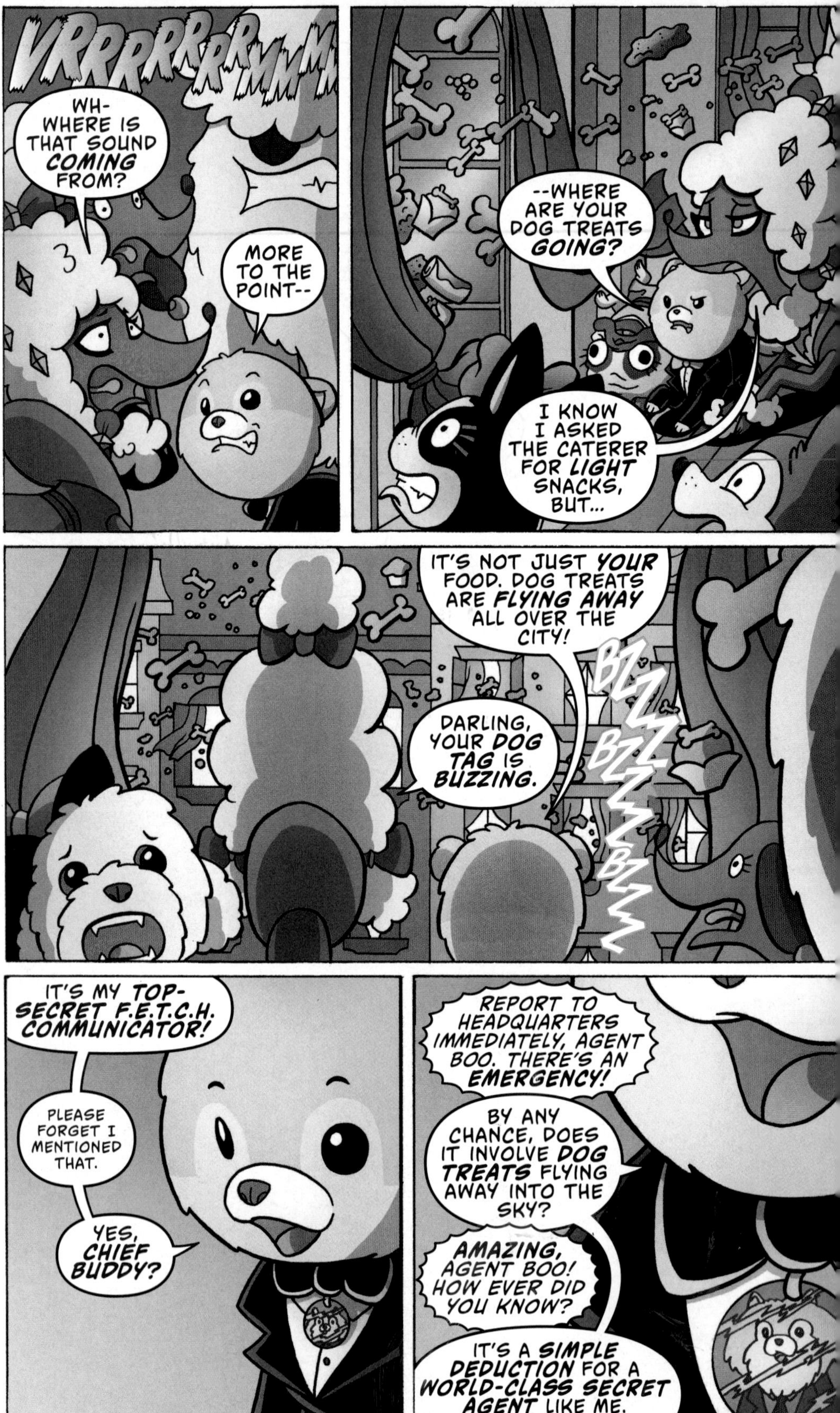
VRRRRRRRMMM
WH- WHERE IS THAT SOUND COMING FROM?
MORE TO THE POINT--
--WHERE ARE YOUR DOG TREATS GOING?
I KNOW I ASKED THE CATERER FOR LIGHT SNACKS, BUT...
IT'S NOT JUST YOUR FOOD. DOG TREATS ARE FLYING AWAY ALL OVER THE CITY!
DARLING, YOUR DOG TAG IS BUZZING.
BZZ BZZ BZZ
IT'S MY TOP-SECRET F.E.T.C.H. COMMUNICATOR!
PLEASE FORGET I MENTIONED THAT.
YES, CHIEF BUDDY?
REPORT TO HEADQUARTERS IMMEDIATELY, AGENT BOO. THERE'S AN EMERGENCY!
BY ANY CHANCE, DOES IT INVOLVE DOG TREATS FLYING AWAY INTO THE SKY?
AMAZING, AGENT BOO! HOW EVER DID YOU KNOW?
IT'S A SIMPLE DEDUCTION FOR A WORLD-CLASS SECRET AGENT LIKE ME.

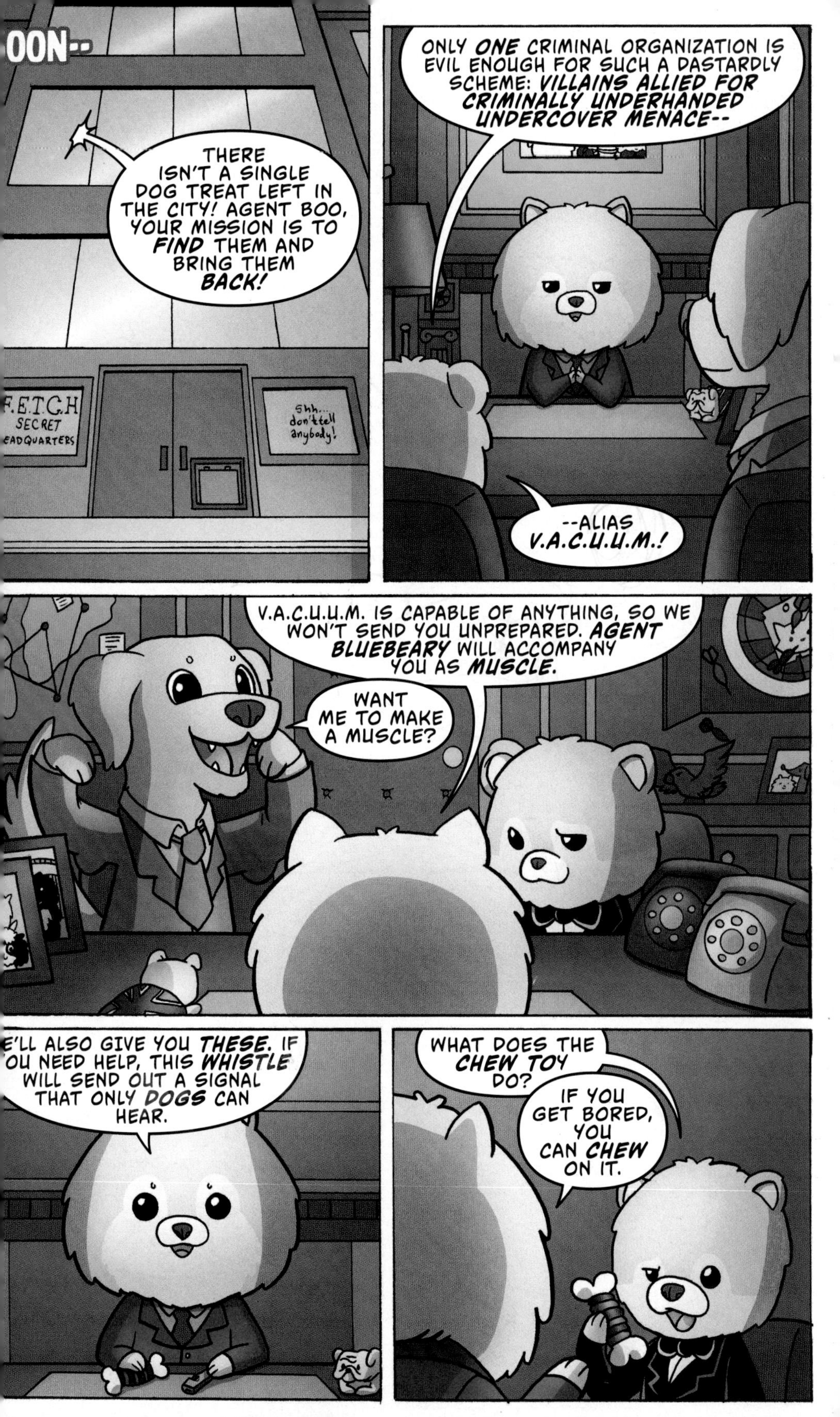
OON--
THERE ISN'T A SINGLE DOG TREAT LEFT IN THE CITY! AGENT BOO, YOUR MISSION IS TO FIND THEM AND BRING THEM BACK!
F.E.T.C.H SECRET EADQUARTERS
Shh... don't tell anybody!
ONLY ONE CRIMINAL ORGANIZATION IS EVIL ENOUGH FOR SUCH A DASTARDLY SCHEME: VILLAINS ALLIED FOR CRIMINALLY UNDERHANDED UNDERCOVER MENACE--
--ALIAS V.A.C.U.U.M.!
V.A.C.U.U.M. IS CAPABLE OF ANYTHING, SO WE WON'T SEND YOU UNPREPARED. AGENT BLUEBEARY WILL ACCOMPANY YOU AS MUSCLE.
WANT ME TO MAKE A MUSCLE?
E'LL ALSO GIVE YOU THESE. IF OU NEED HELP, THIS WHISTLE WILL SEND OUT A SIGNAL THAT ONLY DOGS CAN HEAR.
WHAT DOES THE CHEW TOY DO?
IF YOU GET BORED, YOU CAN CHEW ON IT.

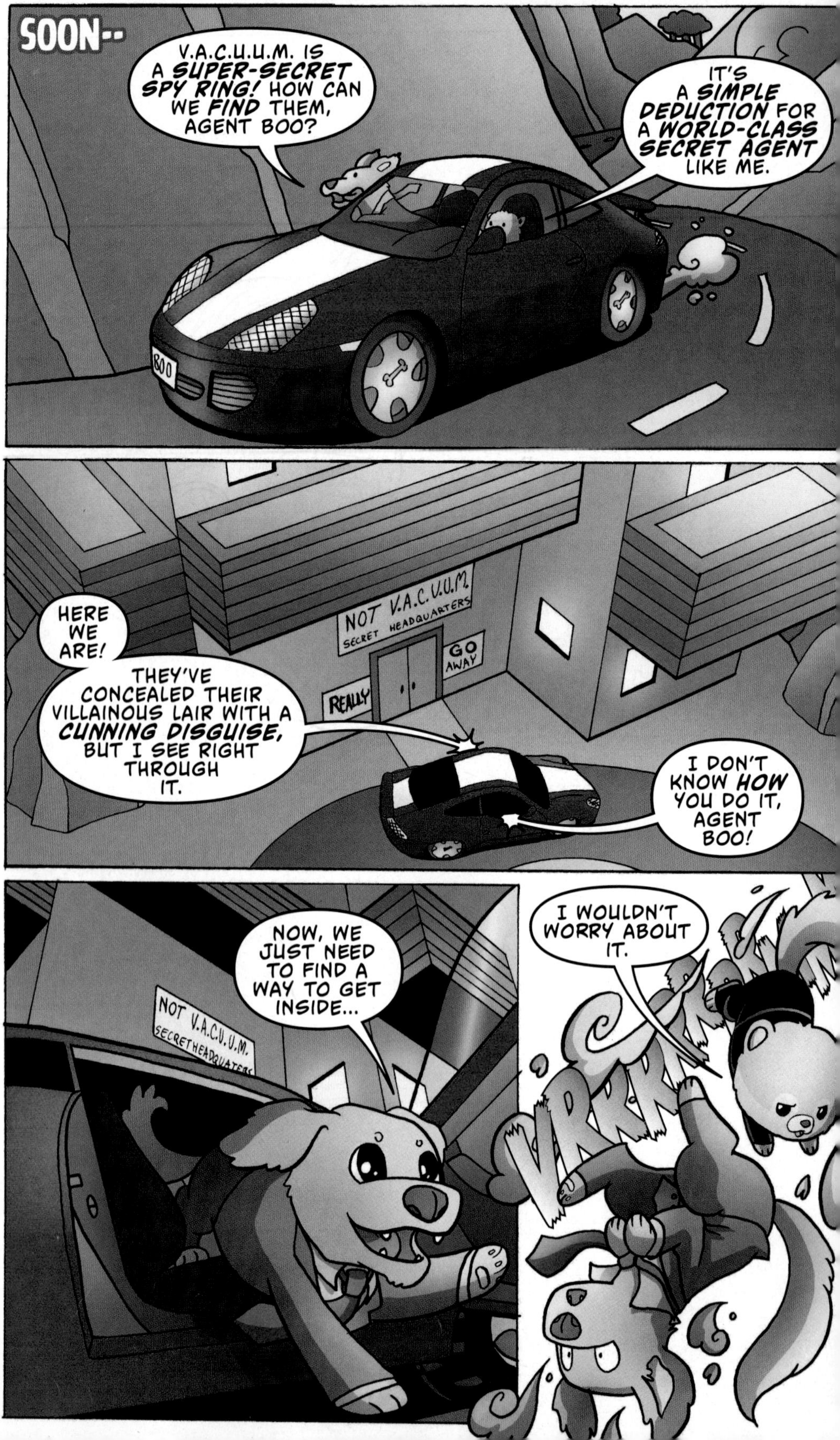
SOON--
V.A.C.U.U.M. IS A SUPER-SECRET SPY RING! HOW CAN WE FIND THEM, AGENT BOO?
IT'S A SIMPLE DEDUCTION FOR A WORLD-CLASS SECRET AGENT LIKE ME.
BOO
NOT V.A.C.U.U.M. SECRET HEADQUARTERS
GO AWAY
REALLY
HERE WE ARE!
THEY'VE CONCEALED THEIR VILLAINOUS LAIR WITH A CUNNING DISGUISE, BUT I SEE RIGHT THROUGH IT.
I DON'T KNOW HOW YOU DO IT, AGENT BOO!
NOT V.A.C.U.U.M. SECRETHEADQUATERS
NOW, WE JUST NEED TO FIND A WAY TO GET INSIDE...
I WOULDN'T WORRY ABOUT IT.
VRRRR

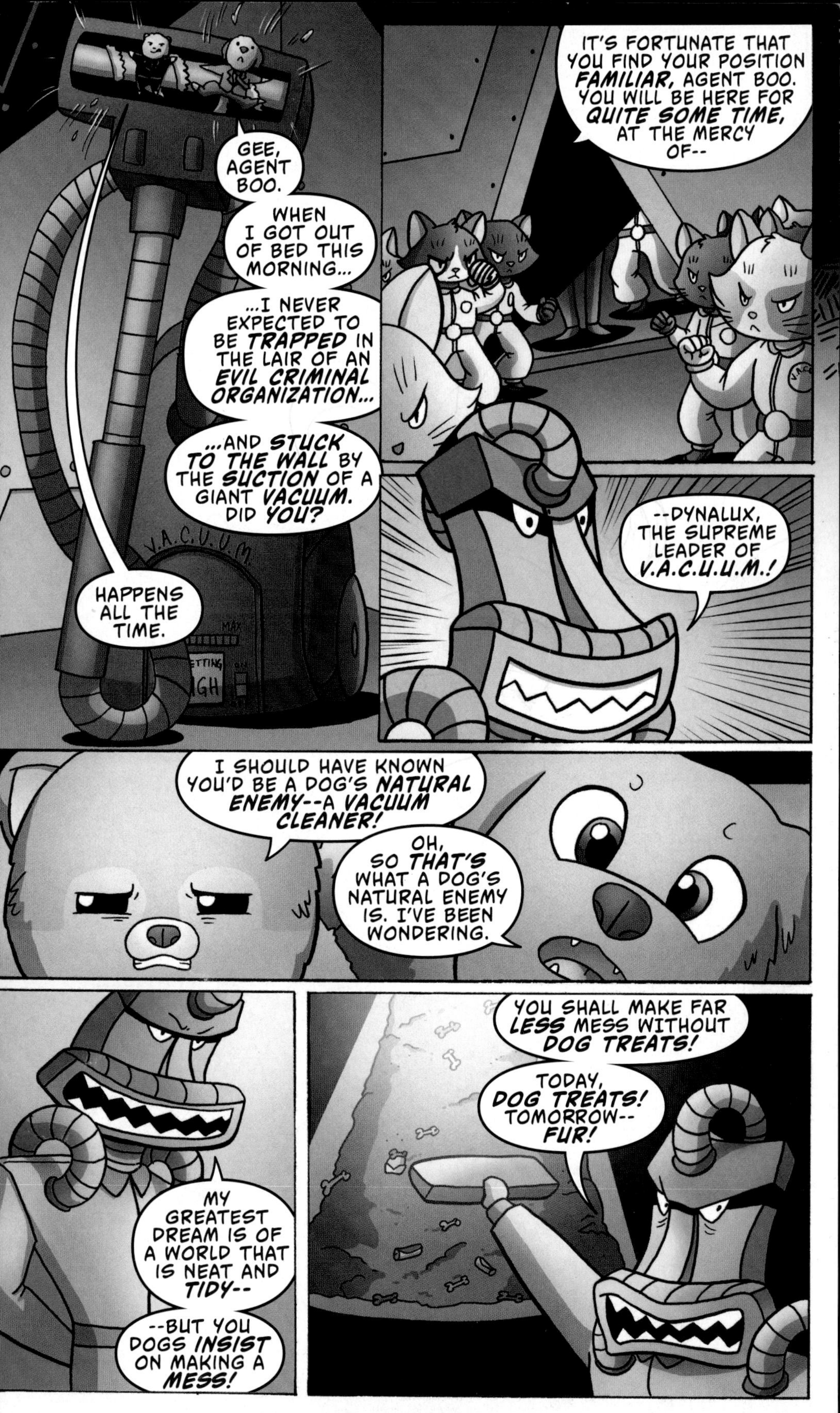
GEE, AGENT BOO.
WHEN I GOT OUT OF BED THIS MORNING...
...I NEVER EXPECTED TO BE TRAPPED IN THE LAIR OF AN EVIL CRIMINAL ORGANIZATION...
...AND STUCK TO THE WALL BY THE SUCTION OF A GIANT VACUUM. DID YOU?
HAPPENS ALL THE TIME.
V.A.C.U.U.M.
MAX
IT'S FORTUNATE THAT YOU FIND YOUR POSITION FAMILIAR, AGENT BOO. YOU WILL BE HERE FOR QUITE SOME TIME, AT THE MERCY OF--
--DYNALUX, THE SUPREME LEADER OF V.A.C.U.U.M.!
I SHOULD HAVE KNOWN YOU'D BE A DOG'S NATURAL ENEMY--A VACUUM CLEANER!
OH, SO THAT'S WHAT A DOG'S NATURAL ENEMY IS. I'VE BEEN WONDERING.
MY GREATEST DREAM IS OF A WORLD THAT IS NEAT AND TIDY--
--BUT YOU DOGS INSIST ON MAKING A MESS!
YOU SHALL MAKE FAR LESS MESS WITHOUT DOG TREATS!
TODAY, DOG TREATS! TOMORROW-- FUR!

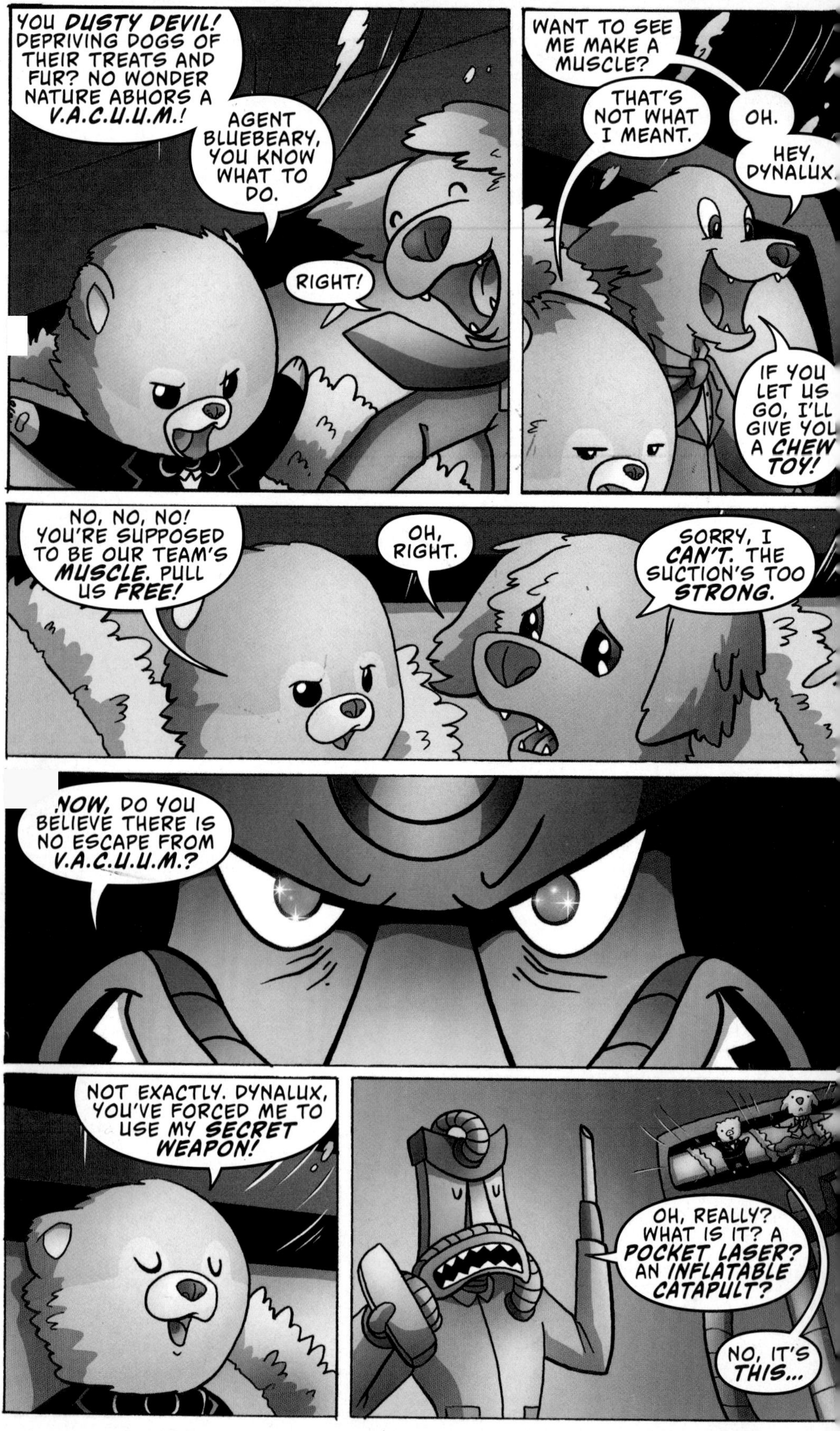
YOU DUSTY DEVIL! DEPRIVING DOGS OF THEIR TREATS AND FUR? NO WONDER NATURE ABHORS A V.A.C.U.U.M.!
AGENT BLUEBEARY, YOU KNOW WHAT TO DO.
RIGHT!
WANT TO SEE ME MAKE A MUSCLE?
THAT'S NOT WHAT I MEANT.
OH.
HEY, DYNALUX.
IF YOU LET US GO, I'LL GIVE YOU A CHEW TOY!
NO, NO, NO! YOU'RE SUPPOSED TO BE OUR TEAM'S MUSCLE. PULL US FREE!
OH, RIGHT.
SORRY, I CAN'T. THE SUCTION'S TOO STRONG.
NOW, DO YOU BELIEVE THERE IS NO ESCAPE FROM V.A.C.U.U.M.?
NOT EXACTLY. DYNALUX, YOU'VE FORCED ME TO USE MY SECRET WEAPON!
OH, REALLY? WHAT IS IT? A POCKET LASER? AN INFLATABLE CATAPULT?
NO, IT'S THIS...

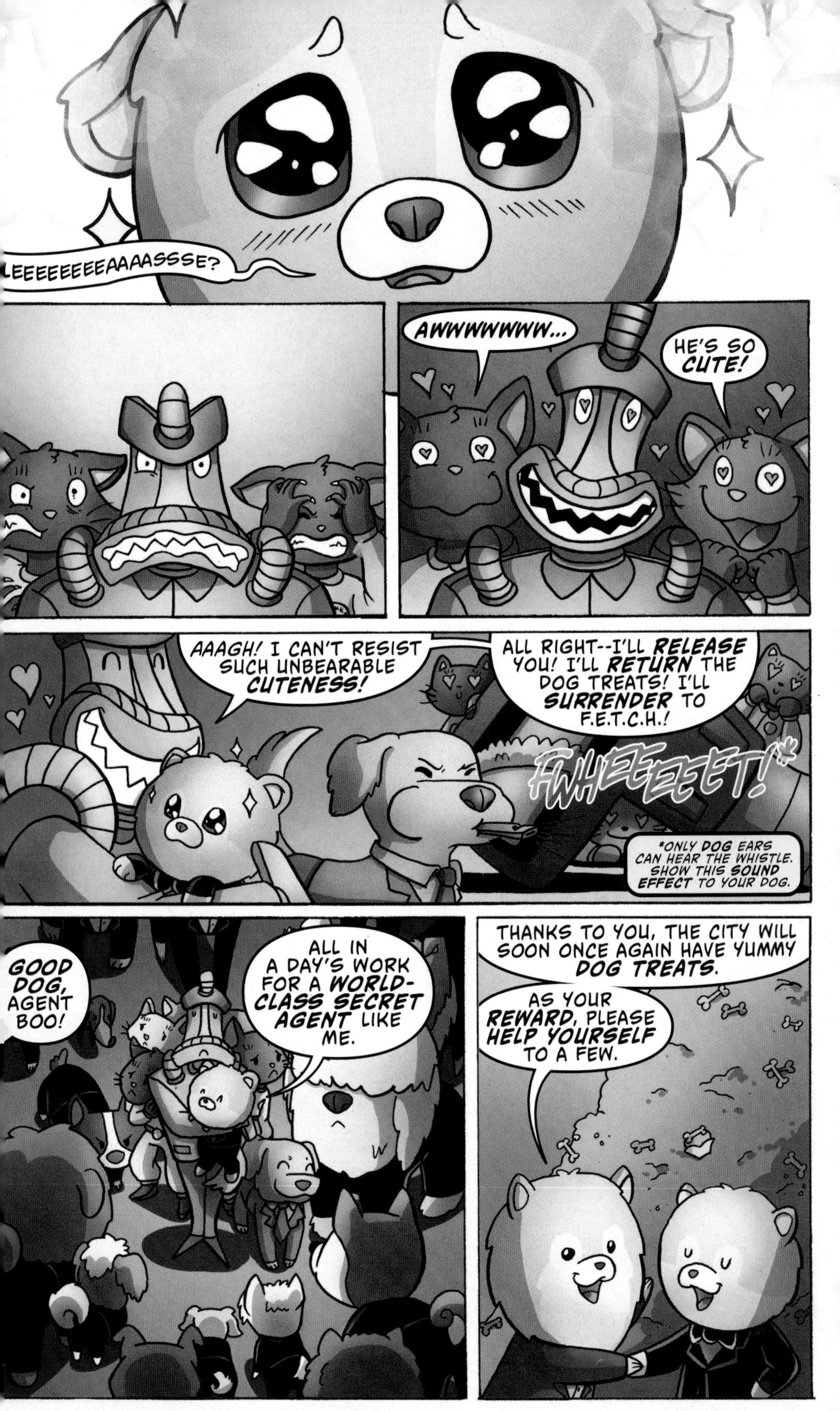
LEEEEEEEEAAAASSSE?
AWWWWWWW...
HE'S SO CUTE!
AAAGH! I CAN'T RESIST SUCH UNBEARABLE CUTENESS!
ALL RIGHT--I'LL RELEASE YOU! I'LL RETURN THE DOG TREATS! I'LL SURRENDER TO F.E.T.C.H.!
FWHEEEEEET!*
*ONLY DOG EARS CAN HEAR THE WHISTLE. SHOW THIS SOUND EFFECT TO YOUR DOG.
GOOD DOG, AGENT BOO!
ALL IN A DAY'S WORK FOR A WORLD-CLASS SECRET AGENT LIKE ME.
THANKS TO YOU, THE CITY WILL SOON ONCE AGAIN HAVE YUMMY DOG TREATS.
AS YOUR REWARD, PLEASE HELP YOURSELF TO A FEW.

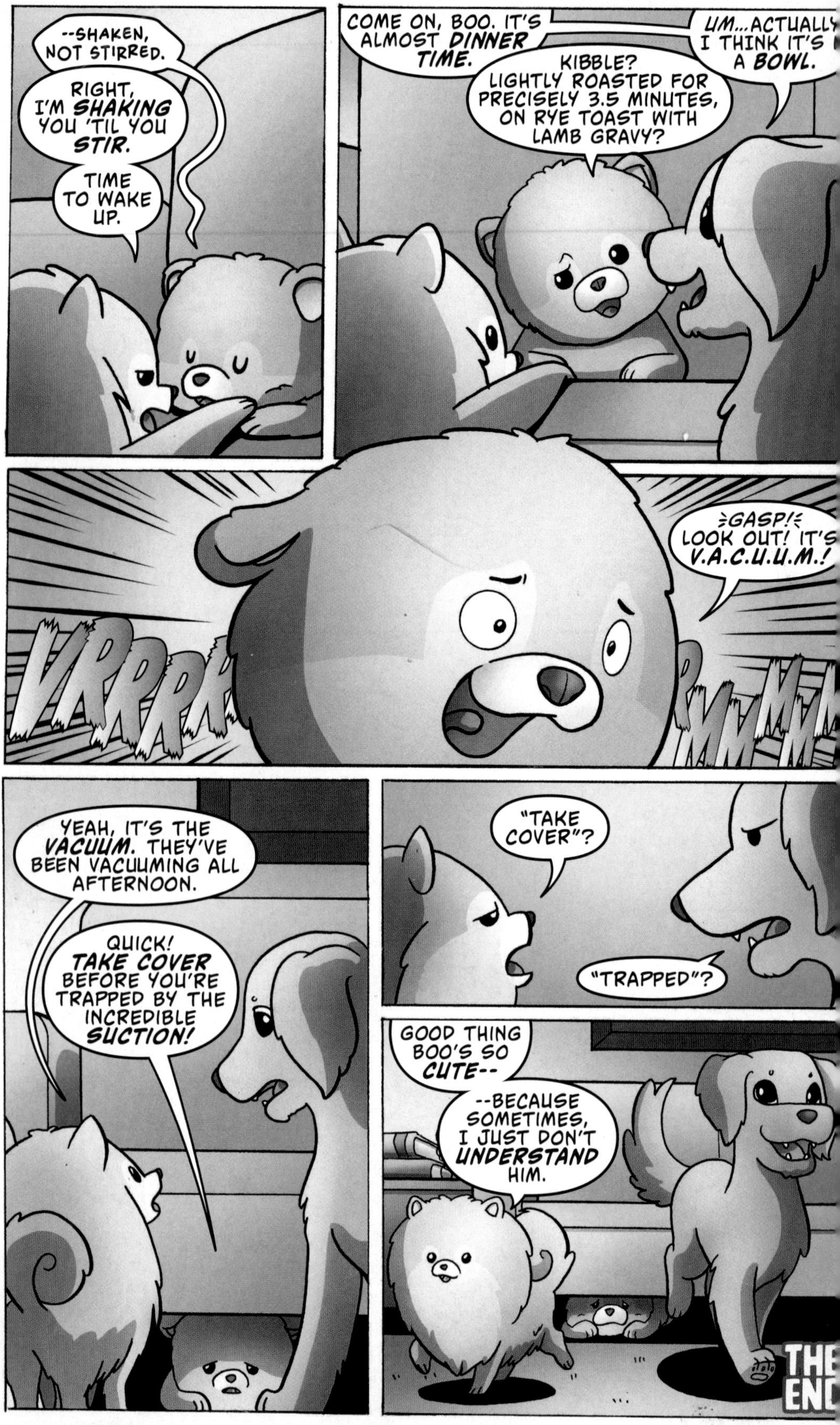
--SHAKEN, NOT STIRRED.
RIGHT, I'M SHAKING YOU 'TIL YOU STIR.
TIME TO WAKE UP.
COME ON, BOO. IT'S ALMOST DINNER TIME.
KIBBLE? LIGHTLY ROASTED FOR PRECISELY 3.5 MINUTES, ON RYE TOAST WITH LAMB GRAVY?
UM...ACTUALLY I THINK IT'S A BOWL.
VRRRR
RMMMM
GASP! LOOK OUT! IT'S V.A.C.U.U.M.!
YEAH, IT'S THE VACUUM. THEY'VE BEEN VACUUMING ALL AFTERNOON.
QUICK! TAKE COVER BEFORE YOU'RE TRAPPED BY THE INCREDIBLE SUCTION!
"TAKE COVER"?
"TRAPPED"?
GOOD THING BOO'S SO CUTE--
--BECAUSE SOMETIMES, I JUST DON'T UNDERSTAND HIM.
THE END

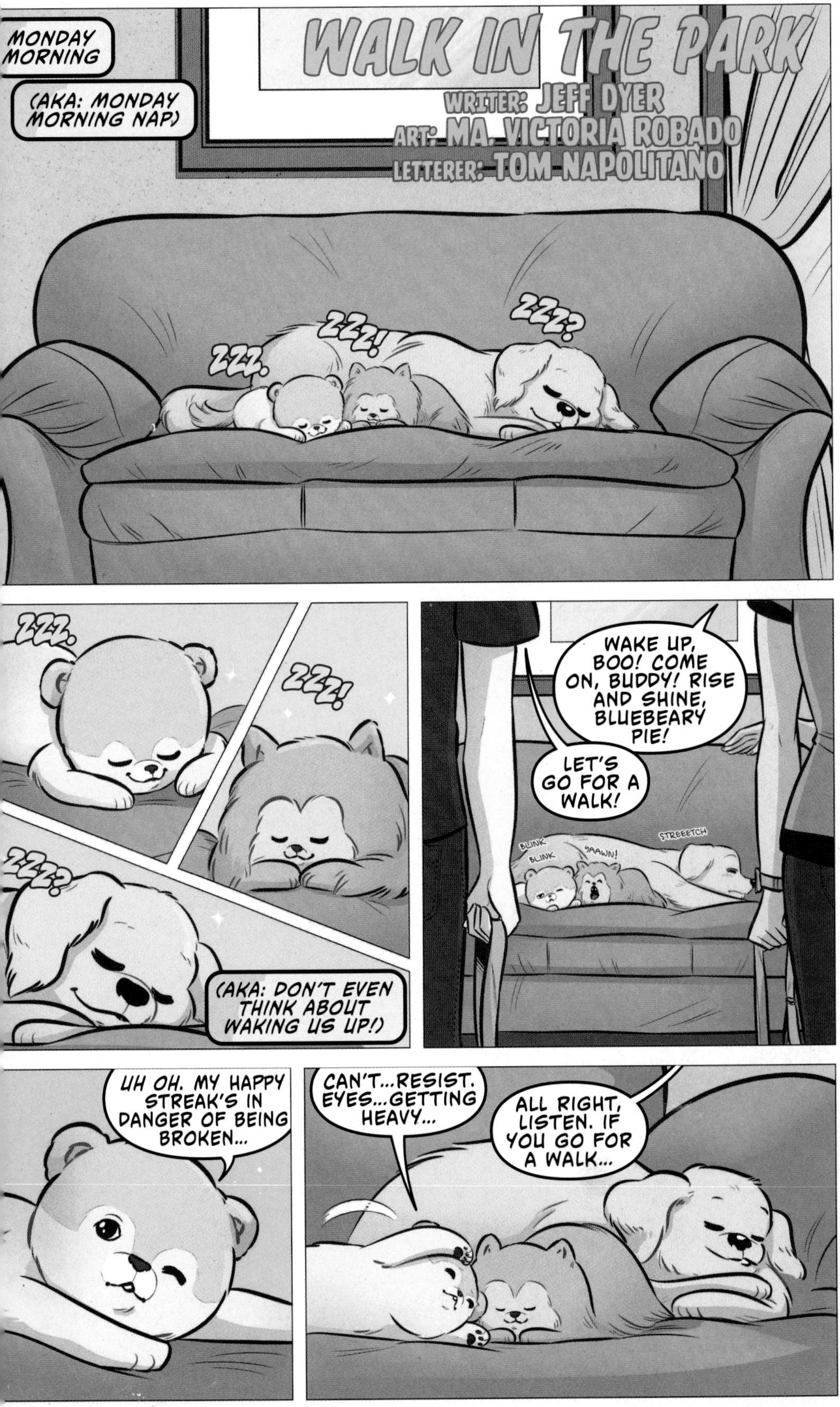
MONDAY MORNING
(AKA: MONDAY MORNING NAP)
WALK IN THE PARK
WRITER: JEFF DYER
ART: MA. VICTORIA ROBADO
LETTERER: TOM NAPOLITANO
ZZZ.
ZZZ!
ZZZ?
ZZZ.
ZZZ!
ZZZ?
(AKA: DON'T EVEN THINK ABOUT WAKING US UP!)
WAKE UP, BOO! COME ON, BUDDY! RISE AND SHINE, BLUEBEARY PIE!
LET'S GO FOR A WALK!
BLINK
BLINK
YAAWN!
STREEETCH
UH OH. MY HAPPY STREAK'S IN DANGER OF BEING BROKEN...
CAN'T...RESIST. EYES...GETTING HEAVY...
ALL RIGHT, LISTEN. IF YOU GO FOR A WALK...

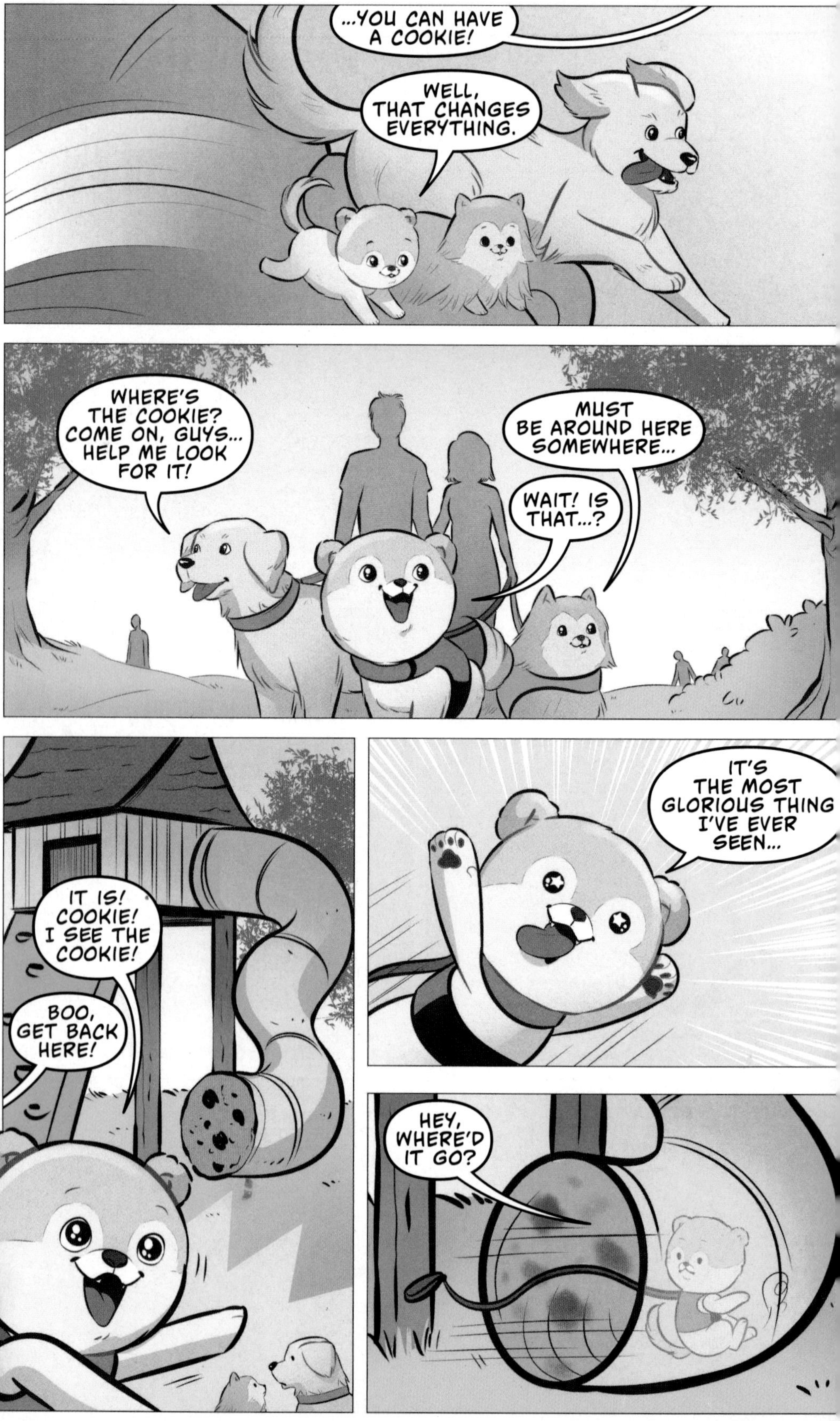
...YOU CAN HAVE A COOKIE!
WELL, THAT CHANGES EVERYTHING.
WHERE'S THE COOKIE? COME ON, GUYS... HELP ME LOOK FOR IT!
MUST BE AROUND HERE SOMEWHERE...
WAIT! IS THAT...?
IT IS! COOKIE! I SEE THE COOKIE!
BOO, GET BACK HERE!
IT'S THE MOST GLORIOUS THING I'VE EVER SEEN...
HEY, WHERE'D IT GO?

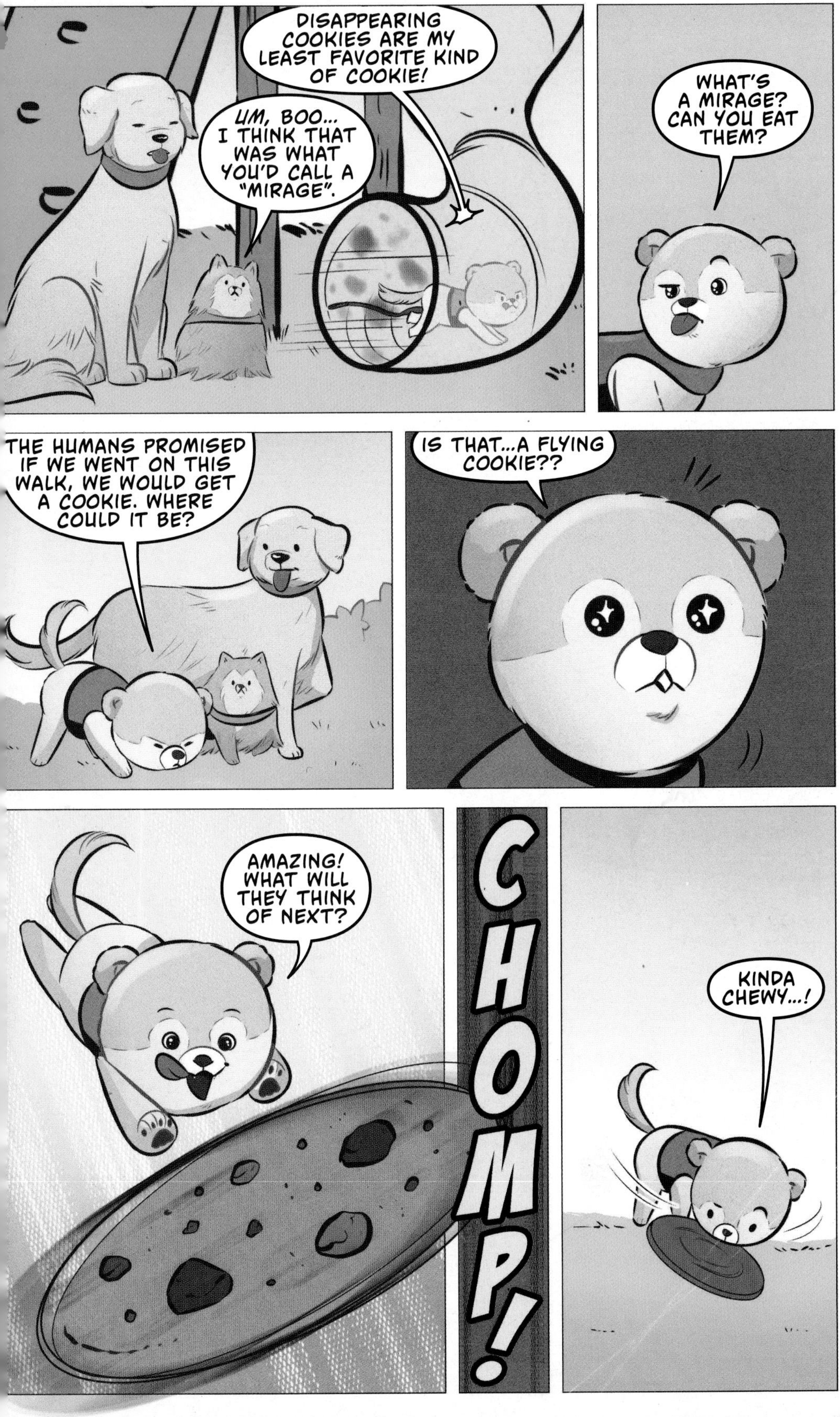
UM, BOO... I THINK THAT WAS WHAT YOU'D CALL A "MIRAGE".
DISAPPEARING COOKIES ARE MY LEAST FAVORITE KIND OF COOKIE!
WHAT'S A MIRAGE? CAN YOU EAT THEM?
THE HUMANS PROMISED IF WE WENT ON THIS WALK, WE WOULD GET A COOKIE. WHERE COULD IT BE?
IS THAT...A FLYING COOKIE??
AMAZING! WHAT WILL THEY THINK OF NEXT?
CHOMP!
KINDA CHEWY...!

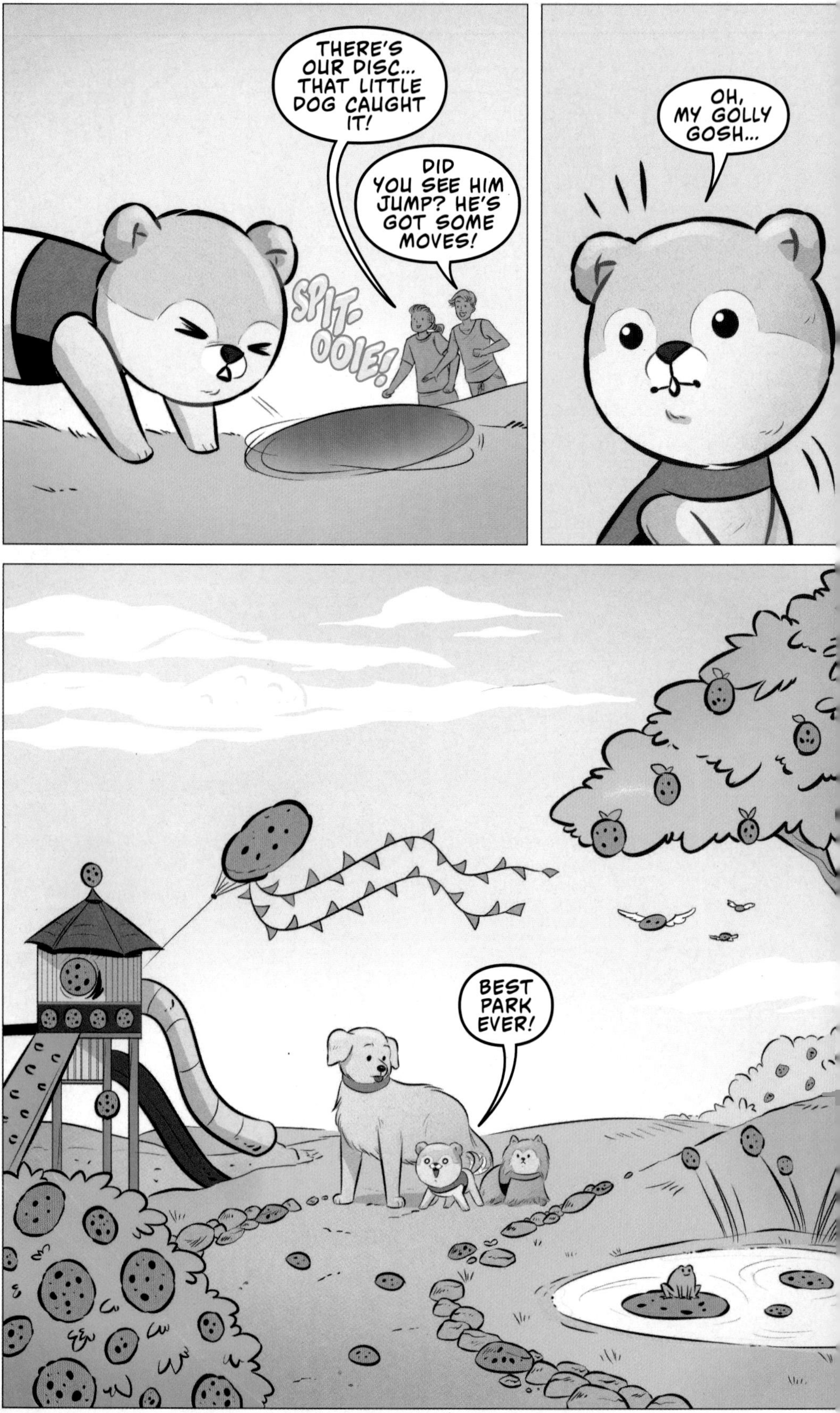
THERE'S OUR DISC... THAT LITTLE DOG CAUGHT IT!
DID YOU SEE HIM JUMP? HE'S GOT SOME MOVES!
SPIT-OOIE!
OH, MY GOLLY GOSH...
BEST PARK EVER!

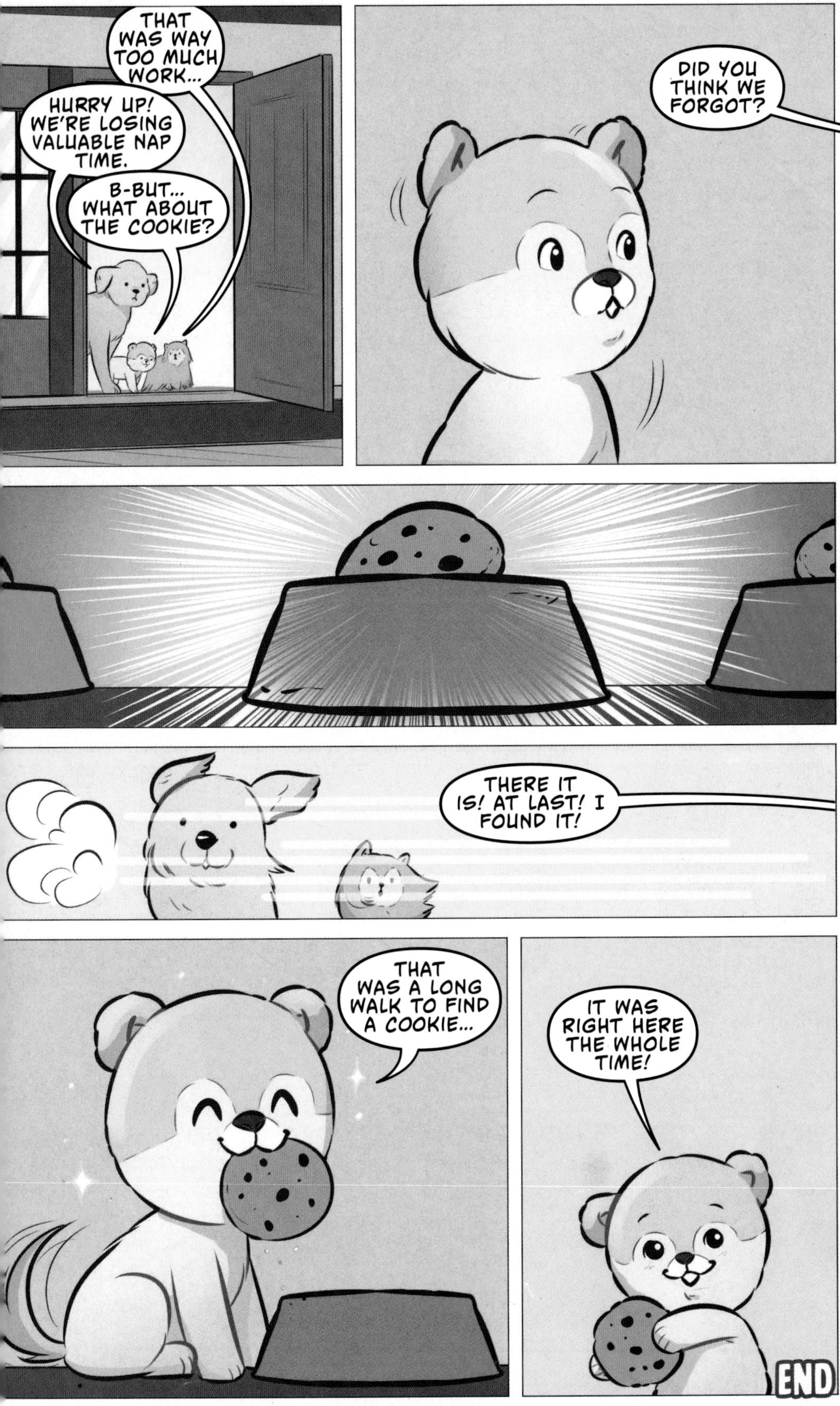
THAT WAS WAY TOO MUCH WORK...
HURRY UP! WE'RE LOSING VALUABLE NAP TIME.
B-BUT... WHAT ABOUT THE COOKIE?
DID YOU THINK WE FORGOT?
THERE IT IS! AT LAST! I FOUND IT!
THAT WAS A LONG WALK TO FIND A COOKIE...
IT WAS RIGHT HERE THE WHOLE TIME!
END

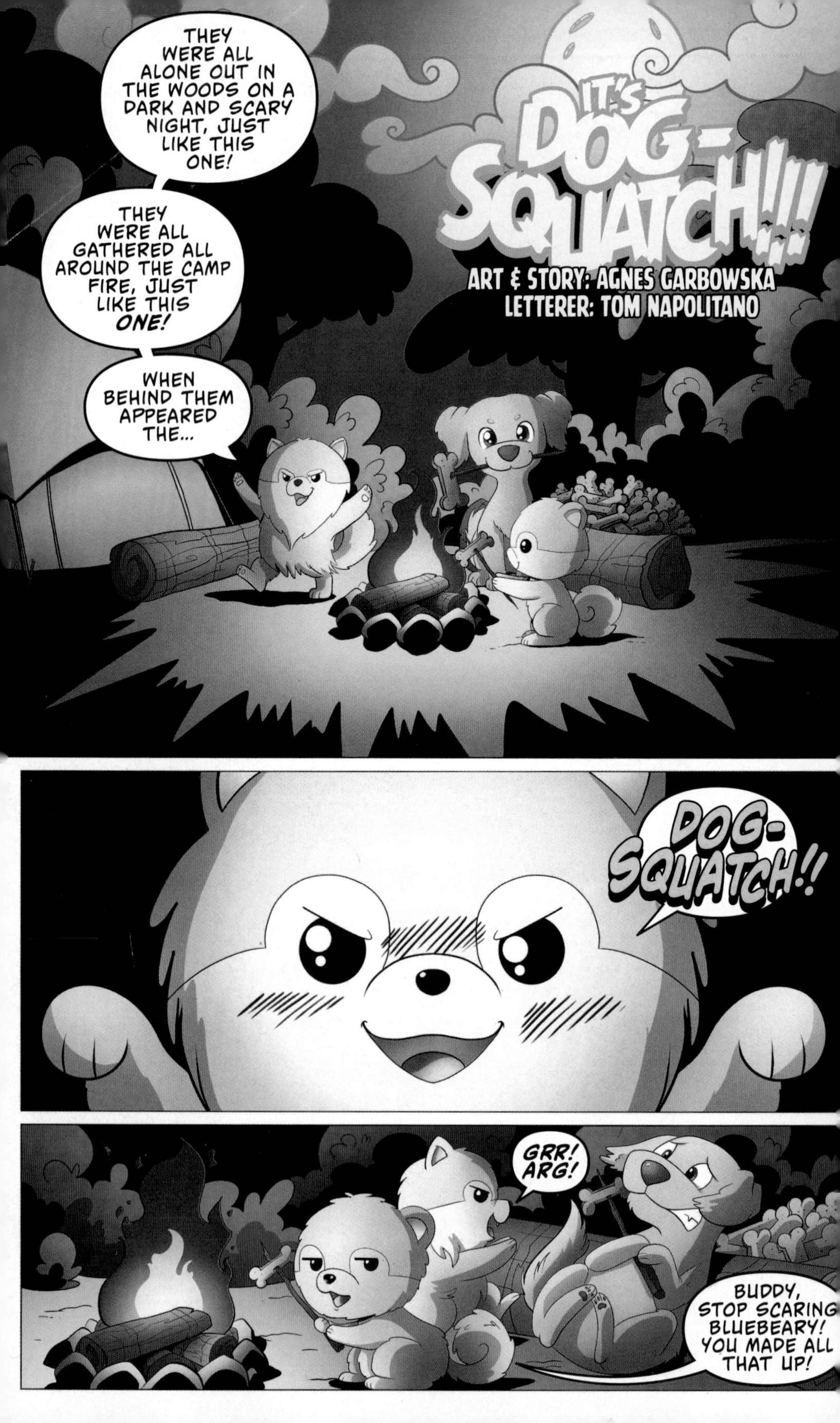
IT'S DOG-SQUATCH!!!
ART & STORY: AGNES GARBOWSKA
LETTERER: TOM NAPOLITANO
THEY WERE ALL ALONE OUT IN THE WOODS ON A DARK AND SCARY NIGHT, JUST LIKE THIS ONE!
THEY WERE ALL GATHERED ALL AROUND THE CAMP FIRE, JUST LIKE THIS ONE!
WHEN BEHIND THEM APPEARED THE...
DOG-SQUATCH!!
GRR! ARG!
BUDDY, STOP SCARING BLUEBEARY! YOU MADE ALL THAT UP!

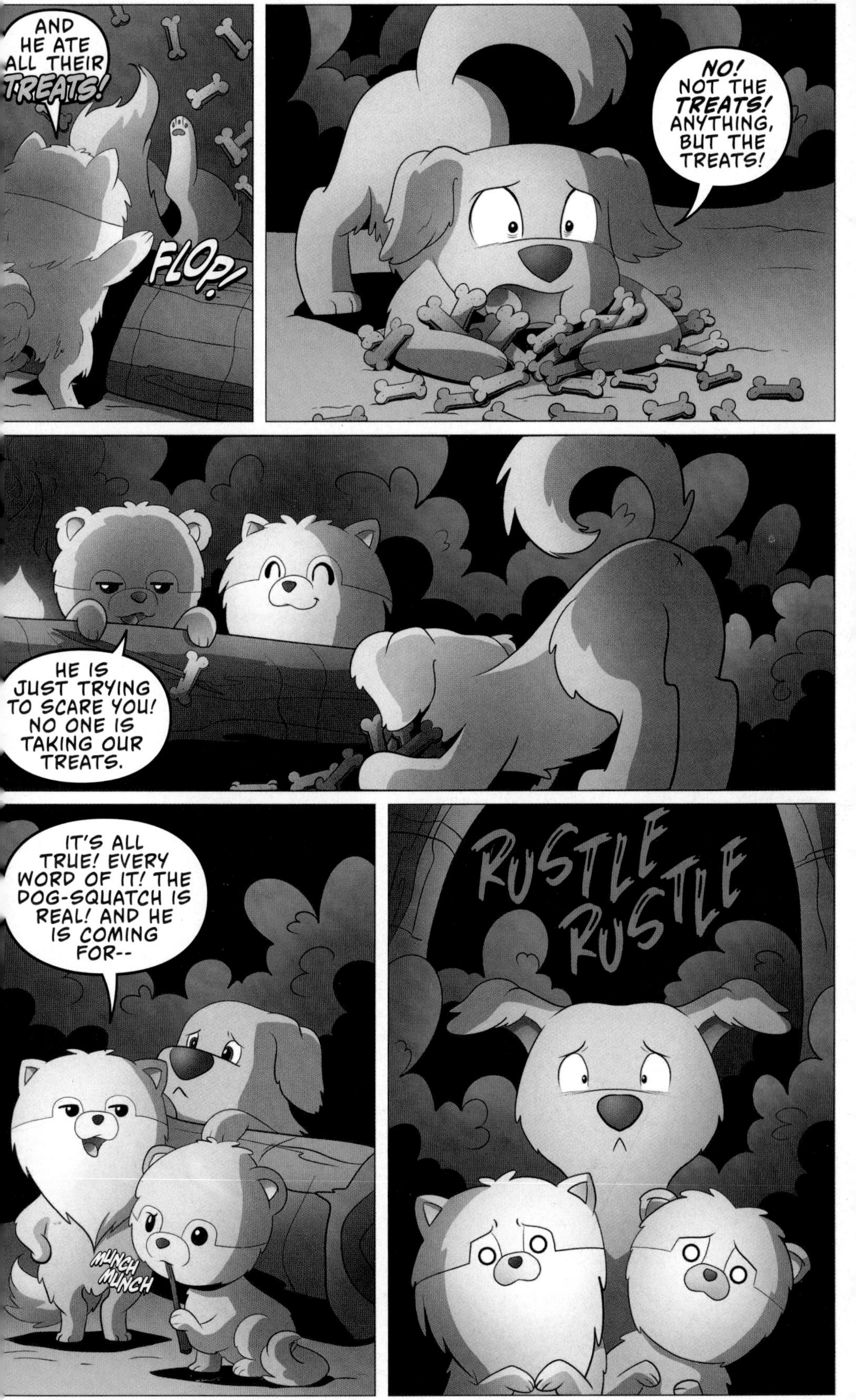
AND HE ATE ALL THEIR TREATS!
FLOP!
NO! NOT THE TREATS! ANYTHING, BUT THE TREATS!
HE IS JUST TRYING TO SCARE YOU! NO ONE IS TAKING OUR TREATS.
IT'S ALL TRUE! EVERY WORD OF IT! THE DOG-SQUATCH IS REAL! AND HE IS COMING FOR--
MUNCH MUNCH
RUSTLE RUSTLE

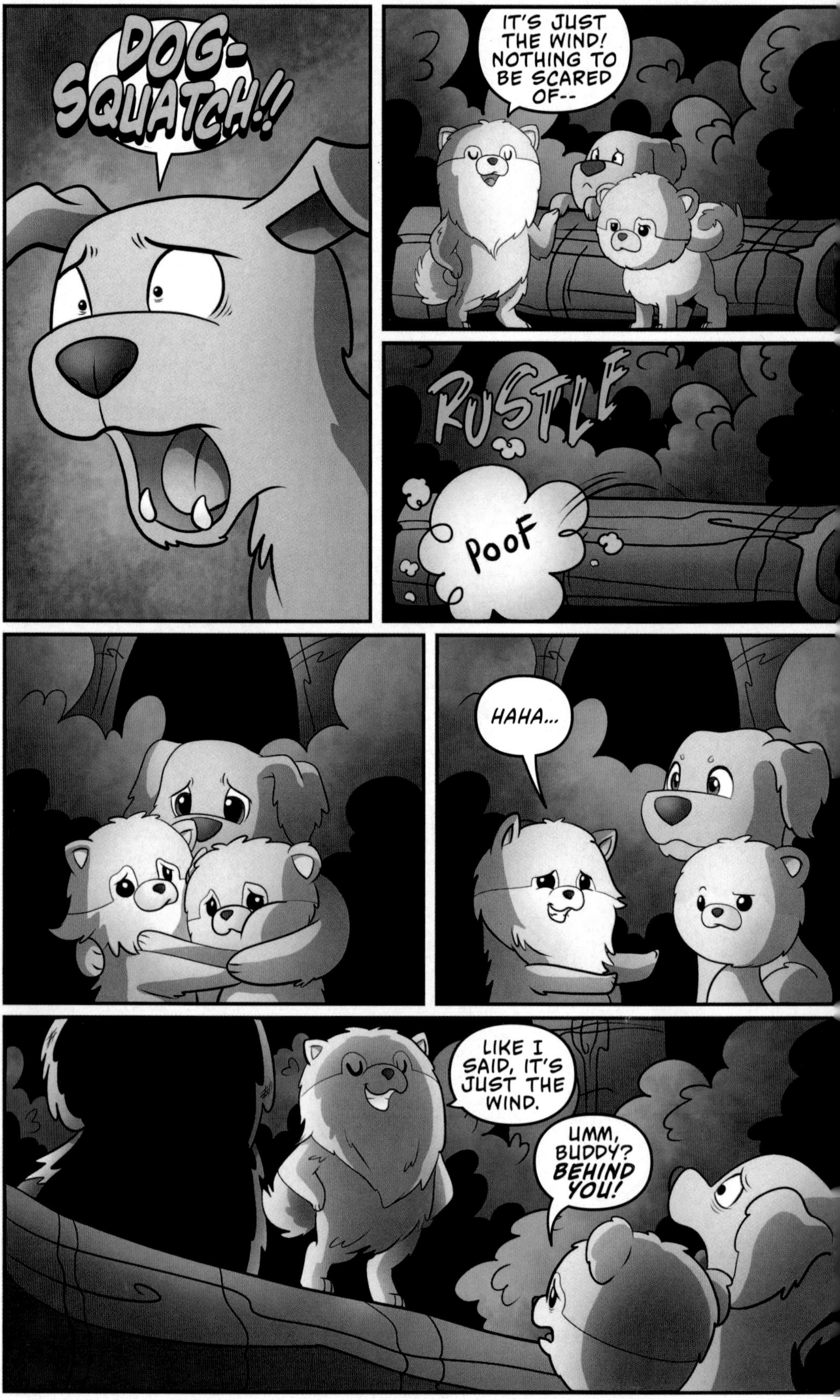
DOG-SQUATCH!!
IT'S JUST THE WIND! NOTHING TO BE SCARED OF--
RUSTLE
POOF
HAHA...
LIKE I SAID, IT'S JUST THE WIND.
UMM, BUDDY? BEHIND YOU!

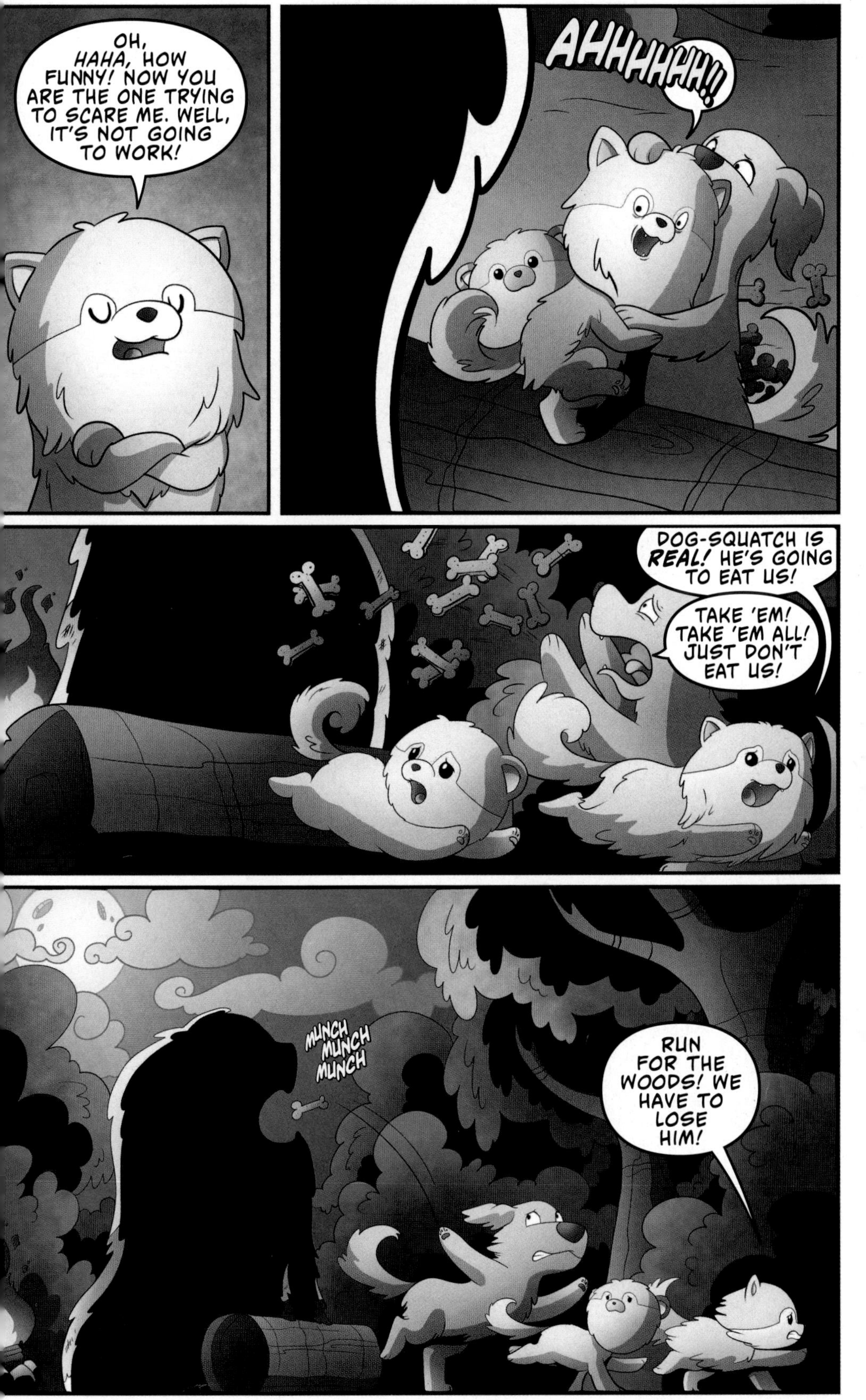
OH, HAHA, HOW FUNNY! NOW YOU ARE THE ONE TRYING TO SCARE ME. WELL, IT'S NOT GOING TO WORK!
AHHHHHH!!
DOG-SQUATCH IS REAL! HE'S GOING TO EAT US!
TAKE 'EM! TAKE 'EM ALL! JUST DON'T EAT US!
MUNCH MUNCH MUNCH
RUN FOR THE WOODS! WE HAVE TO LOSE HIM!

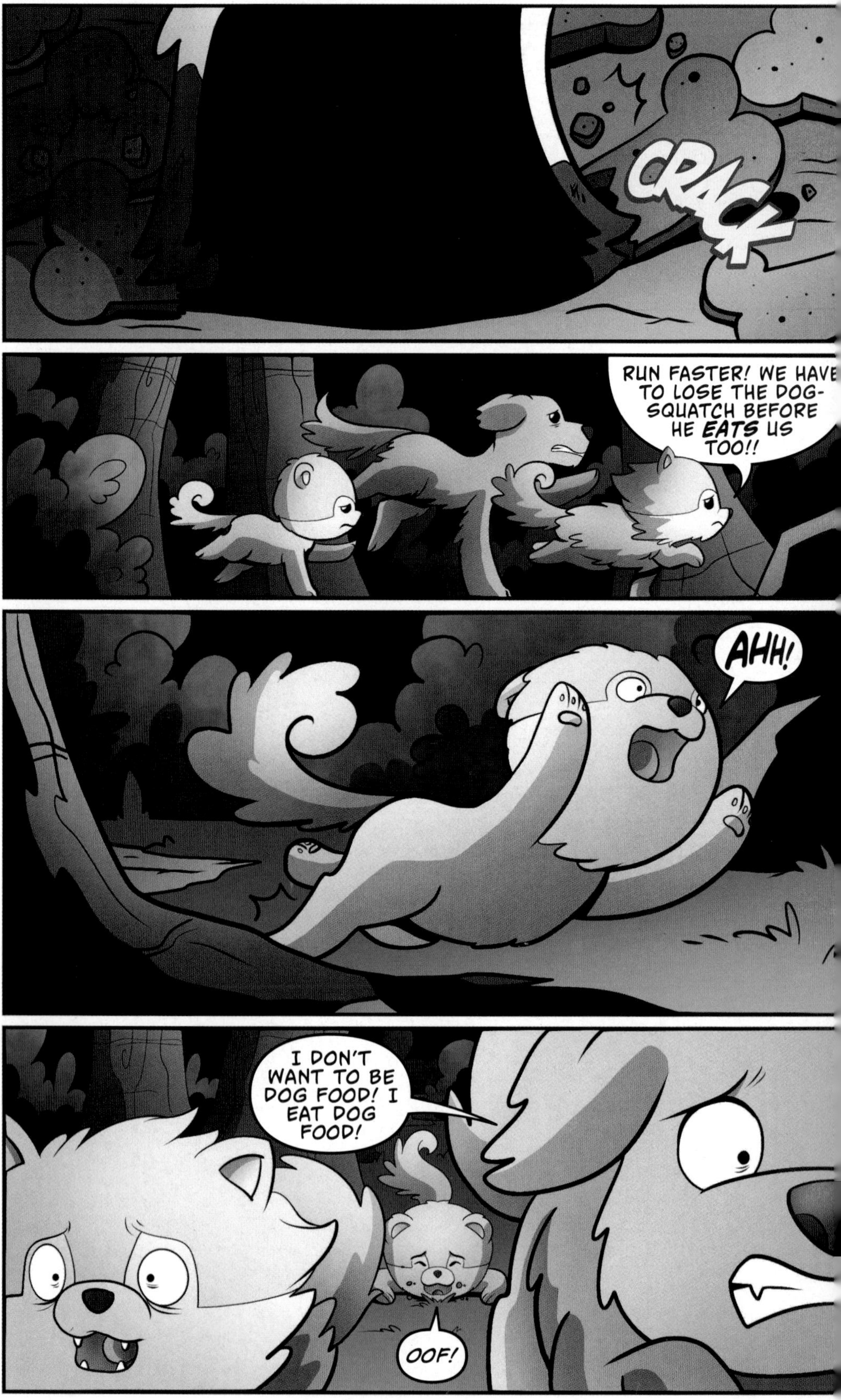
CRACK
RUN FASTER! WE HAVE TO LOSE THE DOG-SQUATCH BEFORE HE EATS US TOO!!
AHH!
I DON'T WANT TO BE DOG FOOD! I EAT DOG FOOD!
OOF!

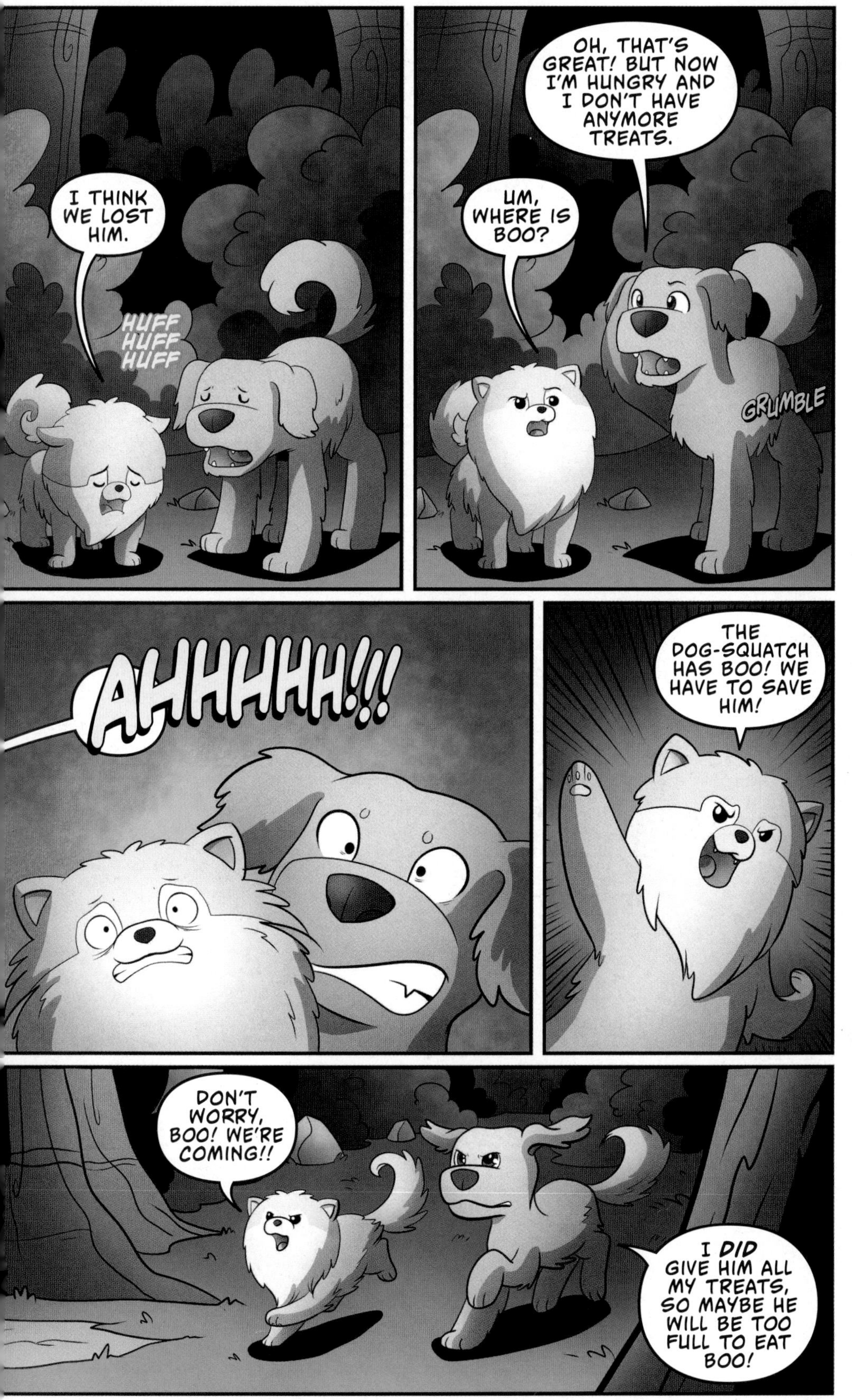
I THINK WE LOST HIM.
HUFF HUFF HUFF
OH, THAT'S GREAT! BUT NOW I'M HUNGRY AND I DON'T HAVE ANYMORE TREATS.
UM, WHERE IS BOO?
GRUMBLE
AHHHHH!!!
THE DOG-SQUATCH HAS BOO! WE HAVE TO SAVE HIM!
DON'T WORRY, BOO! WE'RE COMING!!
I DID GIVE HIM ALL MY TREATS, SO MAYBE HE WILL BE TOO FULL TO EAT BOO!

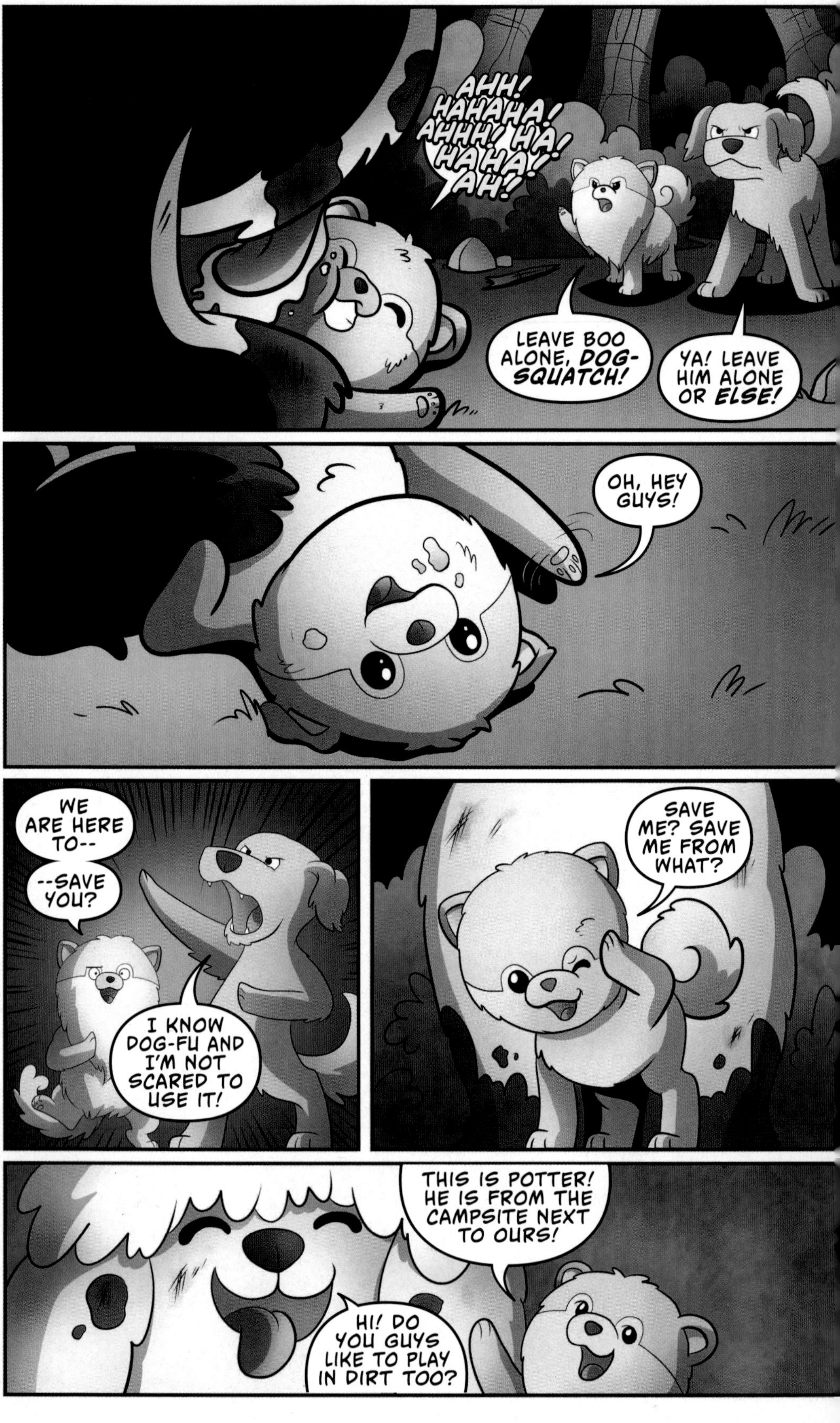
AHH! HAHAHA! AHHH! HA! HAHA! AH!
LEAVE BOO ALONE, DOG-SQUATCH!
YA! LEAVE HIM ALONE OR ELSE!
OH, HEY GUYS!
WE ARE HERE TO--
--SAVE YOU?
I KNOW DOG-FU AND I'M NOT SCARED TO USE IT!
SAVE ME? SAVE ME FROM WHAT?
THIS IS POTTER! HE IS FROM THE CAMPSITE NEXT TO OURS!
HI! DO YOU GUYS LIKE TO PLAY IN DIRT TOO?

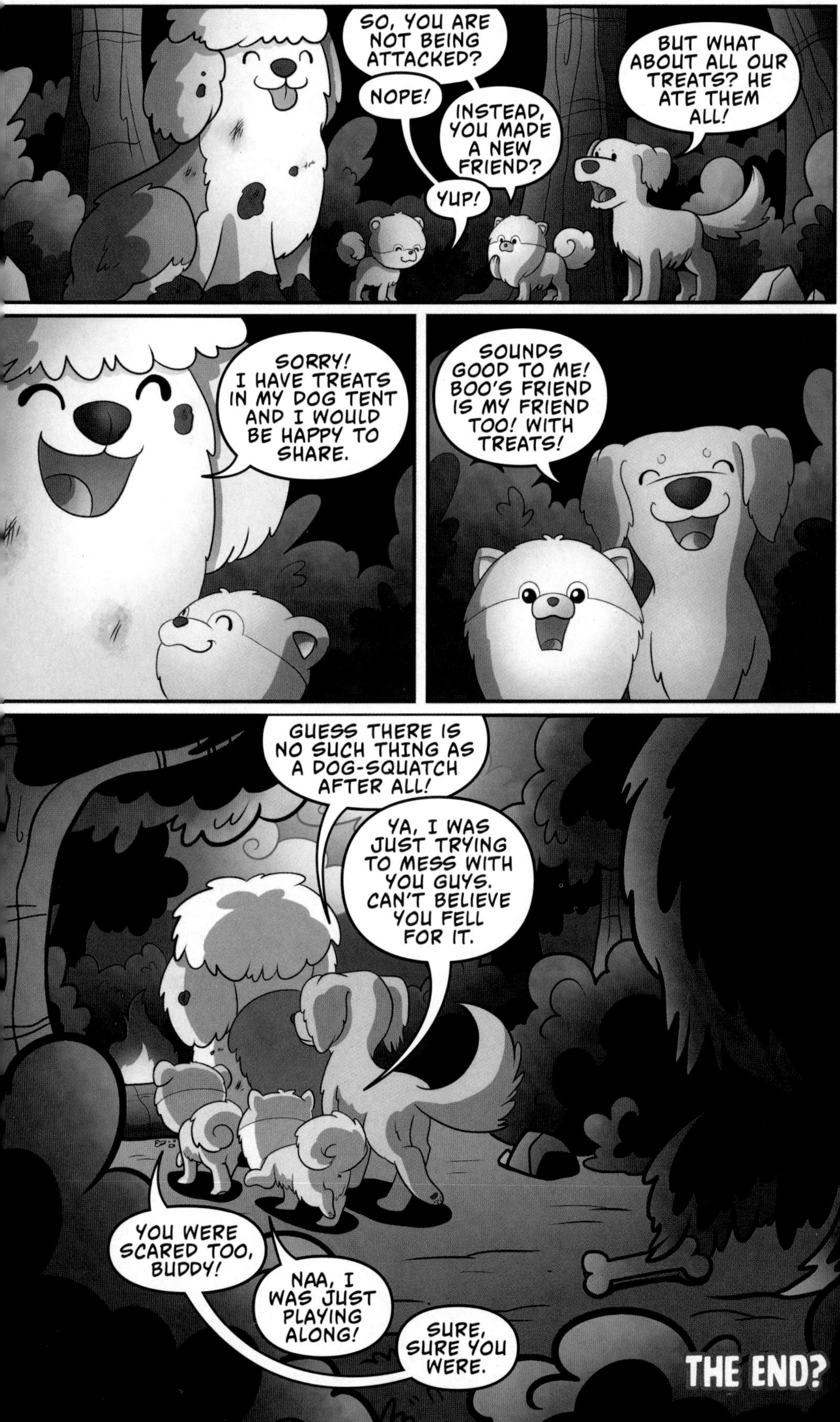
SO, YOU ARE NOT BEING ATTACKED?
NOPE!
INSTEAD, YOU MADE A NEW FRIEND?
YUP!
BUT WHAT ABOUT ALL OUR TREATS? HE ATE THEM ALL!
SORRY! I HAVE TREATS IN MY DOG TENT AND I WOULD BE HAPPY TO SHARE.
SOUNDS GOOD TO ME! BOO'S FRIEND IS MY FRIEND TOO! WITH TREATS!
GUESS THERE IS NO SUCH THING AS A DOG-SQUATCH AFTER ALL!
YA, I WAS JUST TRYING TO MESS WITH YOU GUYS. CAN'T BELIEVE YOU FELL FOR IT.
YOU WERE SCARED TOO, BUDDY!
NAA, I WAS JUST PLAYING ALONG!
SURE, SURE YOU WERE.
THE END?

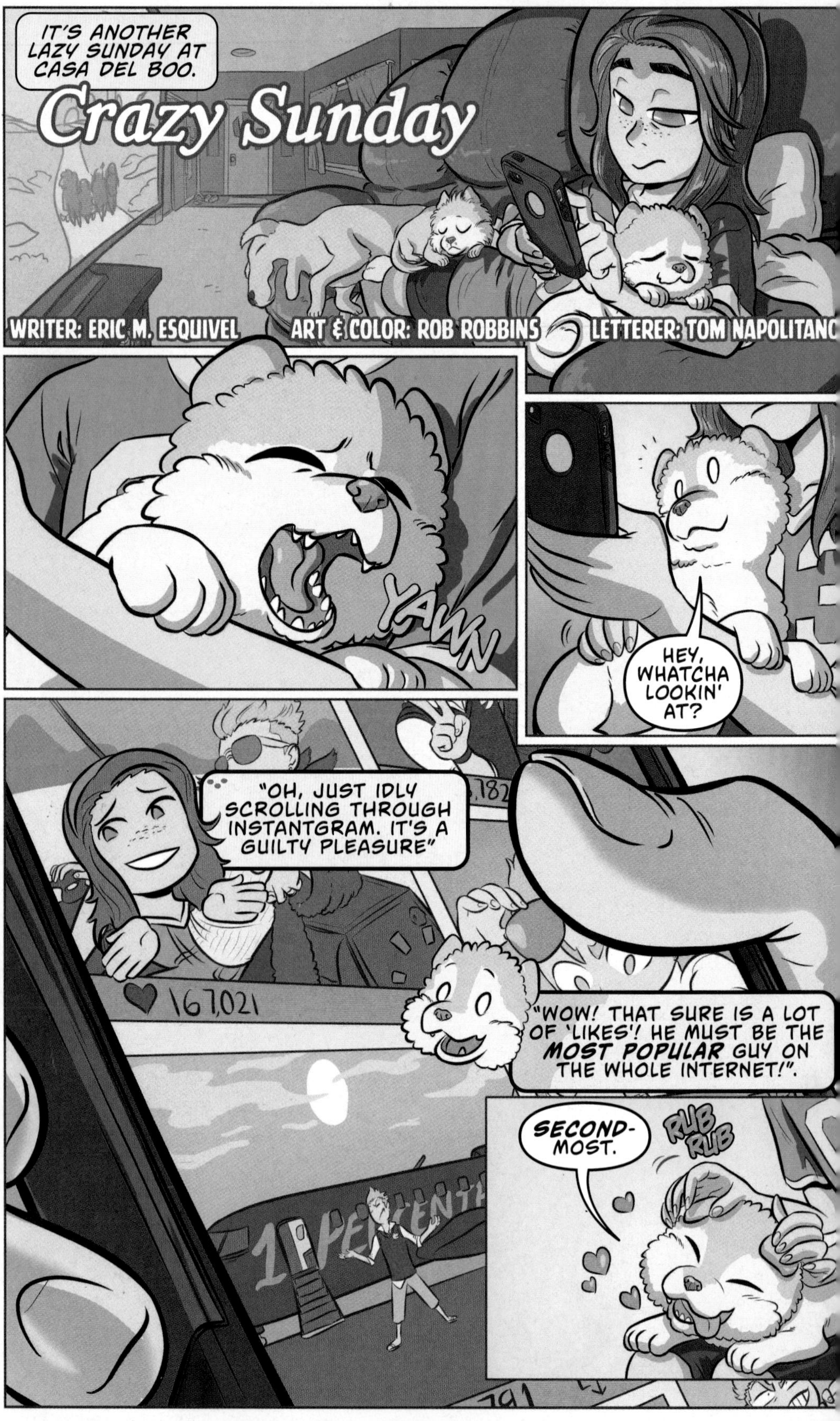
IT'S ANOTHER LAZY SUNDAY AT CASA DEL BOO.
Crazy Sunday
WRITER: ERIC M. ESQUIVEL
ART & COLOR: ROB ROBBINS
LETTERER: TOM NAPOLITANO
YAWN
HEY, WHATCHA LOOKIN' AT?
"OH, JUST IDLY SCROLLING THROUGH INSTANTGRAM. IT'S A GUILTY PLEASURE"
167,021
"WOW! THAT SURE IS A LOT OF 'LIKES'! HE MUST BE THE MOST POPULAR GUY ON THE WHOLE INTERNET!".
SECOND-MOST.
RUB RUB

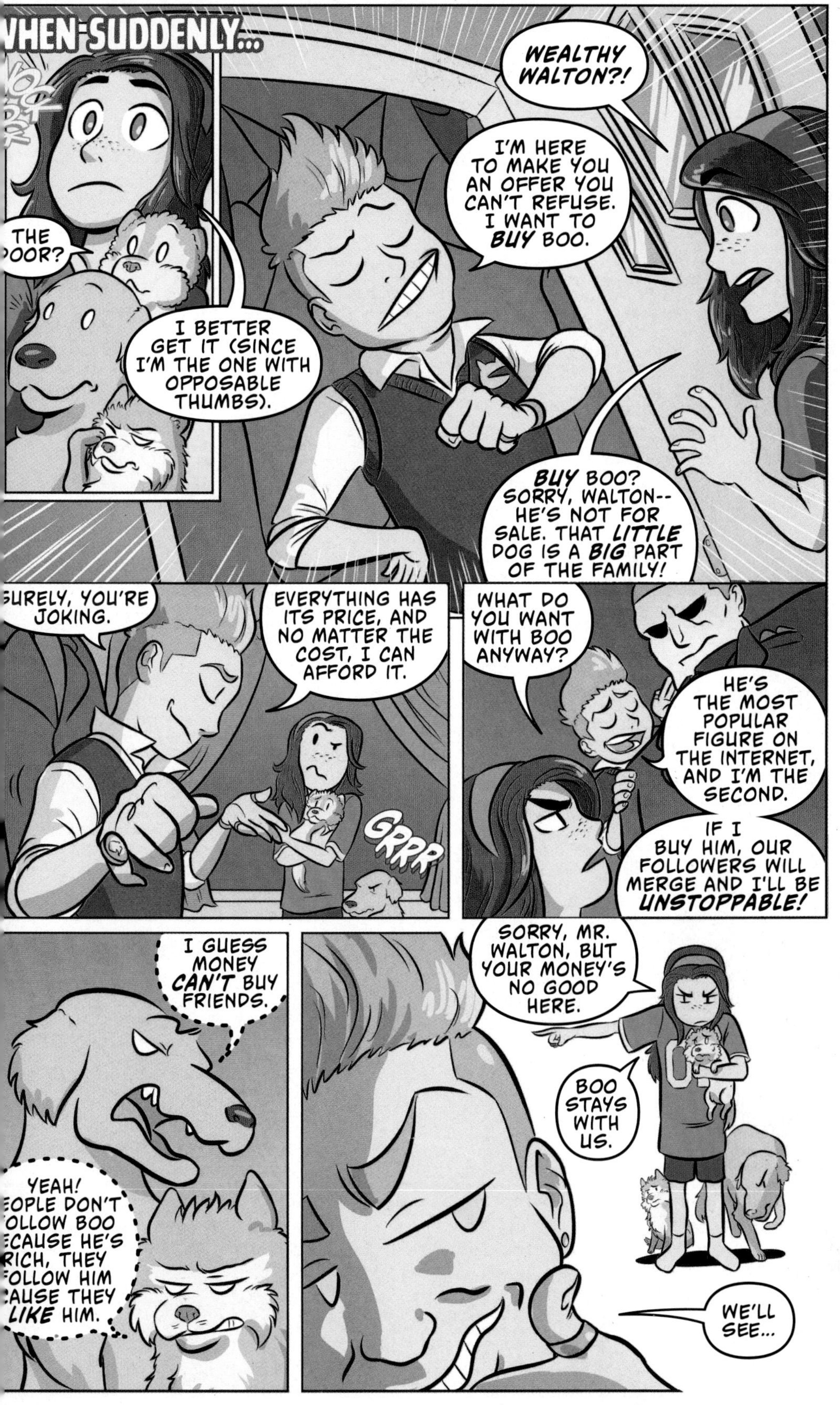
WHEN-SUDDENLY...
THE DOOR?
I BETTER GET IT (SINCE I'M THE ONE WITH OPPOSABLE THUMBS).
WEALTHY WALTON?!
I'M HERE TO MAKE YOU AN OFFER YOU CAN'T REFUSE. I WANT TO BUY BOO.
BUY BOO? SORRY, WALTON-- HE'S NOT FOR SALE. THAT LITTLE DOG IS A BIG PART OF THE FAMILY!
SURELY, YOU'RE JOKING.
EVERYTHING HAS ITS PRICE, AND NO MATTER THE COST, I CAN AFFORD IT.
GRRR
WHAT DO YOU WANT WITH BOO ANYWAY?
HE'S THE MOST POPULAR FIGURE ON THE INTERNET, AND I'M THE SECOND.
IF I BUY HIM, OUR FOLLOWERS WILL MERGE AND I'LL BE UNSTOPPABLE!
I GUESS MONEY CAN'T BUY FRIENDS.
YEAH! PEOPLE DON'T FOLLOW BOO BECAUSE HE'S RICH, THEY FOLLOW HIM 'CAUSE THEY LIKE HIM.
SORRY, MR. WALTON, BUT YOUR MONEY'S NO GOOD HERE.
BOO STAYS WITH US.
WE'LL SEE...

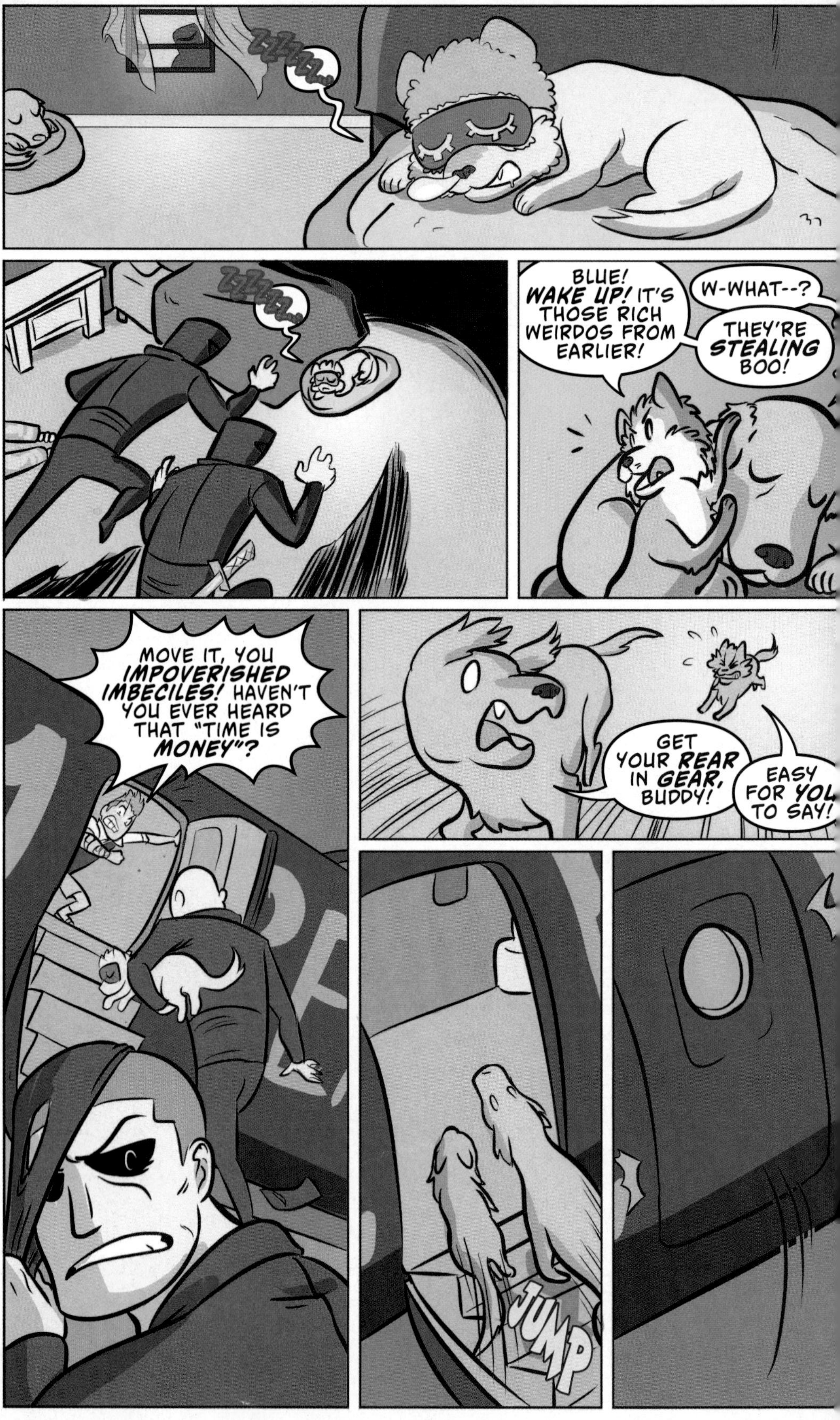
ZZZZZZZ...
ZZZZZZZ...
BLUE! WAKE UP! IT'S THOSE RICH WEIRDOS FROM EARLIER!
W-WHAT--?
THEY'RE STEALING BOO!
MOVE IT, YOU IMPOVERISHED IMBECILES! HAVEN'T YOU EVER HEARD THAT "TIME IS MONEY"?
GET YOUR REAR IN GEAR, BUDDY!
EASY FOR YOU TO SAY!
JUMP

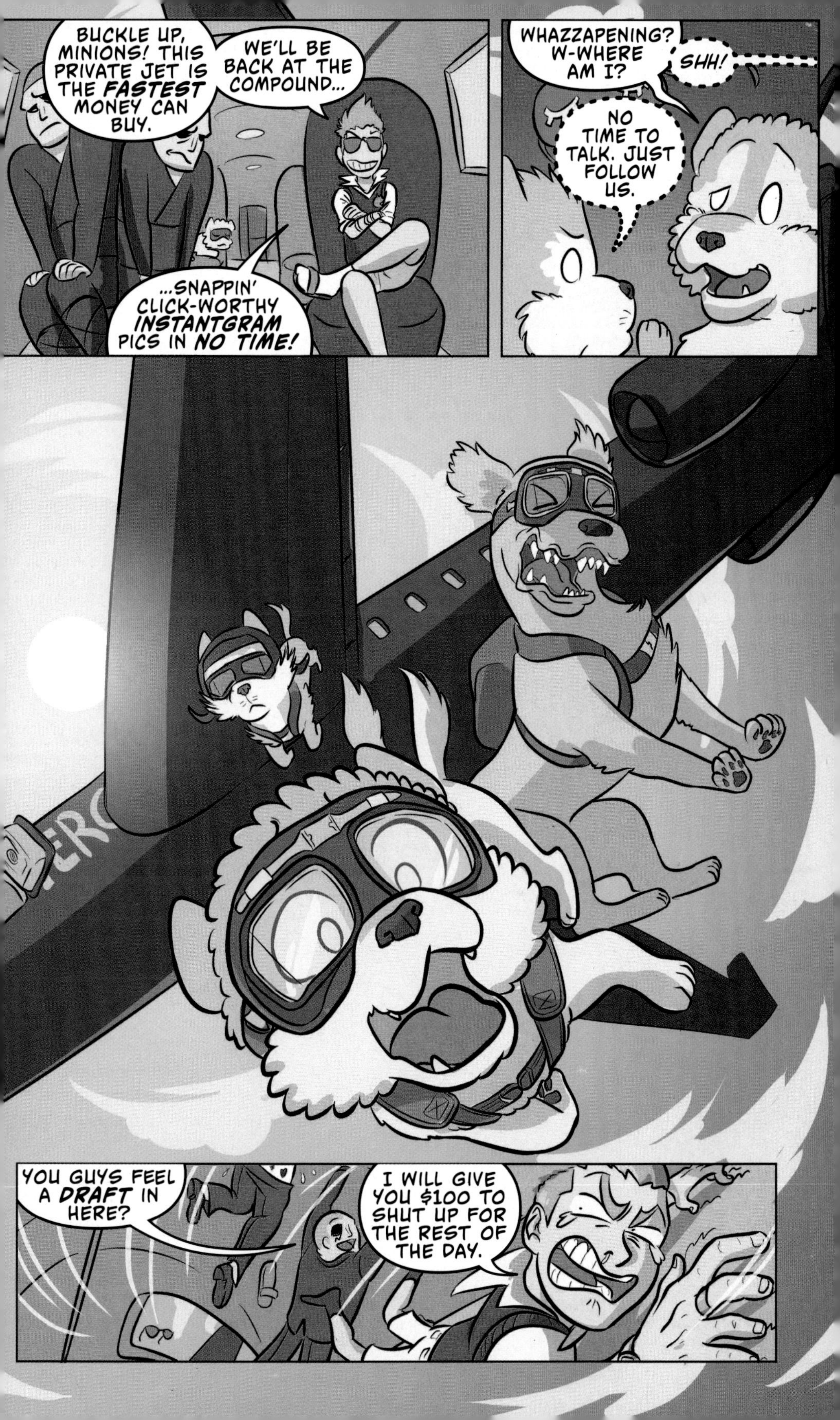
BUCKLE UP, MINIONS! THIS PRIVATE JET IS THE FASTEST MONEY CAN BUY.
WE'LL BE BACK AT THE COMPOUND...
...SNAPPIN' CLICK-WORTHY INSTANTGRAM PICS IN NO TIME!
WHAZZAPENING? W-WHERE AM I?
SHH!
NO TIME TO TALK. JUST FOLLOW US.
YOU GUYS FEEL A DRAFT IN HERE?
I WILL GIVE YOU $100 TO SHUT UP FOR THE REST OF THE DAY.

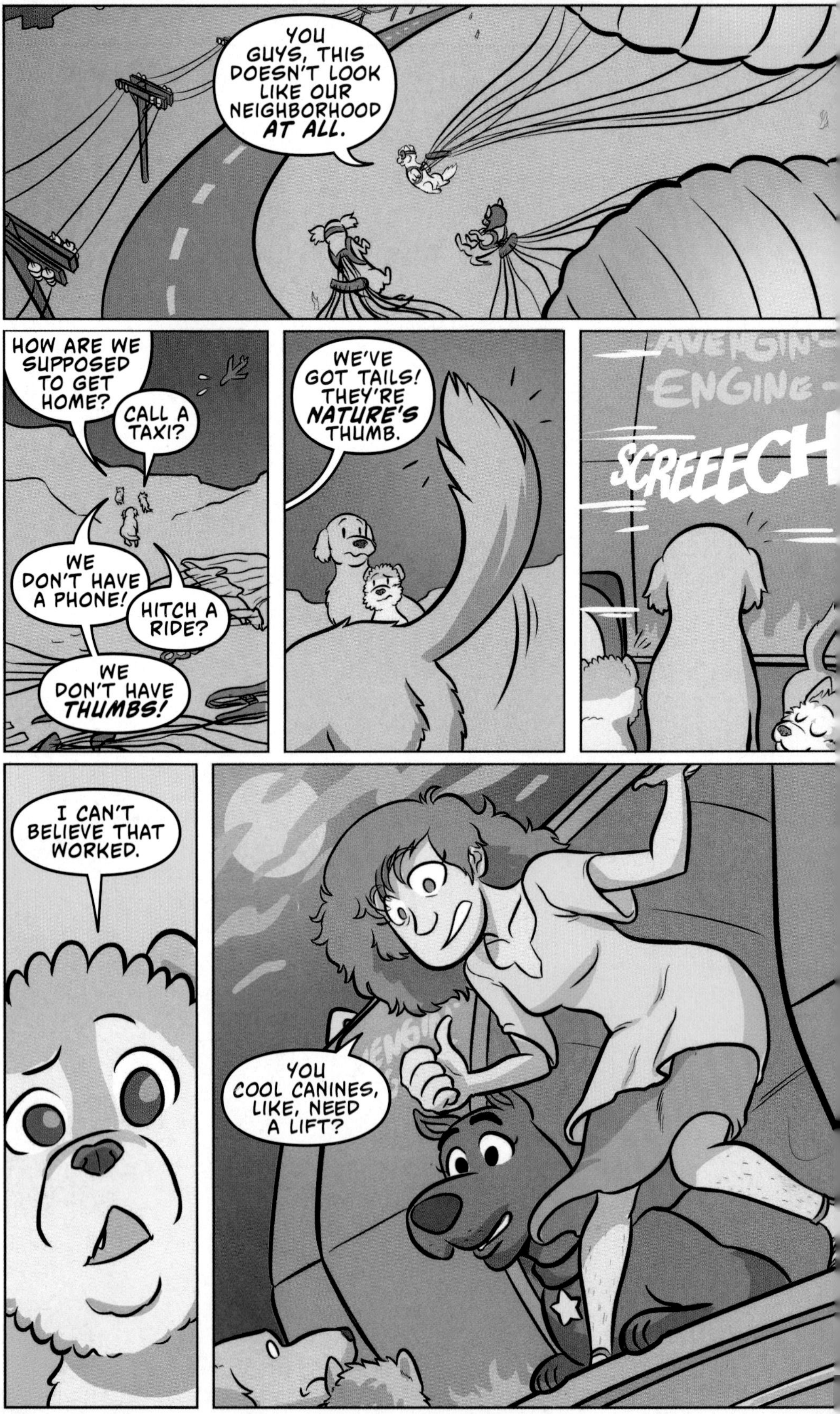
YOU GUYS, THIS DOESN'T LOOK LIKE OUR NEIGHBORHOOD AT ALL.
HOW ARE WE SUPPOSED TO GET HOME?
CALL A TAXI?
WE DON'T HAVE A PHONE!
HITCH A RIDE?
WE DON'T HAVE THUMBS!
WE'VE GOT TAILS! THEY'RE NATURE'S THUMB.
AVENGIN-ENGINE
SCREEECH
I CAN'T BELIEVE THAT WORKED.
YOU COOL CANINES, LIKE, NEED A LIFT?

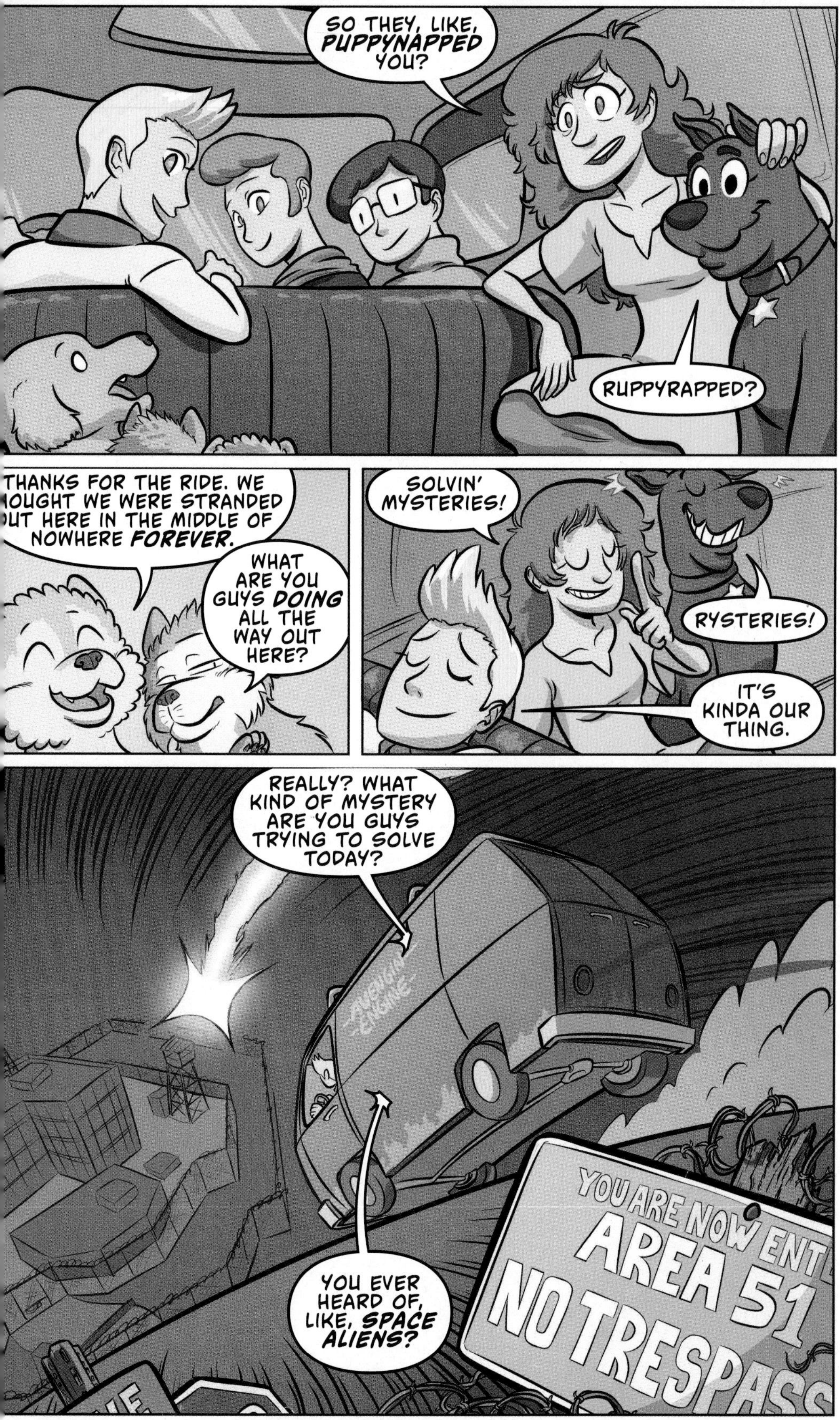
SO THEY, LIKE, *PUPPYNAPPED* YOU?
RUPPYRAPPED?
THANKS FOR THE RIDE. WE HOUGHT WE WERE STRANDED UT HERE IN THE MIDDLE OF NOWHERE *FOREVER.*
WHAT ARE YOU GUYS *DOING* ALL THE WAY OUT HERE?
SOLVIN' MYSTERIES!
RYSTERIES!
IT'S KINDA OUR THING.
REALLY? WHAT KIND OF MYSTERY ARE YOU GUYS TRYING TO SOLVE TODAY?
AVENGIN' ENGINE
YOU EVER HEARD OF, LIKE, *SPACE ALIENS?*
YOU ARE NOW ENT
AREA 51
NO TRESPASS

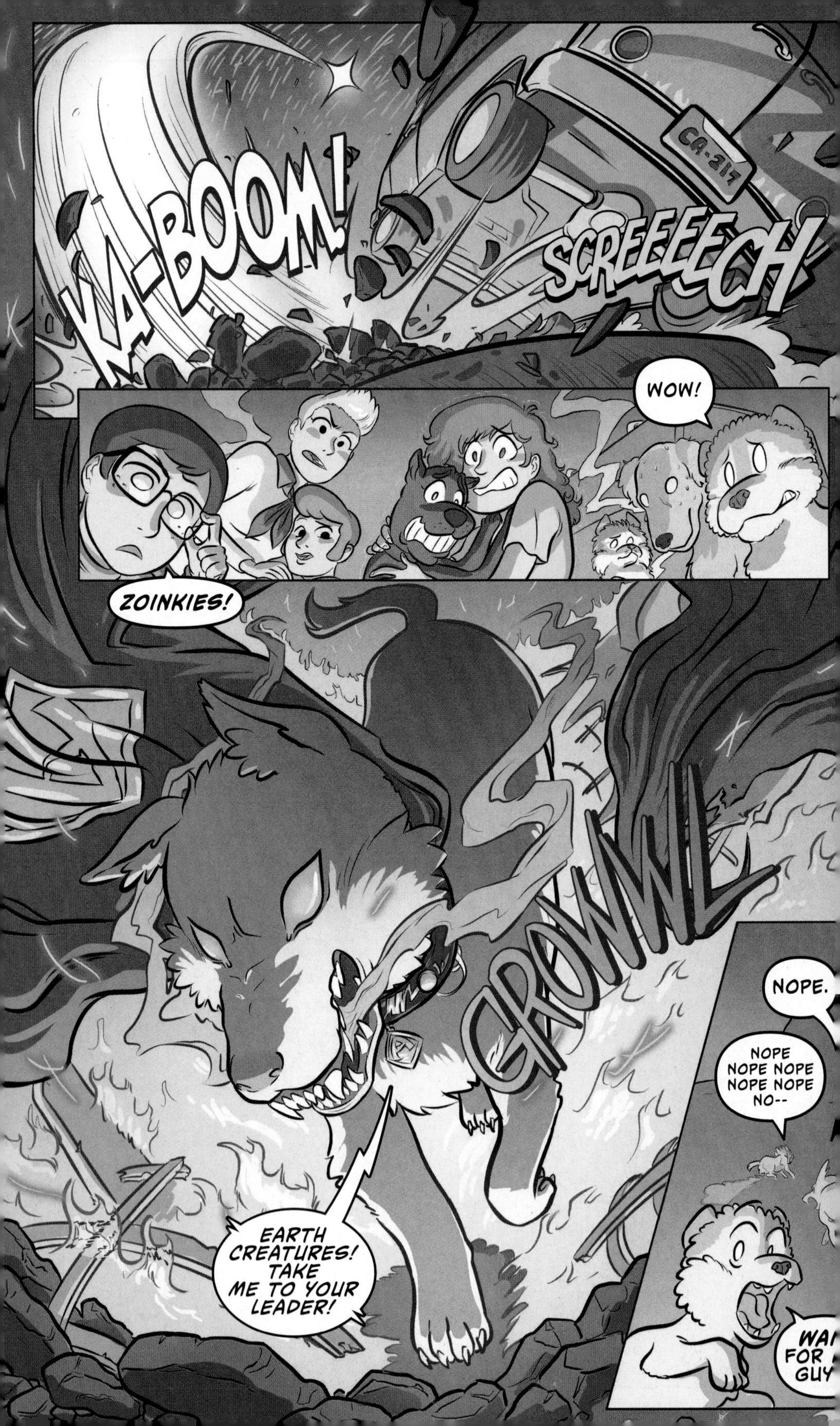
KA-BOOM!
SCREEEEECH
CA-217
WOW!
ZOINKIES!
GROWWL
EARTH CREATURES! TAKE ME TO YOUR LEADER!
NOPE.
NOPE NOPE NOPE NOPE NOPE NO--

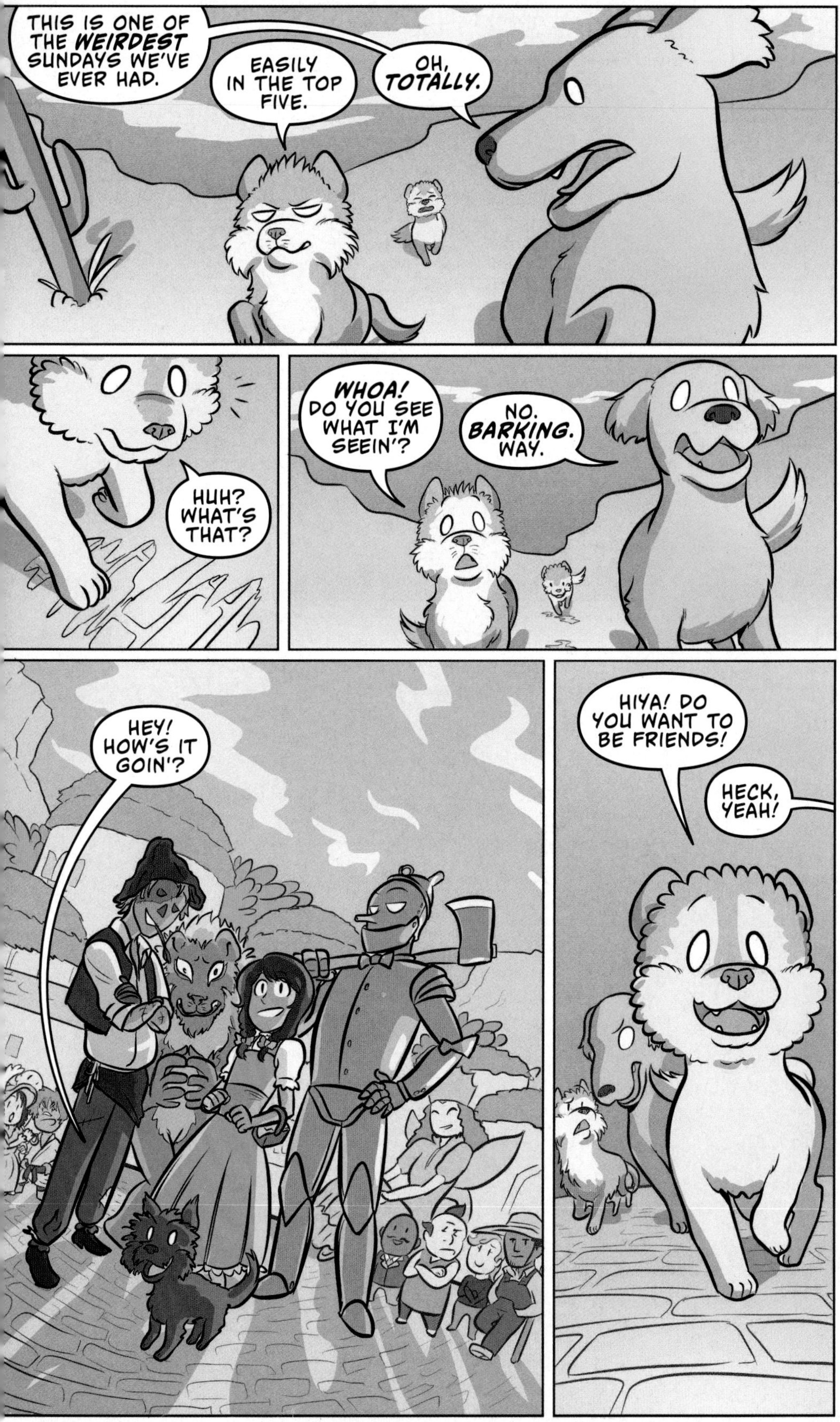
THIS IS ONE OF THE *WEIRDEST* SUNDAYS WE'VE EVER HAD.
EASILY IN THE TOP FIVE.
OH, *TOTALLY.*
HUH? WHAT'S THAT?
WHOA! DO YOU SEE WHAT I'M SEEIN'?
NO. *BARKING.* WAY.
HEY! HOW'S IT GOIN'?
HIYA! DO YOU WANT TO BE FRIENDS!
HECK, YEAH!

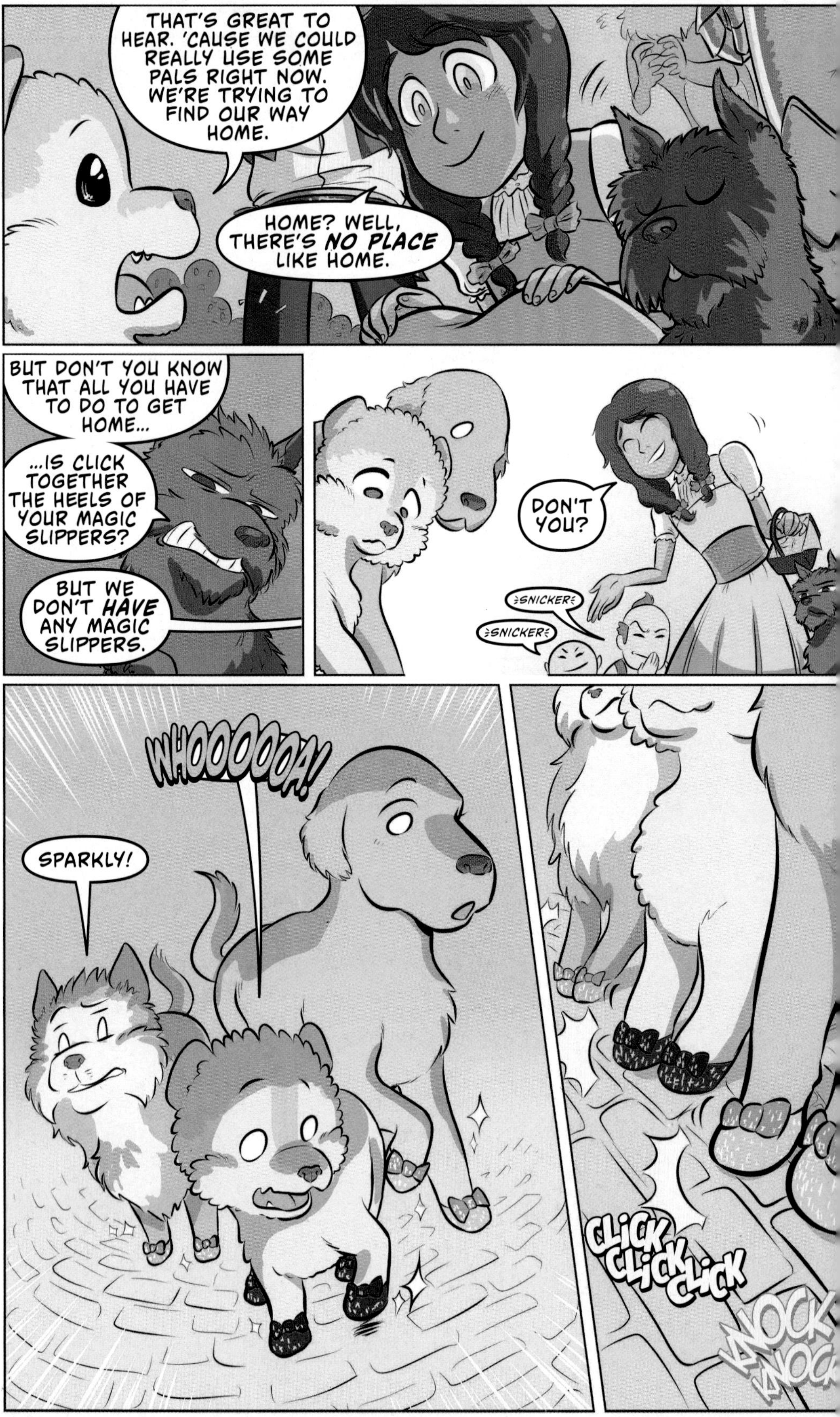

THAT'S GREAT TO HEAR. 'CAUSE WE COULD REALLY USE SOME PALS RIGHT NOW. WE'RE TRYING TO FIND OUR WAY HOME.
HOME? WELL, THERE'S NO PLACE LIKE HOME.
BUT DON'T YOU KNOW THAT ALL YOU HAVE TO DO TO GET HOME...
...IS CLICK TOGETHER THE HEELS OF YOUR MAGIC SLIPPERS?
BUT WE DON'T HAVE ANY MAGIC SLIPPERS.
DON'T YOU?
SNICKER
SNICKER
WHOOOOOOA!
SPARKLY!
CLICK CLICK CLICK
KNOCK KNOCK

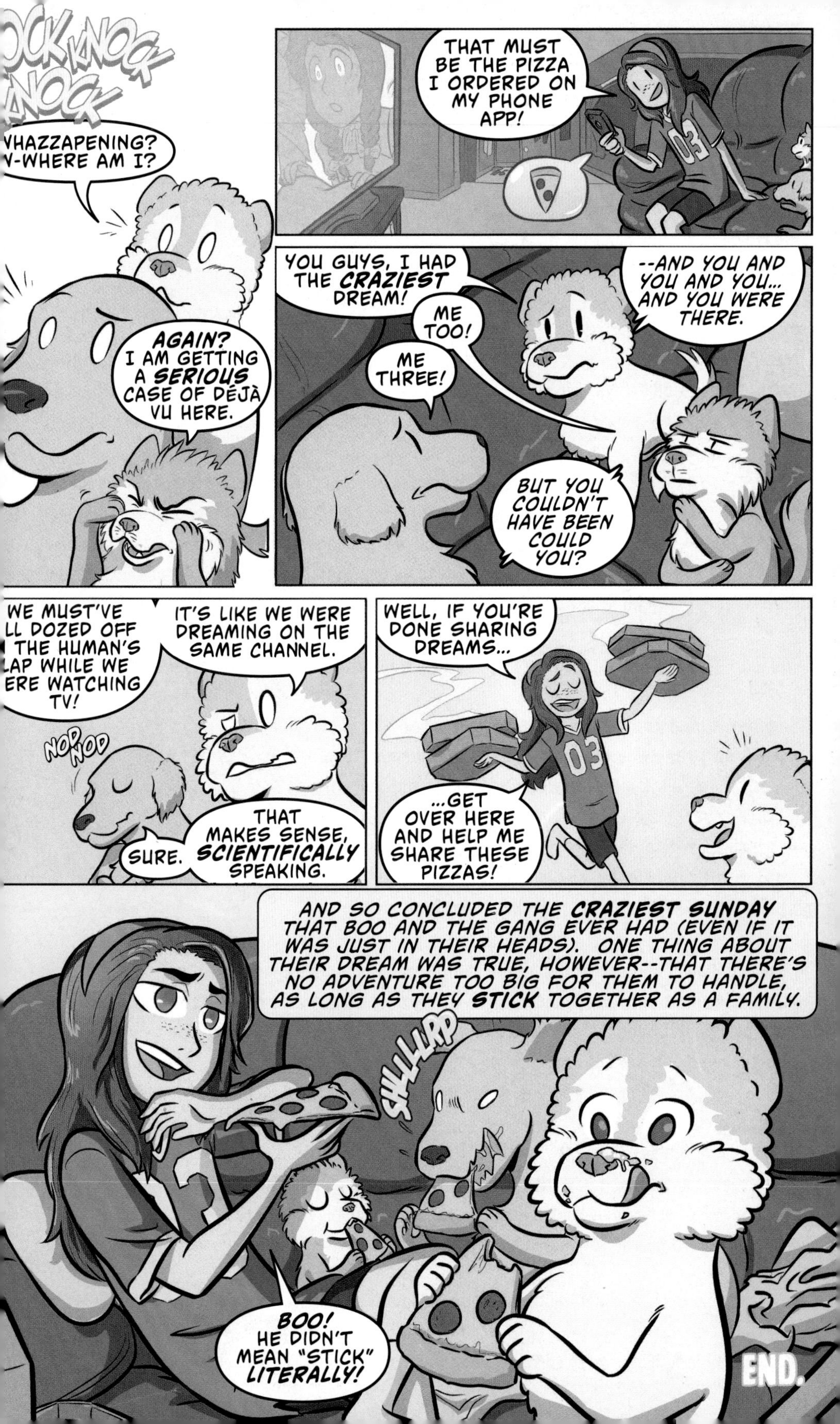
OCK KNOCK KNOCK
VHAZZAPENING? V-WHERE AM I?
THAT MUST BE THE PIZZA I ORDERED ON MY PHONE APP!
AGAIN? I AM GETTING A SERIOUS CASE OF DÉJÀ VU HERE.
YOU GUYS, I HAD THE CRAZIEST DREAM!
--AND YOU AND YOU AND YOU... AND YOU WERE THERE.
ME TOO!
ME THREE!
BUT YOU COULDN'T HAVE BEEN COULD YOU?
WE MUST'VE LL DOZED OFF THE HUMAN'S LAP WHILE WE ERE WATCHING TV!
IT'S LIKE WE WERE DREAMING ON THE SAME CHANNEL.
NOD NOD
SURE.
THAT MAKES SENSE, SCIENTIFICALLY SPEAKING.
WELL, IF YOU'RE DONE SHARING DREAMS...
...GET OVER HERE AND HELP ME SHARE THESE PIZZAS!
AND SO CONCLUDED THE CRAZIEST SUNDAY THAT BOO AND THE GANG EVER HAD (EVEN IF IT WAS JUST IN THEIR HEADS). ONE THING ABOUT THEIR DREAM WAS TRUE, HOWEVER--THAT THERE'S NO ADVENTURE TOO BIG FOR THEM TO HANDLE, AS LONG AS THEY STICK TOGETHER AS A FAMILY.
SHLLLRP
BOO! HE DIDN'T MEAN "STICK" LITERALLY!
END.

FRIDAY:

Sometimes Human loves to watch television. She likes to watch shows with dogs on them and especially shows with very smart dogs that can do tricks. I was sitting on her lap on the couch watching one of these shows with her tonight. We watched a little dog walking around on his hind paws. Human seemed to really like it, but I wasn't too impressed. I'm sure I can do that too!

SATURDAY:

This morning during our walk in the park, Human unleashed me so I could run freely on the park's doggy trails.

I decided I was going to impress Human by showing her that I can walk on my back paws too, like those dogs on TV last night. I hopped up on my hind legs and started towards her. Keeping my balance on two legs was a lot harder than I thought. I don't know how Human does it.

When I got to her, I fell forward but I managed to hold myself up by leaning my front two paws on Human. More specifically, I landed my front two paws on Human's long white skirt. What I hadn't noticed was how muddy the doggy trails were that day. I left some very good paw prints on Human's skirt, but judging by her reaction, I don't think she approved of my sense of design.

I thought it best to give her some alone time so she could cool off, so I ran away from her. This didn't seem to help her cool off at all. I guess it was because I ran back onto the muddy trails. She kept yelling at me to come back to her, but I didn't want to get her muddy, so I stayed where I was...in the mud. Finally, she marched into the mud and picked me up. That didn't seem to help her mood either.

It seemed Human had this thing about mud. Now to be honest, my paws were caked in the stuff and somewhere along the way, a splotch or two did stick to me here and there. I knew Human would be livid if I brought any mud into the house, so once we got into her car, I gave myself good shake to get it all off me.

Strangely, this didn't cheer Human up at all.

SUNDAY:

This morning, Buddy, Bluebeary and I got up very early. Human was still asleep and we were hungry. Since she'd had a bad day yesterday, we decided to let her sleep and we would get our own food. Bluebeary knew where Human kept a big box of doggy treats in the kitchen. It was up on a counter, so of the three of us only Bluebeary could reach it.

Ol' Blue reached up, and with his long nose, he knocked the box right off the counter. It hit the floor and it exploded. Doggy treats were everywhere. I thought this was great! Human could sleep all day long if she wanted! We had enough food to eat for the whole weekend!

uess the commotion woke up
man because we heard her coming
wn the hall towards the kitchen. I
ured she would be pleased with our
-ourcefulness. My pals, Buddy and
ebeary, must've wanted to give me
the credit because they took off
ining and left me alone there in a
: of spilled dog food.

man must not have slept very well because she was still in a bad mood when she got into the
chen and saw me. I tried wagging my tail, but it was wasted on her.

)NDAY:

day, Human announced that I needed to learn better behavior, so she was going to take me to
edience School. I wasn't sure how I felt about this, so I turned to my pal, Buddy. Buddy, after
. knew everything! He knew all about how schools worked from watching television. He told me
: most important thing I needed to do was to get in good with the "cool kids." I asked him how
/ould know who the cool kids were and he told me I'd know them when I saw them.

ddy was sure right! When Human and I got to the Obedience School, I saw some of my
ssmates right away. There was this big Doberman named "Prince" and a handsome German
epherd named "Duke." I knew right off that they couldn't be the "cool kids." They sat very still
the ends of their human's leashes and did nothing. How boring! There was this other dog
ough, named Stanley. Stanley was much more interesting than Prince or Duke.

He was short like me, but I couldn't tell what his breed was. He
looked like he was made of all of them! He also couldn't sit still at all.

He chased his own tail for hours and
kept licking a spot on the ground. He
said he was sure it was gum.

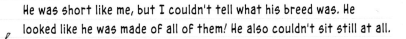

:new Stanley had to be in with the cool kids. Later on he told me he liked to chew on the ends of
ffee tables and to drink toilet water. Suddenly, I wasn't so sure who the cool kids were again.

ESDAY:

e honestly had mixed feelings about this Obedience School business.

ter all, I have a busy schedule, what with taking ten naps a day and hours of sniffing things,
I initially saw this Obedience School thing as a huge interruption to my day. Today, however,
edience School justified itself because today we started learning tricks!

is is the stuff I've been wanting to learn all my life. With this knowledge, the sky's the limit! I
ild be a police dog or maybe act in movies.

I could even be one of those internet sensations with videos on Puptube!

I checked out the competition to see what the other dogs could do. Prince could keep a ball in the air with his nose for five minutes. He looked like a big seal. Then, Duke came along and blew that away! Duke could count! His human would say a number and he would bark that many time I was stunned. How did he learn to do that? He must be a dog from the future or another plan I was going to impress everybody with my ability to chase my own shadow, but after seeing th wizard, Duke, do veritable magic, I didn't think shadow-chasing was going to do the trick.

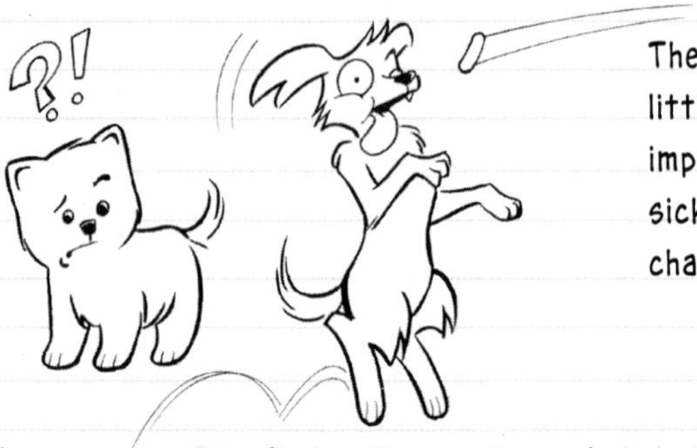
?!

Then, Stanley did his trick. Stanley could swallow little sausages whole. I had to admit, I was impressed. He did his trick six times. Then he got sick. I felt a little better about my shadow chasing.

WEDNESDAY:

Today at Obedience School, I fell in love. Her name was Bae. She's a Pomeranian and she's the new dog in school. With her long white fur and big red bow, you can tell this girl's used to the finer things in life! She just barks out "clas I've got my work cut out for me because already two big dogs like Prince and that genius, Duk have set their sights on her. During playtime, they chased her all around the park. I waited for her to be alone so I could make my move. Finally, an opportunity presented itself when she sat on the sidelines and scratched herself. She didn't scratch like some flea-bitten tail chaser! She delicately wiped at herself with her dainty little paws. She was mesmerizing! I walked over to h

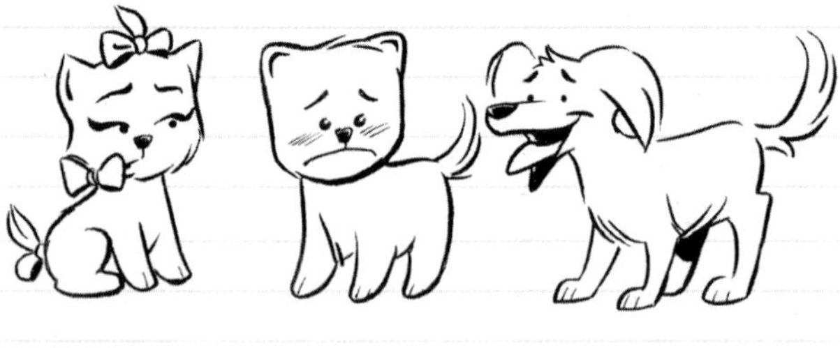

That was when Stanley joined u He said he thought he saw a tic crawling up my tail and offered bite it for me. I thanked him, b told him no. Then I went to the sandbox and buried my head.

THURSDAY:

Today, another new dog joined our class. His name is Spotty and, even though he's covered in spots, I'm not sure which spots are real and which ones are splatters of mud and dirt. Spotty a real mess. We tried our best to make him feel welcome, but we noticed this cloud of tiny spec that seemed to follow him everywhere.

Upon closer look, we caught on that those specks were fleas. We all kept away from him after that, except for Stanley, who liked to eat Spotty's fleas.

Before the day was over, Spotty's human was called to come and pick him up. I'm sure a long flea bath waited for him at home.

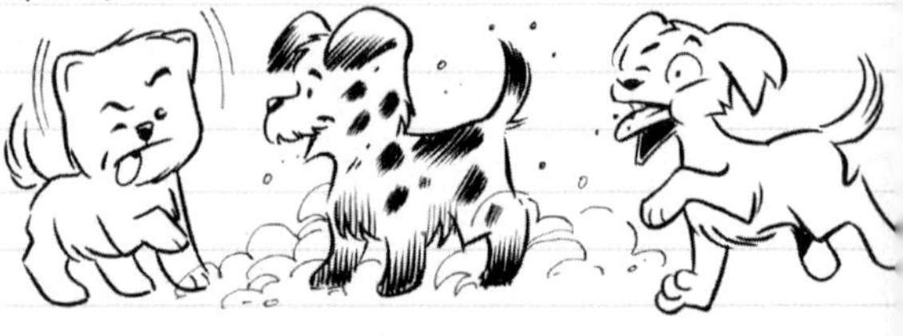

AY:

otty came back today and he looked like a new dog. He was all clean and was wearing a nice ny new collar. He stayed that way until playtime when we were all allowed to run around tside in the school's yard. Spotty found a nice fresh mud puddle and dove in. He rolled in that p and nearly painted himself completely brown! Once playtime was over, we were all called back ide. I told Spotty it was probably best that he **NOT** wait until we got inside before shaking : mud off himself.

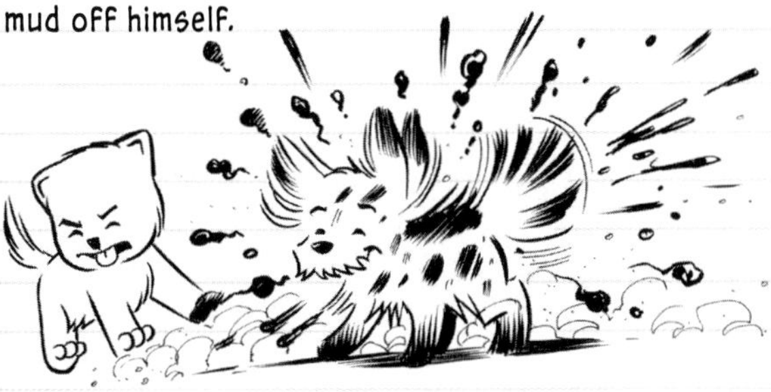

That was a lesson I learned the hard way. He listened and shook himself right there.

I probably saved his life, but in shaking himself, he splattered me.

NDAY:

day at school, we learned that as part of our final exam, we were all going to take part in a ; dog show where we would get to show off all of the tricks and good behavior that we've been arning. A special prize would be awarded to the dog who performed the best. This was great! is was the opportunity I'd been waiting for. If I could win this, I was sure to impress Bae! ıs, winning this thing would look great on my resume when I made my career move to police dog.

ter, I saw Prince and Duke running on the dog track and elegantly leaping over the hurdles. I ticed Bae was watching them. I decided to get her attention by running out and clearing a few rdles. I got her attention alright! On the first hurdle, I didn't make it all the way over. I landed ;ht on the bar and hung there like clothes on a laundry line. I kicked and kicked until I fell off d landed on my tail. I didn't even look her way when I skulked away. Later, Stanley told me he ıs sure no one noticed because everyone was busy laughing.

He tries, that Stanley...

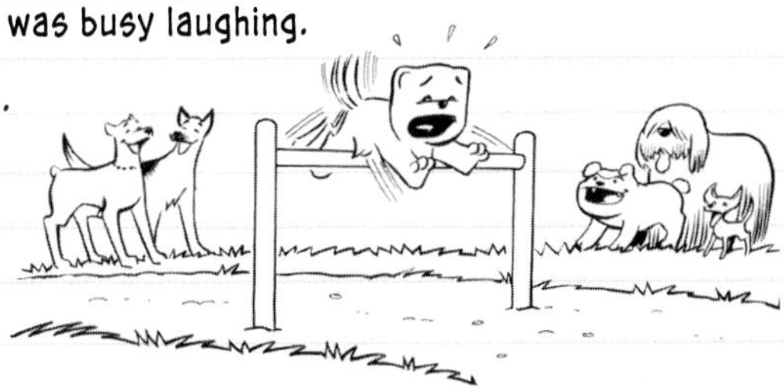

ESDAY:

ıew human joined our school today... d my nightmares!

's a new trainer and even the big dogs like Prince and Duke are afraid of him. They call him arge" and he barks even more than we do. He snaps his fingers and points a lot. I don't even derstand what he's saying since he says a lot of things and says them loudly. Whenever I see n point at me, I wait to see where he points next and then I run in that direction.

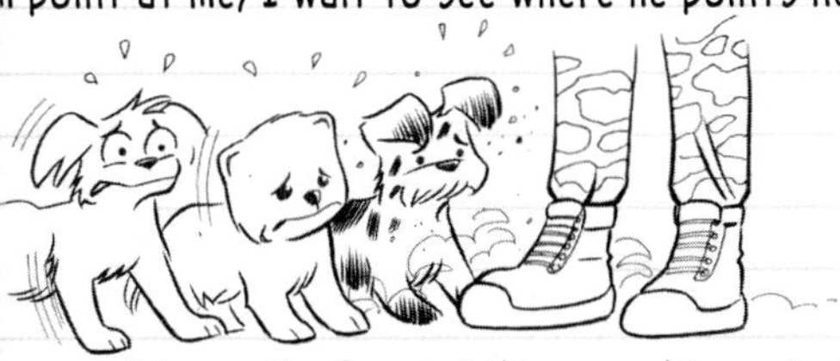

Stanley has a different strategy. When Sarge points at him, he shakes and cries until Sarge yells at him even louder. Good ol' Stanley!

may not be on the Dean's List around here, but I'm not Stanley either. Poor Stanley! When I come a famous police dog, I'm going to come back and give Stanley a job as my sidekick. Maybe can be my butler.

WEDNESDAY:

Sarge made us run a lot of laps today. It may sound like a lot of work, but this was actually a b break. Bae, a pommie like me, has short little legs like me. Neither of us can keep up with those long-legged gazelles like Prince and Duke, so we get to hang back and run together.

This meant plenty of alone-time with the beautiful Bae. We didn't talk much, but we did run together. I made sure to put out the vibe while I hustled my tiny tail. I'm sure she picked up or the signals I was sending.

Later at lunch, I expected her to come and seek me out. I saw her coming toward me, when, once again, Stanley moved in like a bull! The crazy fool was giddy because he'd just chased a cat up a tree. His story sounded fishy to me so I had to investigate. It turned out Stanley's "cat" was Sanchez, a Mexican hairless who was in our very class! Poor Sanchez! He was stuck up in that tree until Sarge got him down. Later, he said to me, "Stanley es muy malo." I don't always understand Sanchez but this time he came across crystal clear.

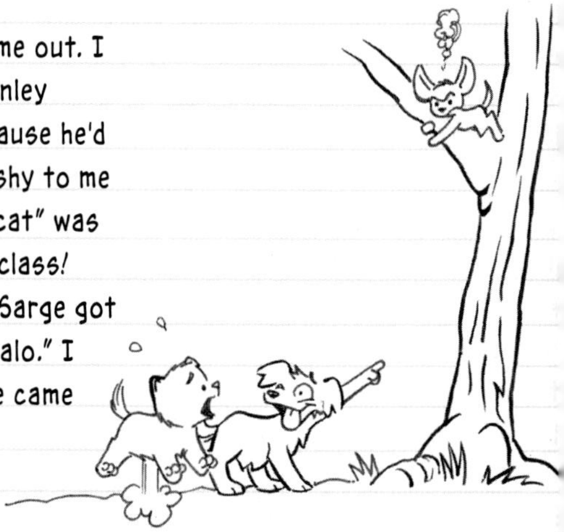

THURSDAY:

Tonight, I practiced a few drills at home with Buddy and Bluebeary. Bless their hearts! These guys have been my rock. I've got to make sure when I become a world famous police dog marrie to Bae that I'll come back for these two. Poor Buddy and Bluebeary can't make it without me. They don't have the higher education that I've been receiving. One day, I'll make sure that my mansion has dog houses in the back for each of them. Maybe even with doggy blankets. Bluebeary likes to chew on his.

FRIDAY:

A great idea for winning over Bae hit me today! Whenever we do a trick right, Sarge throws us a doggy treat. Some of us, of course, get more treats than others. Prince and Duke are masters Those guys get a treat every time. Poor Stanley has to make his own treats by eating the caterpillars he finds in the dirt. That guy gets so many commands wrong, the humans may as w be speaking in "cat" to him.

Dear, sweet Bae is right in the middle. Like me, she gets some and she misses sor

Today, I got the bright idea to save my treats whenever I was given one. I'm going to stash th in a flower pot at the school and once I've built up a good bouquet of treats, I'm going to give them to my darling Bae. That will show her! I don't know why I didn't think of this before! Why was I wasting my time trying to impress her with my personality and intelligence? I was going BUY her love with dog treats!

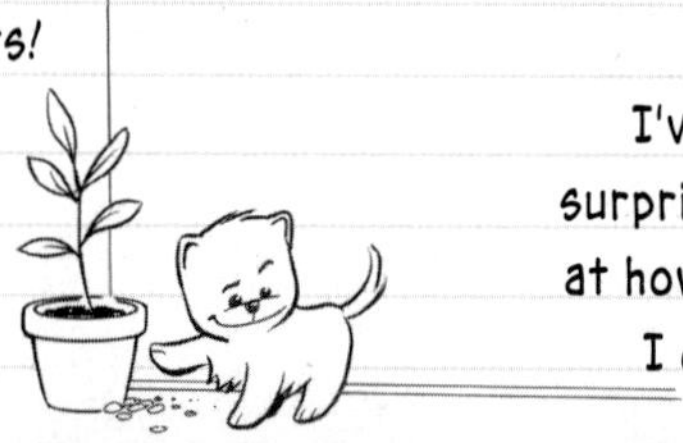

I've really
surprised myself
at how romantic
I can be!

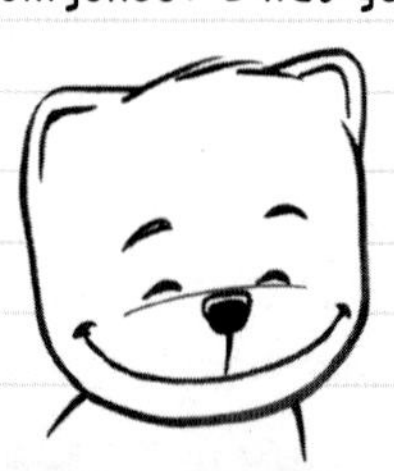

AY:

other new student joined us today. His name was Rolly and he was a big, chubby shar pei. lly was the fattest dog I've ever seen. The poor guy looked like he was going to have ouble following Sarge's commands. I felt sorry for him right away.

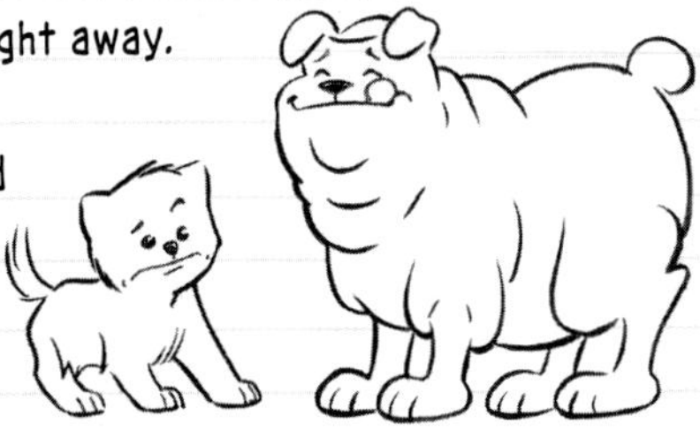

my surprise though, Rolly performed like a champ. He had it of a rocky start, but once he saw that there were ats involved, he pulled out his A game and delivered like best of us. I decided Rolly was going to be someone to ck close to.

ESDAY:

th our finals getting closer, Sarge is stepping up our drills. Prince and Duke nailed their moves e pros. They heel and stay like the best of them. Rolly sits around a lot until the treats get lled out. Then he moves with the best of them. Poor Stanley chased what he thought was a cat to some tall grass. It turned out to be a skunk.

ter the skunk sprayed him, Stanley's human was lled and he was sent home.

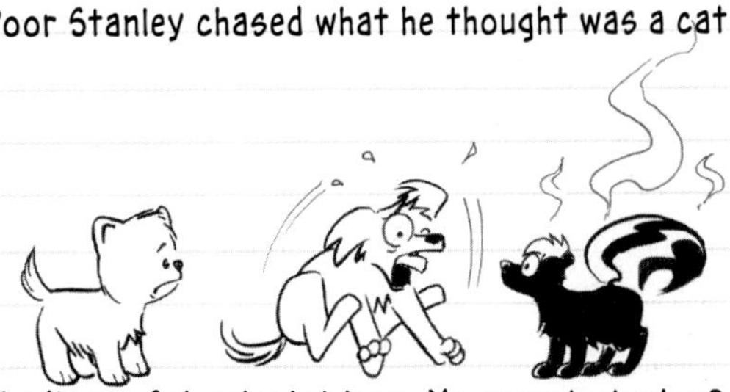

DNESDAY:

w that I have my ace in the hole, I'm sweating Obedience School a lot less. My secret stash of eats continues to grow. By the time I'm ready to make my move, I'm going to have a nice nest g to impress Bae with. There's no way she'll shoot me down. She'll probably want to marry me ht on the spot. After all, here I am, a future police dog, rich in treats! What a catch I am!

e pressure's off! I don't need to win this award anymore. I'm buying my way to happiness!

URSDAY: ***I'm doomed!***

world ended today! As usual, at the end of the class, I went to the flower pot where I've en socking away my treats to deliver whatever I'd saved that day. To my horror, I found that cache of treats was gone! Someone had cleaned me out!

it turned out, that glutton, Rolly, found my stash d gorged himself on my hard-earned savings! He ate em all! The greedy swine! Oh, he apologized to me en he realized they were mine, but the damage has en done. I'll never be able to gather all of those eats again.

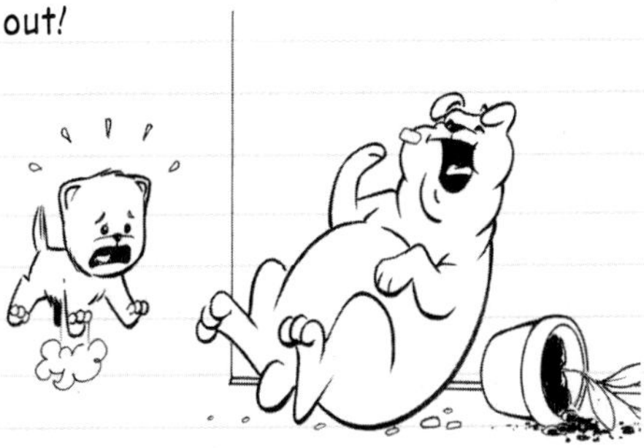

Now how am I going to impress Bae? My charm? My wit?

I'm doomed!

IDAY:

my utter desperation, I decided if I was going to impress Bae, my best bet was to win this mpetition the old fashioned way... through hard work and integrity. That's right! It's come to IAT! Like I said, I'm desperate.

I'm paying attention to Sarge and I'm even working with Stanley, Spotty and the others to see if we can get this training stuff down. It's a long shot, but we're going to do our best.

MONDAY:

Last Friday, we all agreed to practice our drills over the weekend. We got mixed results. Rolly told us he practiced sitting all weekend. I don't know why he did that. He's already an excellent sitter. No one will sit faster than Rolly. He said he sat around so much, he fell asleep. In fact, he fell asleep telling us about it.

Spotty said he tried to practice shaking hands, but he couldn't find anyone that wanted to shake his paw. I got a whiff of him and I could understand why anyone wanted to keep their distance. He smelled like he'd been laying on a pile of old fish.

Stanley showed us he was getting better at chasing his own tail. He'd almost caught it one time he told us. We made him stop before he made himself too dizzy and got sick.

TUESDAY:

With our finals closing, some of the guys and I were practicing our drills. I thought we've been making good progress lately. Even Stanley was learning to heel properly! Then I notice Bae was sitting off to the sidelines watching us. She finally knew we were alive! Should I go over to her? Should I make my move? Just as I was about to go over to her, Rolly bit Spotty. Apparently, Rolly saw a spot on his tail that he mistook for chocolate. Spotty started howling and I had to remind Rolly to take his tail out of his mouth. Then I noticed in all the excitement, I was standing in my own water dish.

I decided maybe it wasn't the best time to approach Bae after all.

WEDNESDAY:

It was the day of the Finals! This was it! This is what we've spent the last two weeks preparing for!

Human even brought Buddy and Bluebeary Pie to the School to watch me take my final test. We were all milling about in the yard before the tests sniffing each other and just generally hanging out. Every dog in our class was there along with their humans and friends of their humans. Suddenly, I bumped into Bae. She looked at me and smiled. "Good luck," she said. Wow! Clearly she was in love with me. I had this in the bag! Maybe I didn't even need to win the special award. Still, I decided to give it my all!

The festivities began by Sarge walking out with each dog and showing a few basic moves... the heeling, the staying, that sort of thing. He took each dog out by their leash, walked them in a circle before the crowd and them handed then off to their respective humans. Sarge started with Prince. The big dobie went out and did his moves perfectly. Then it was Duke's turn. He too was a model of perfect dog behavior. Then Sarge took my leash.

trutted out with my little head held up high and kept a perfect pace alongside Sarge. We did r circle. My posture was perfect. My gait remained even. I was killing it. I'd kept it simple but hought maybe I'd pull a fancy move or two to impress the crowd and leave an impression. I nt into a quick back flip and then a little strut up on two paws. That was always a crowd aser. Then I thought I'd close with a few rolls. Before I could finish my little maneuvers, ough, Sarge spilled across the floor like a giant sack of doggy kibble. Without realizing it, I'd apped my leash around his feet!

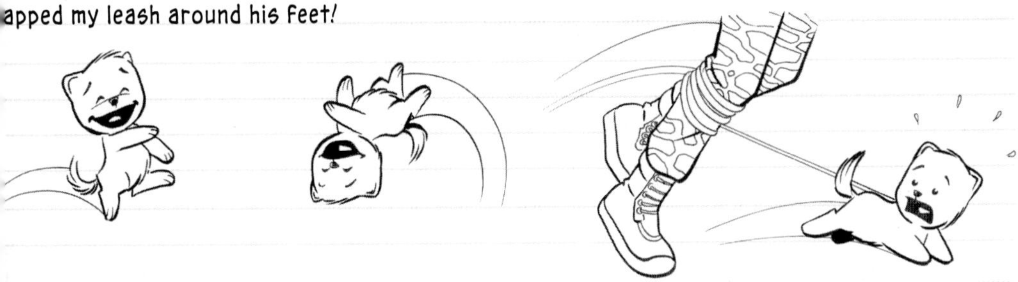

e humans spilled out onto the doggy track and ran over to Sarge. He was okay although his e was very red and his voice was very loud! The other dogs were barking incessantly. When leash was untangled from Sarge's feet, I'd ran as far and as fast as I could. Suddenly, a pair human hands grabbed me and picked me up.

was Human. "It's okay, Boo," she said. "It's okay."

nce won the special award. Duke, of course, came in second. I didn't end up finishing last er all. That dubious honor went to Stanley, who got away from his own human and then tried dig under a fence, but only managed to get his head stuck under it.

ter the exam, we were all allowed to run and play in the yard. I thought I'd be the laughing ock of the whole class. Prince and Duke certainly looked at me pitifully. To my surprise ough, Bae, looking beautiful with freshly smelling long white fur and a new bow, approached . I thought for sure she was going to make fun of me, but she didn't. She actually told me e'd been impressed with me. Oh, she thought I'd made a fool of myself, but she'd noticed how d I'd worked with Stanley, Spotty and the others to help us all make the grade.

e told me it was the sign of a nice dog and a good friend.

en she licked my nose! I was the happiest dog in the World!

ıen Rolly licked my nose too because he thought had a treat stuck to it! **Yeesh!**

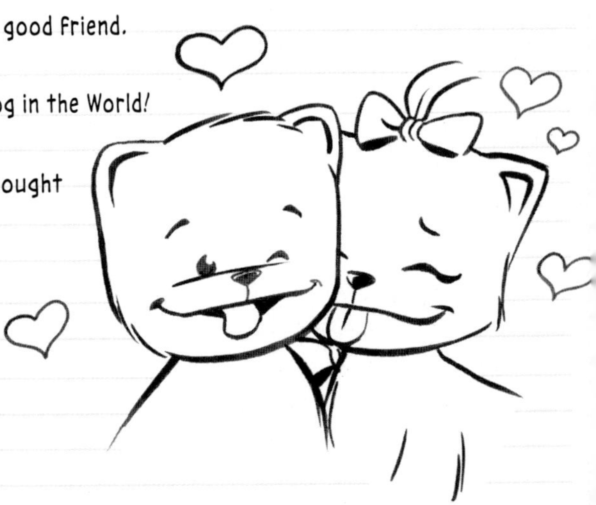

✦COVER GALLERY✦

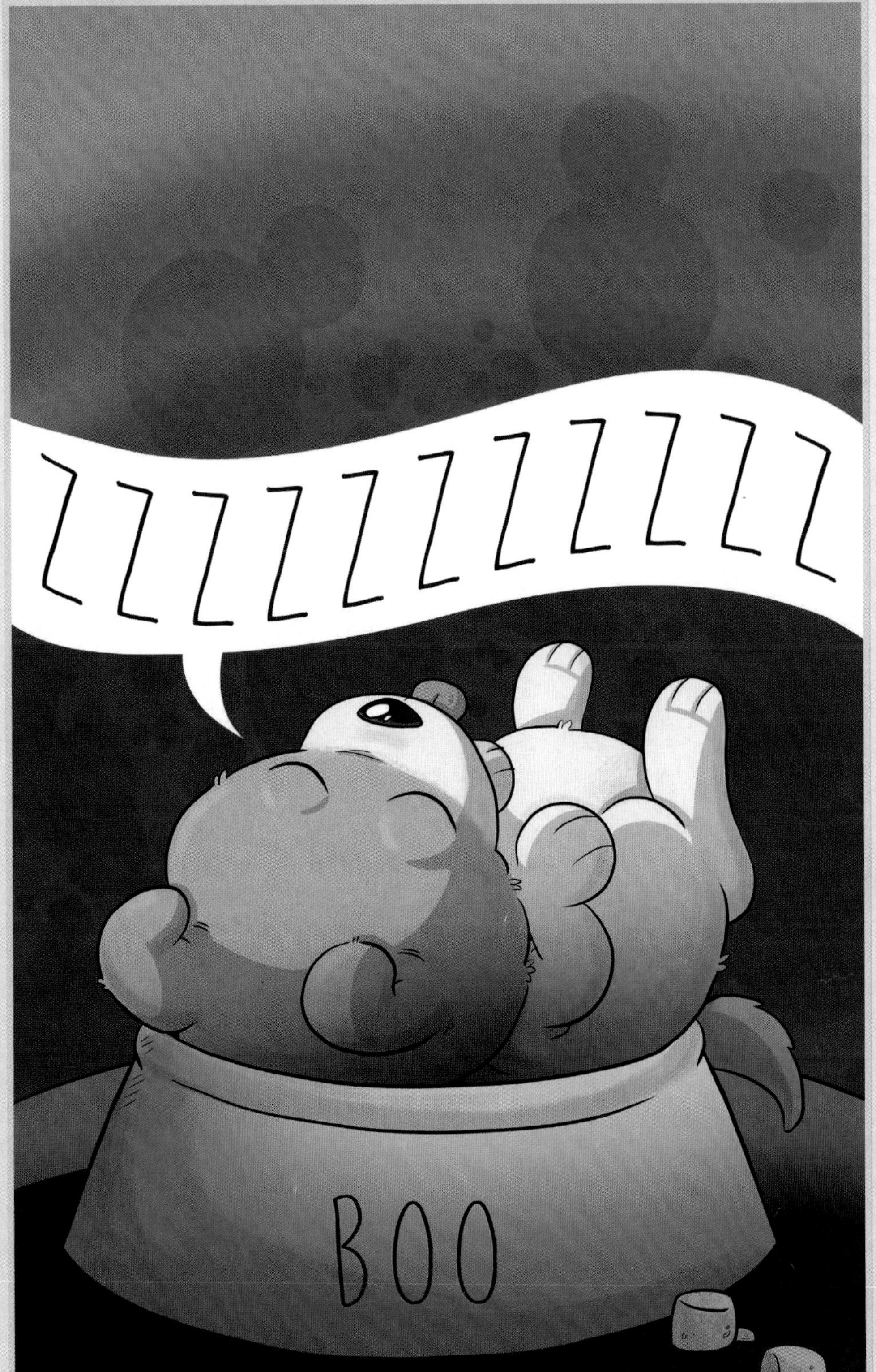
ZZZZZZZZZZZ
BOO

Boo #1 • Cover A • Art & Colors by Katie Cook

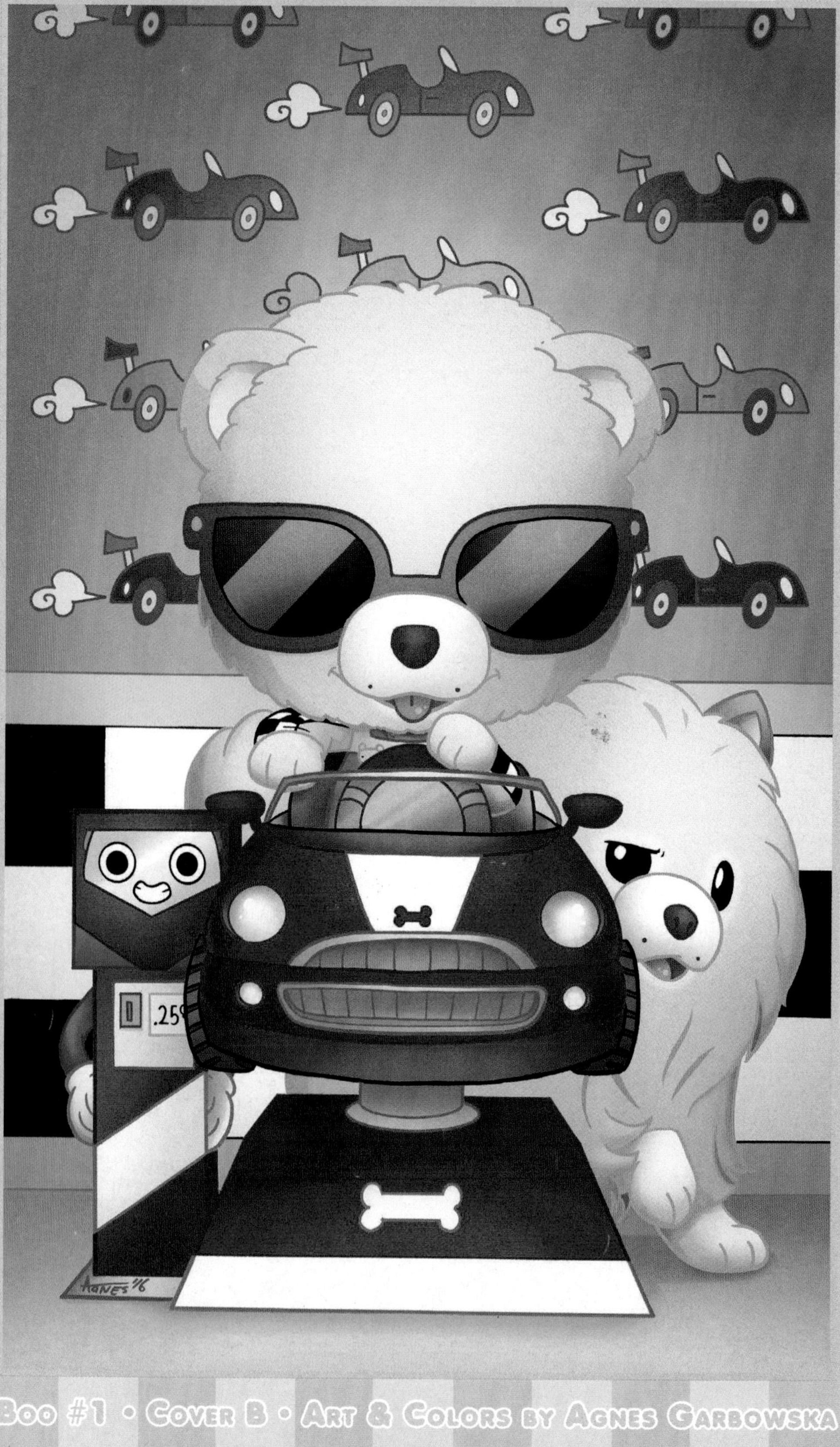

Boo #1 • Cover B • Art & Colors by Agnes Garbowska

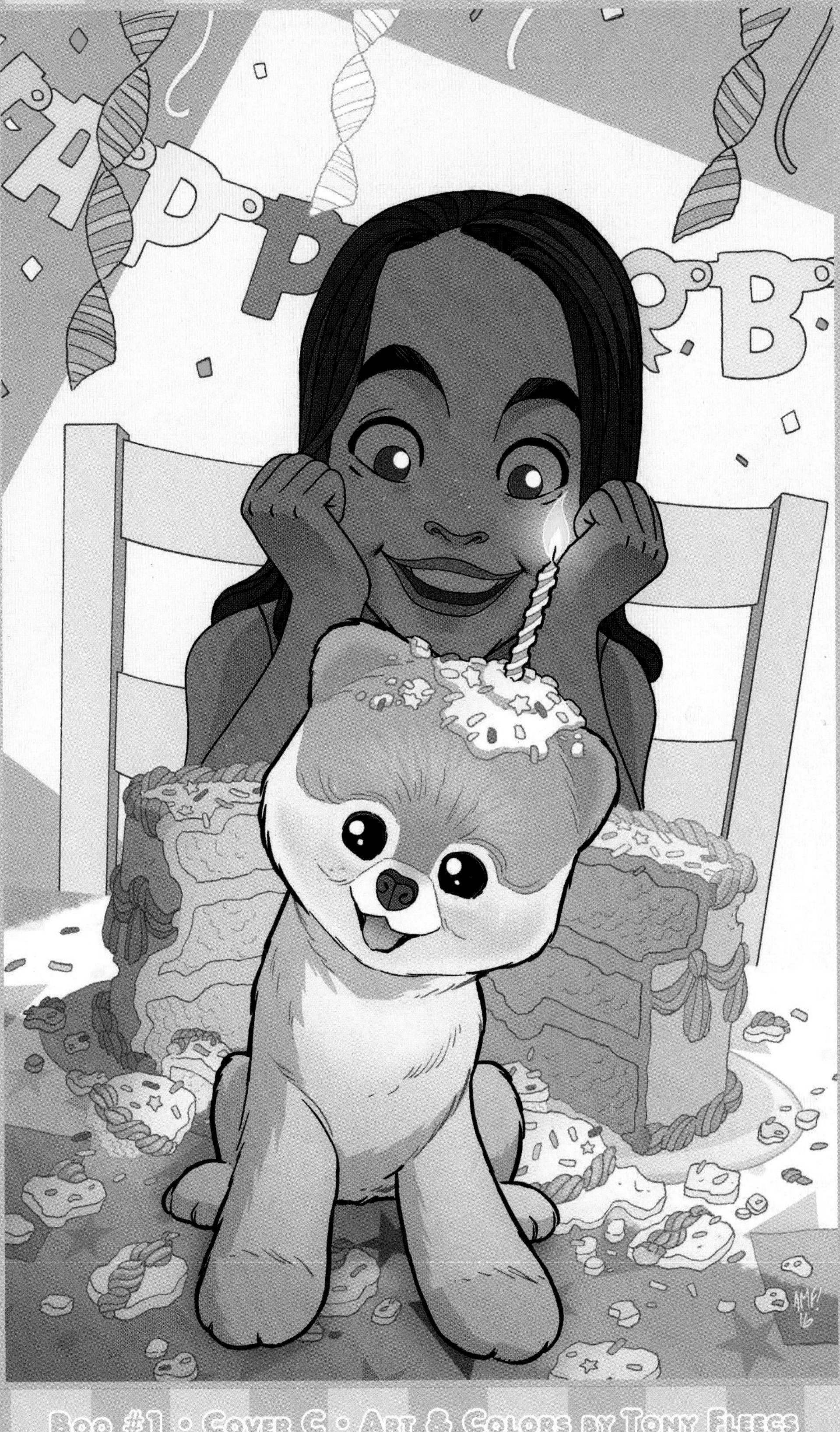

Boo #1 • Cover C • Art & Colors by Tony Fleecs

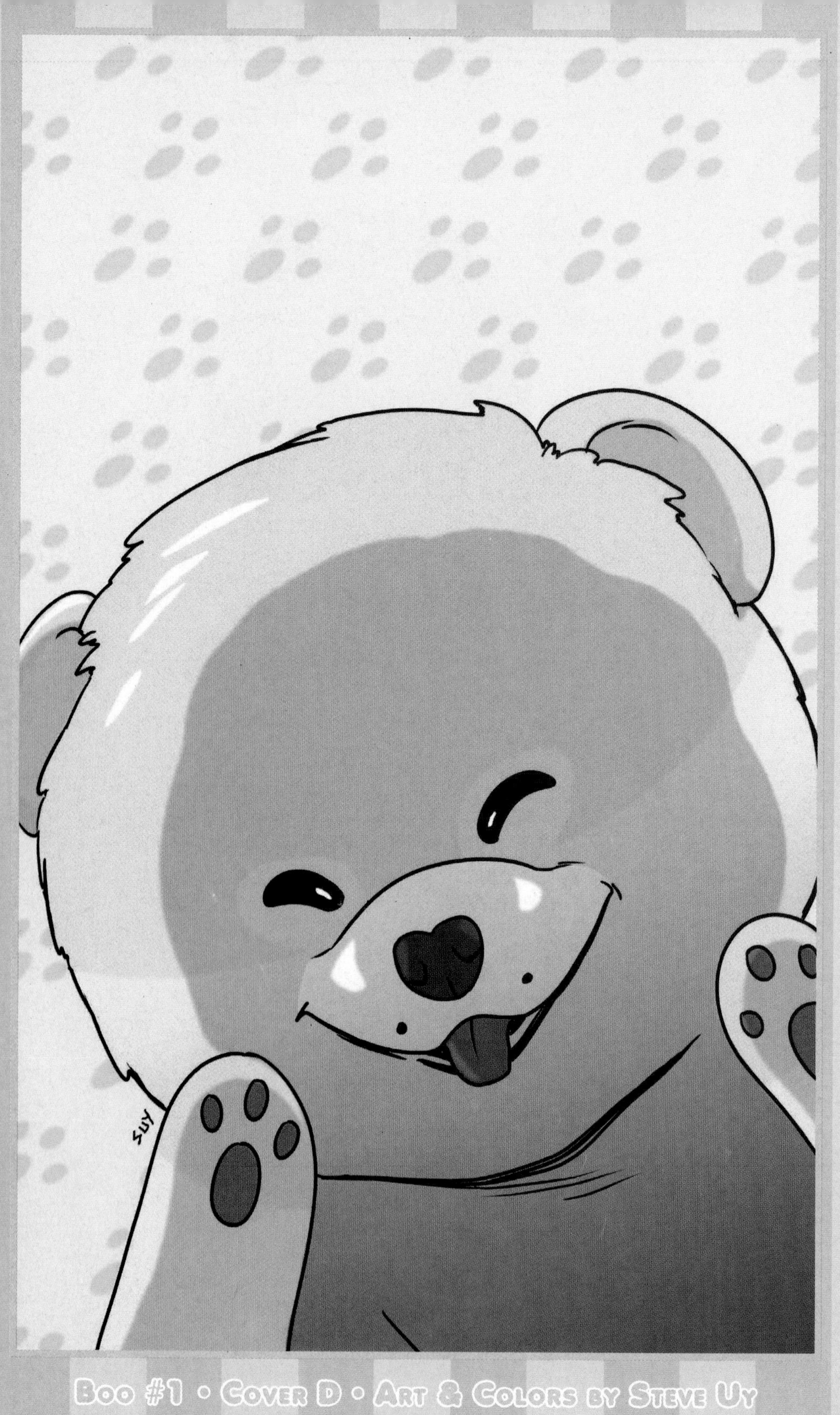
SUY

Boo #1 • Cover D • Art & Colors by Steve Uy

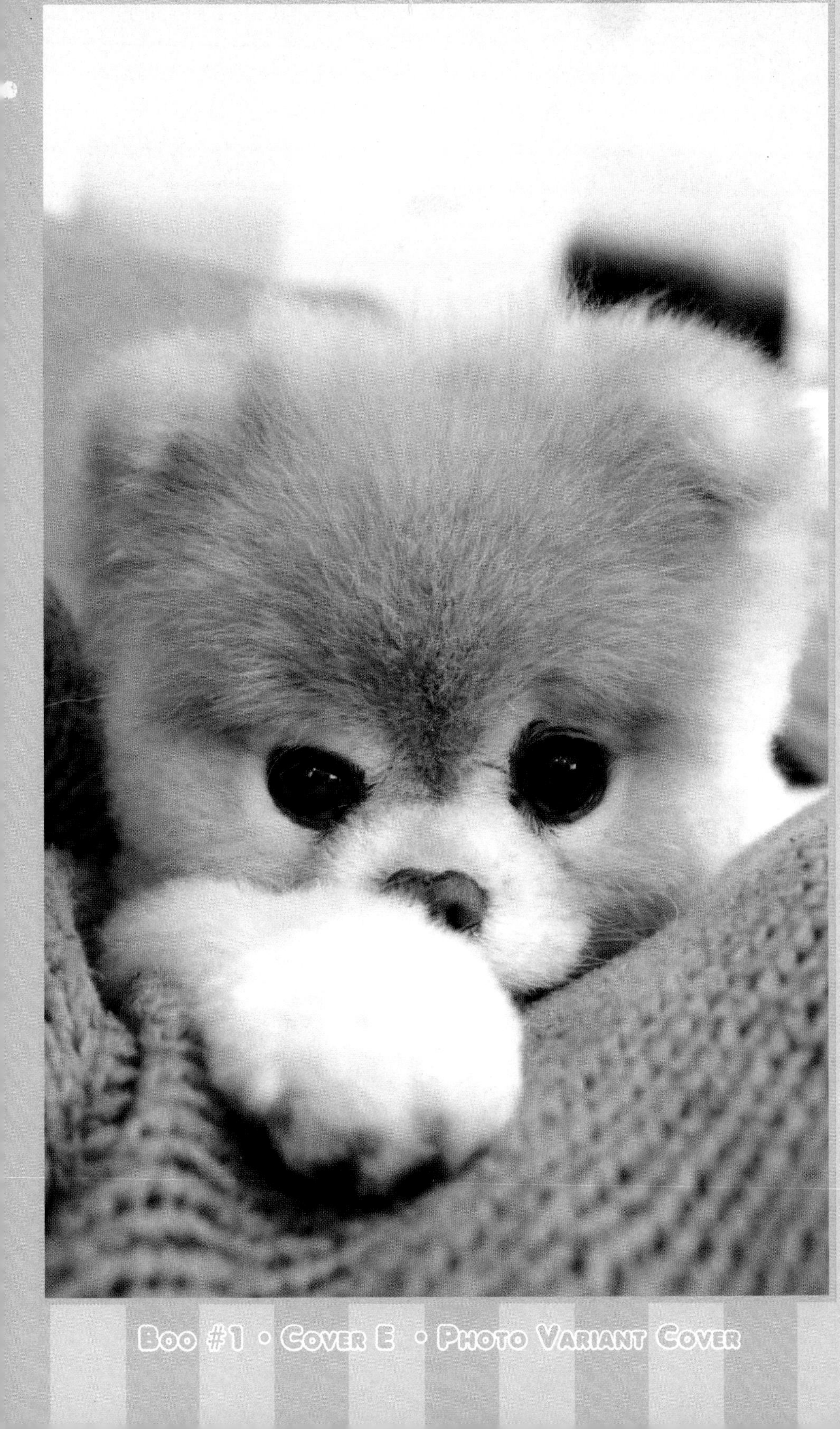

Boo #1 • Cover E • Photo Variant Cover

Boo #1 • Cover G • Art & Colors by Ken Haeser
In Your Dreams Exclusive

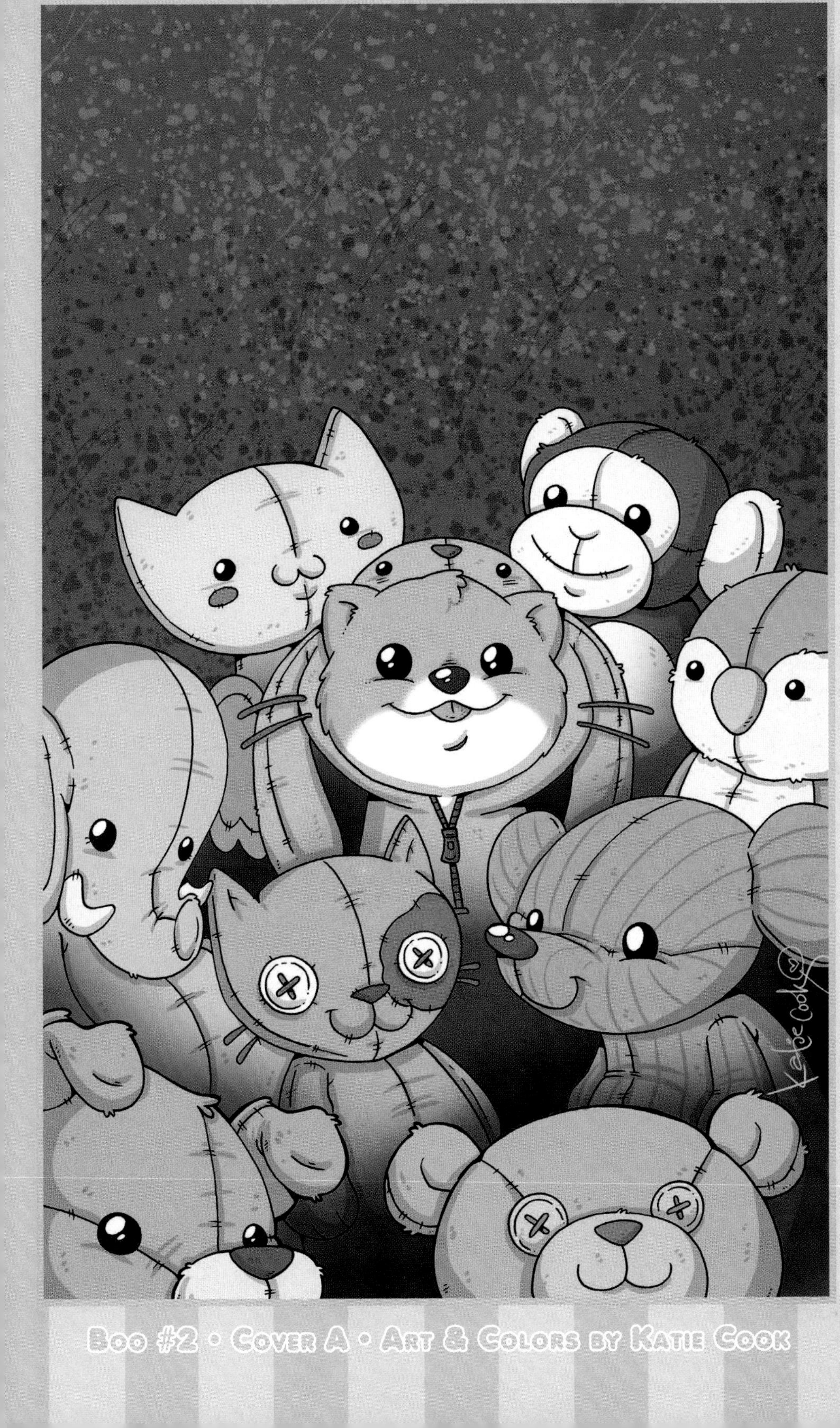
Katie Cook

Boo #2 • Cover A • Art & Colors by Katie Cook

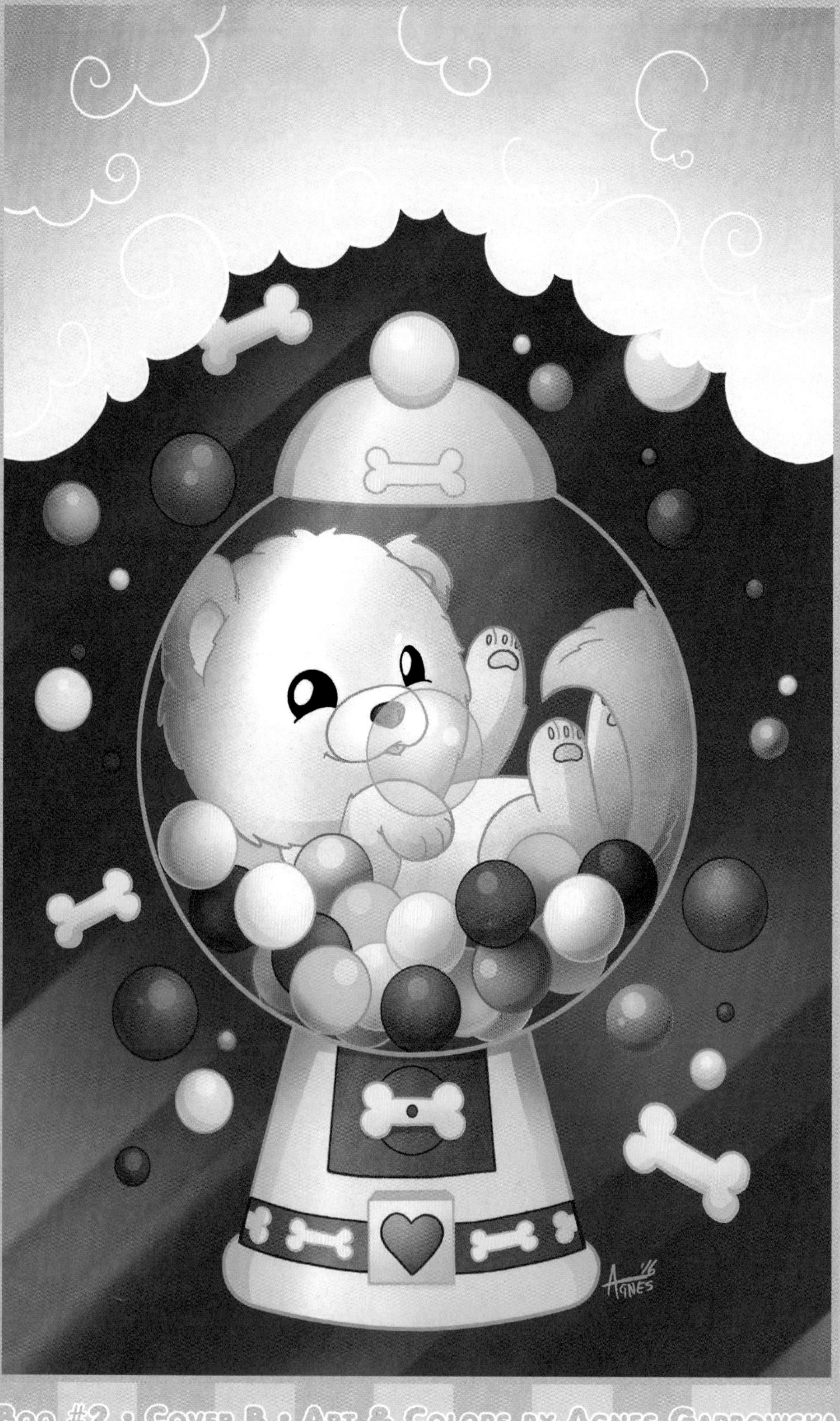
Agnes '16

Boo #2 • Cover B • Art & Colors by Agnes Garbowska

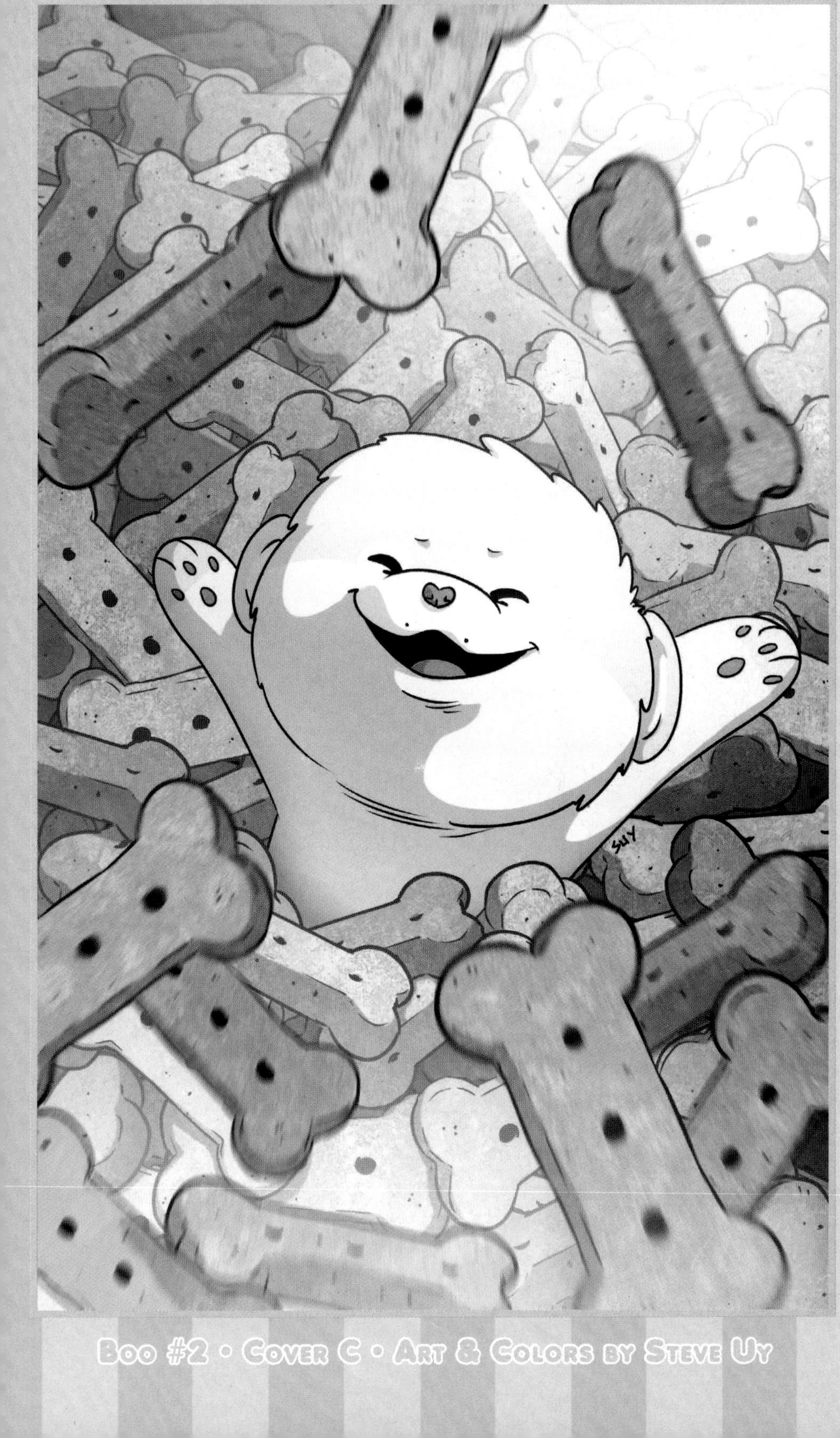

Boo #2 • Cover C • Art & Colors by Steve Uy

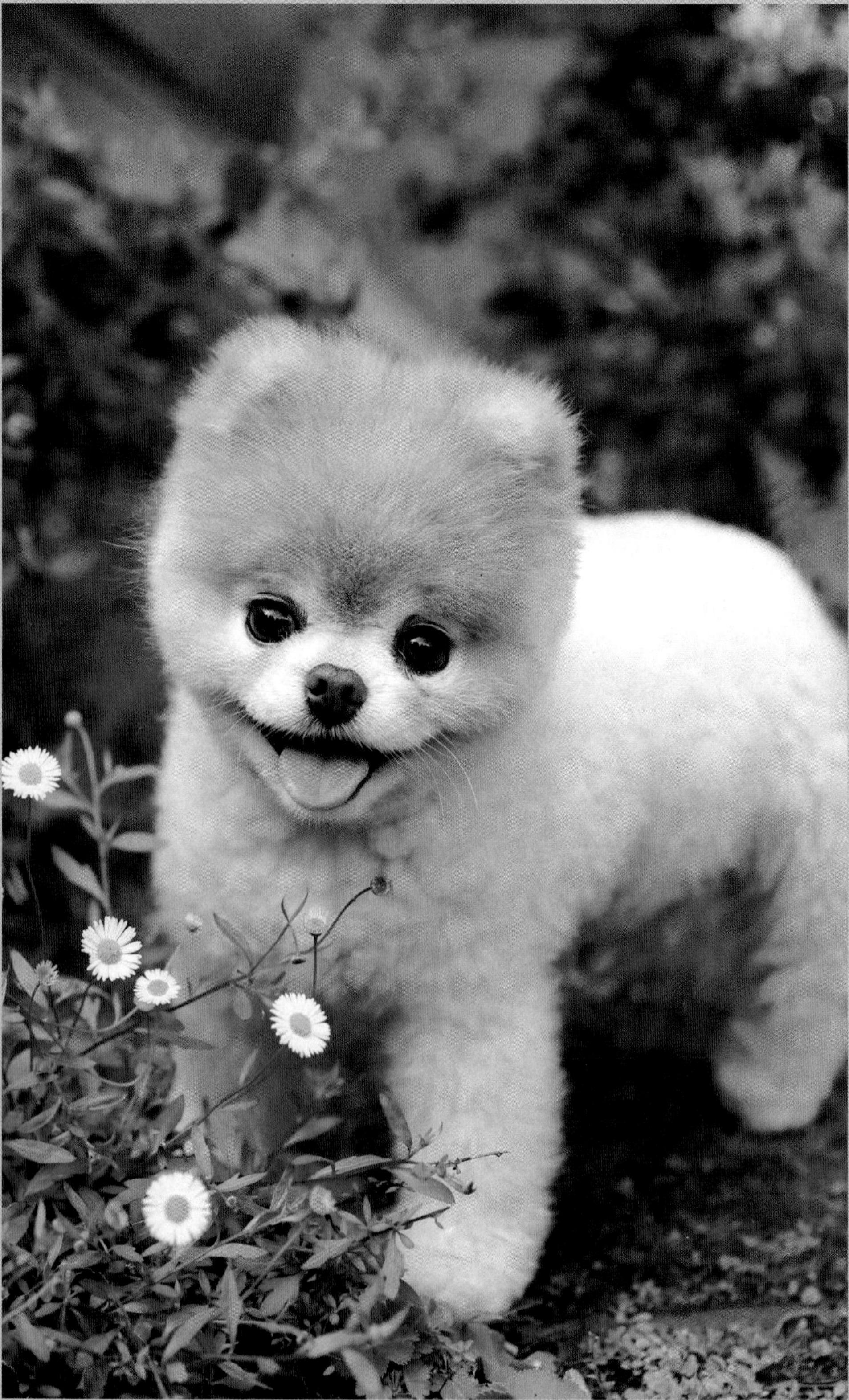

Boo #2 • Cover D • Photo Variant Cover

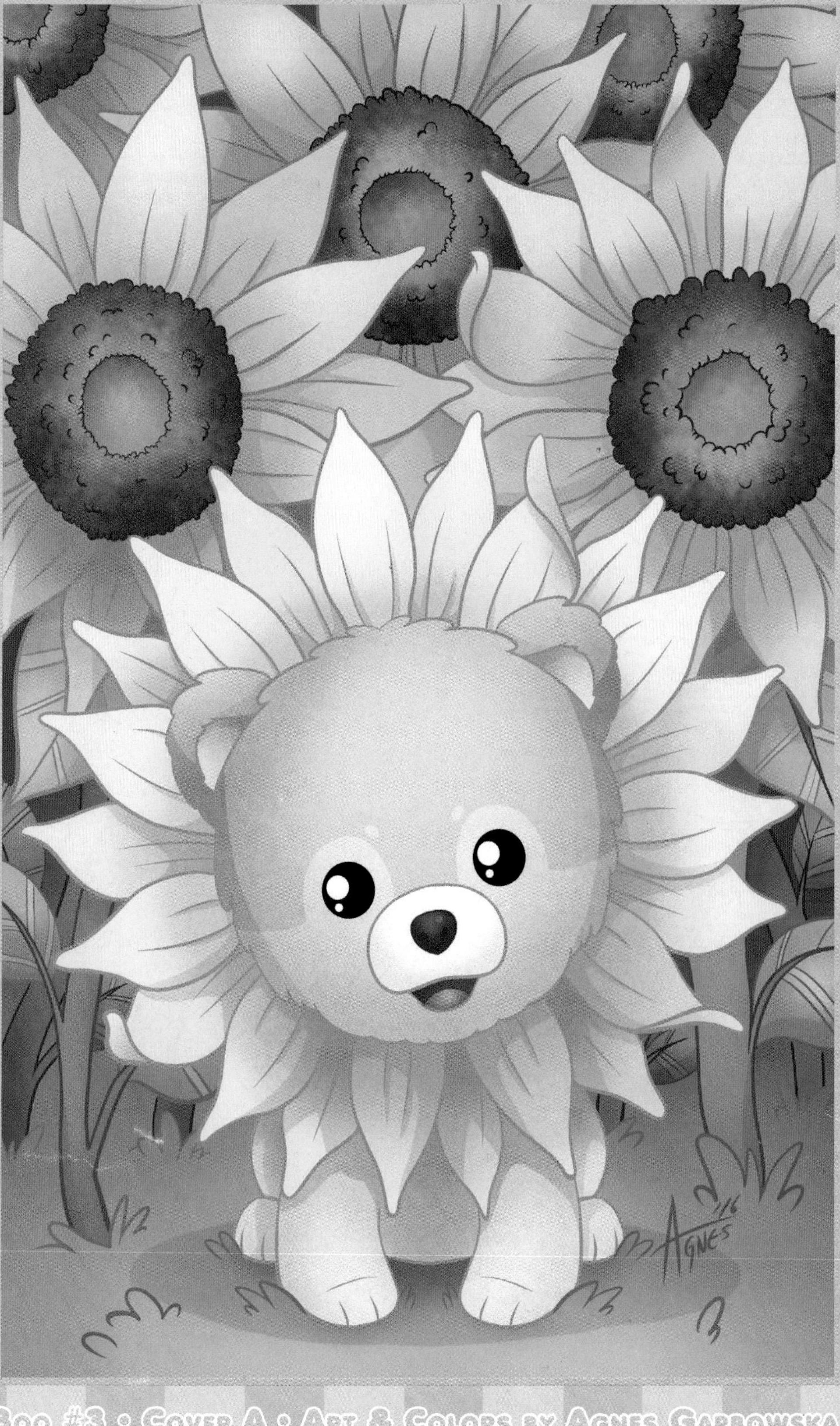
AGNES 1/16

Boo #3 • Cover A • Art & Colors by Agnes Garbowska

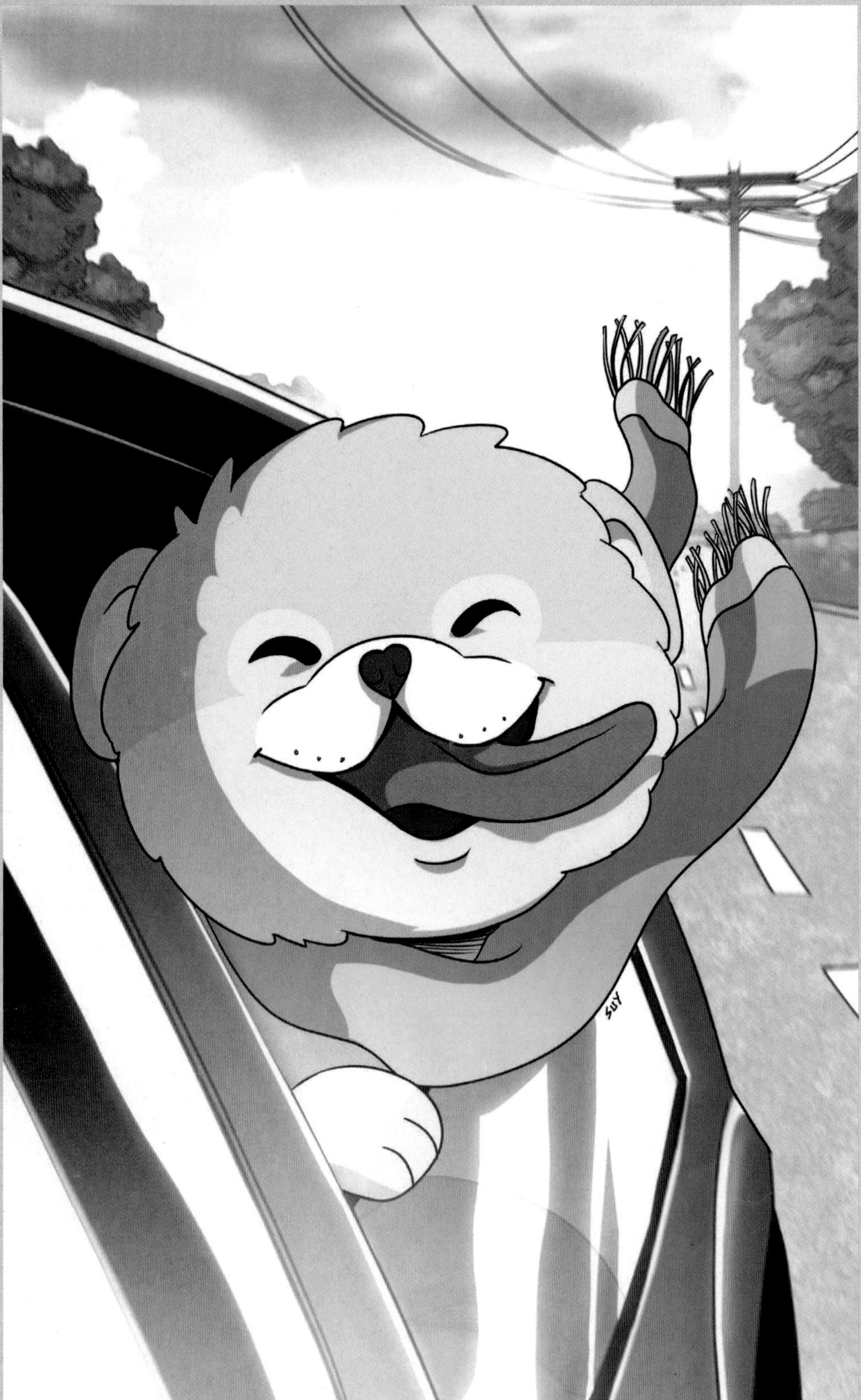
SUY

Boo #3 • Cover B • Art & Colors by Steve Uy

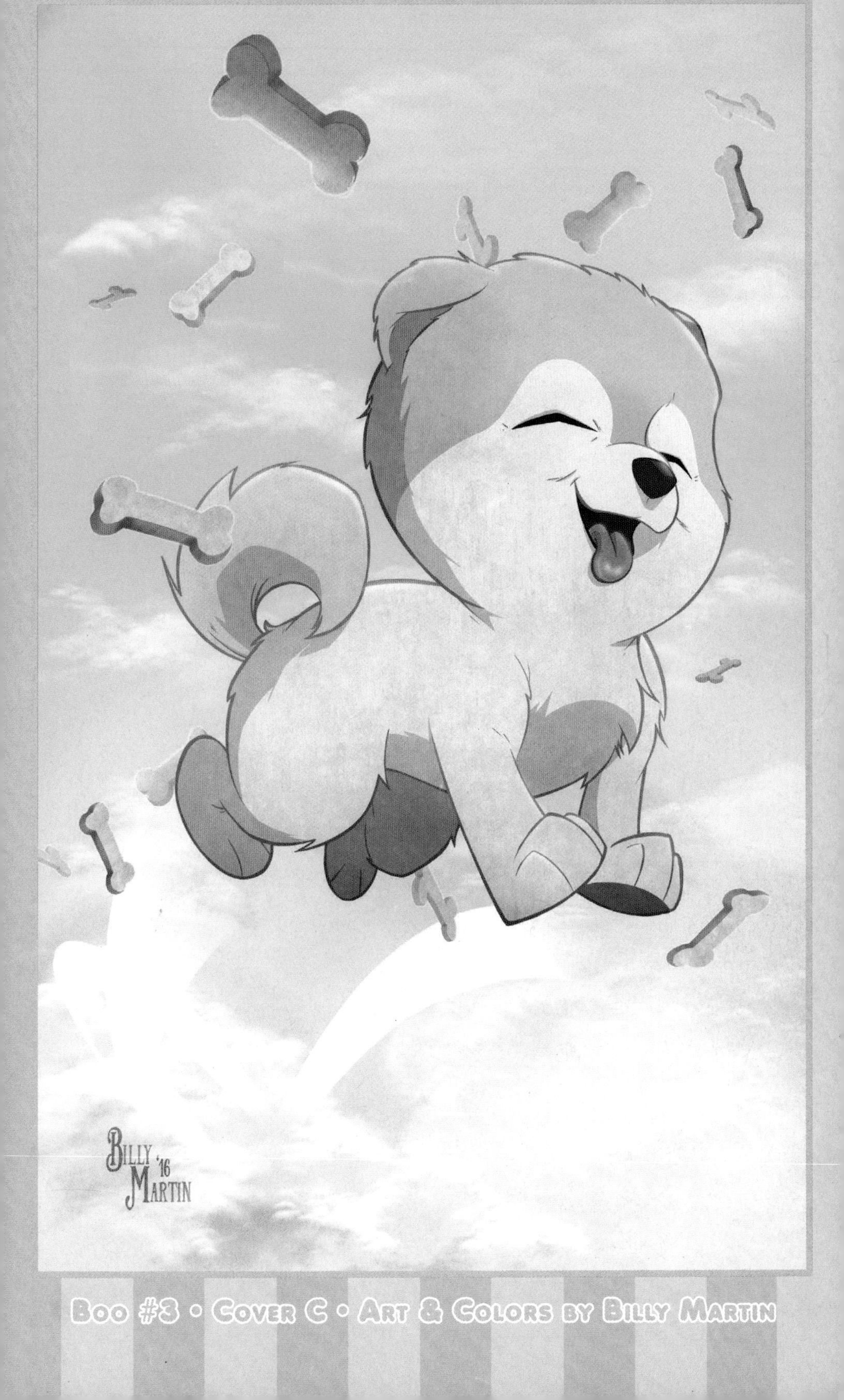
BILLY '16
MARTIN

Boo #3 • Cover C • Art & Colors by Billy Martin

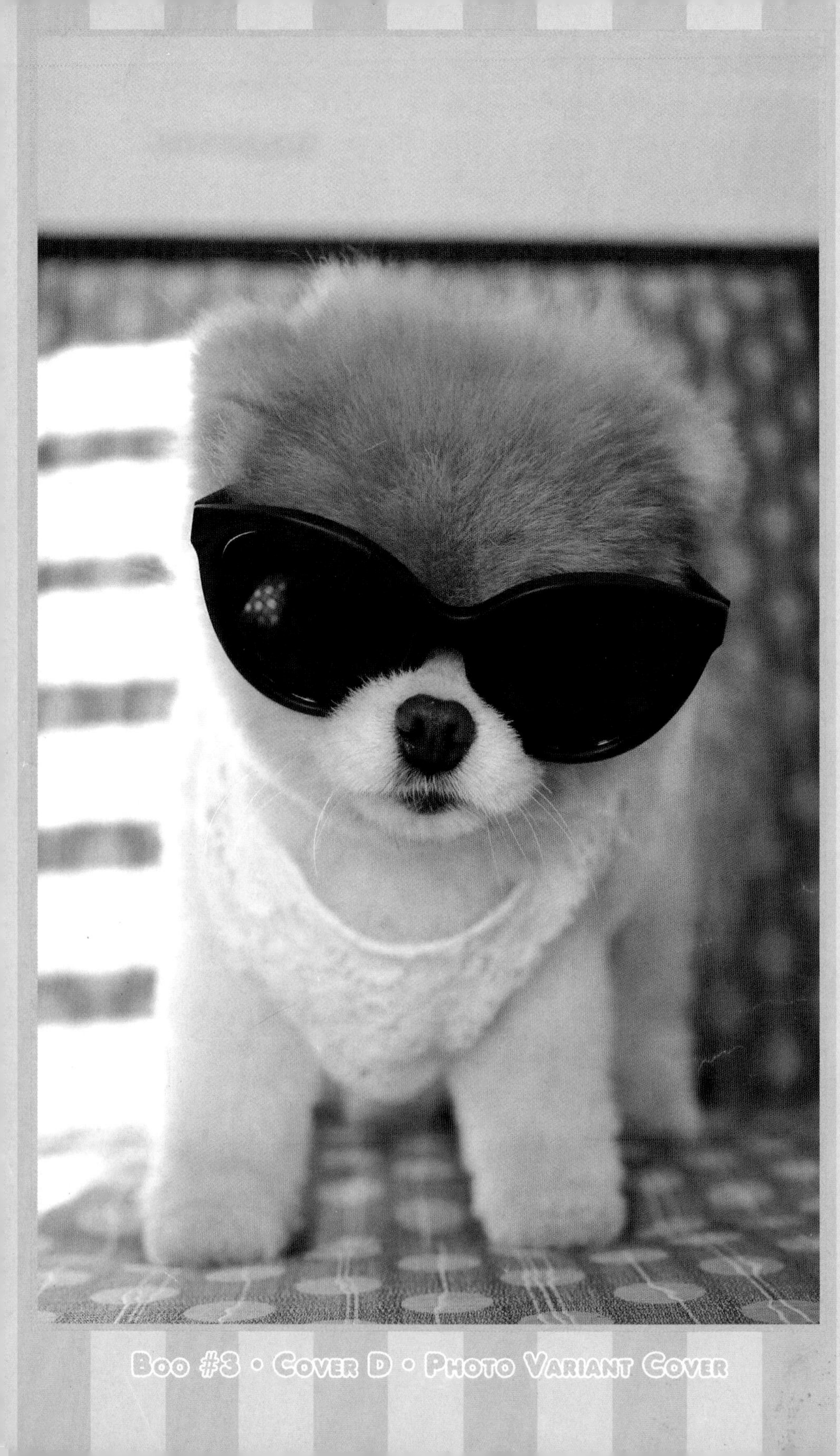

Boo #3 • Cover D • Photo Variant Cover

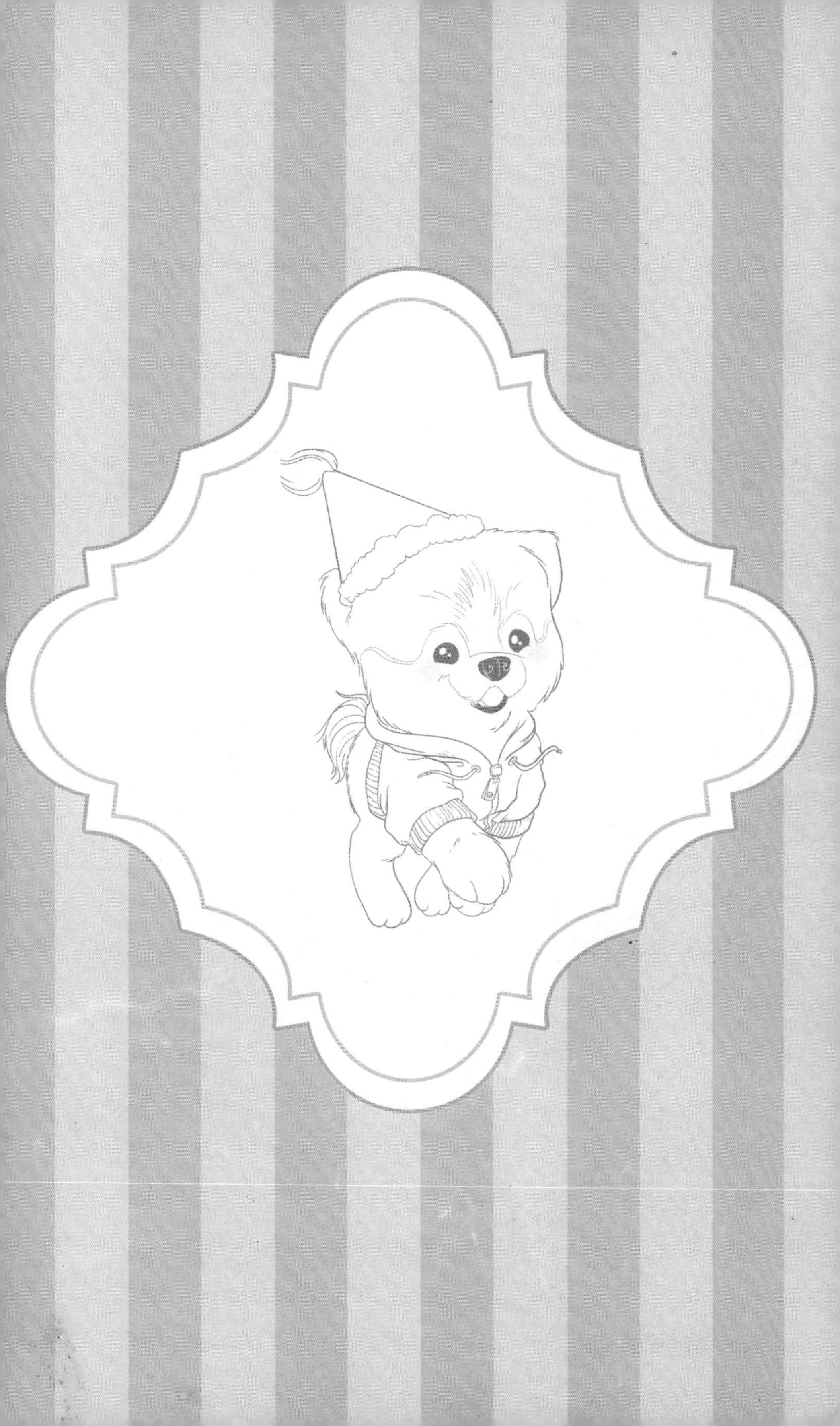

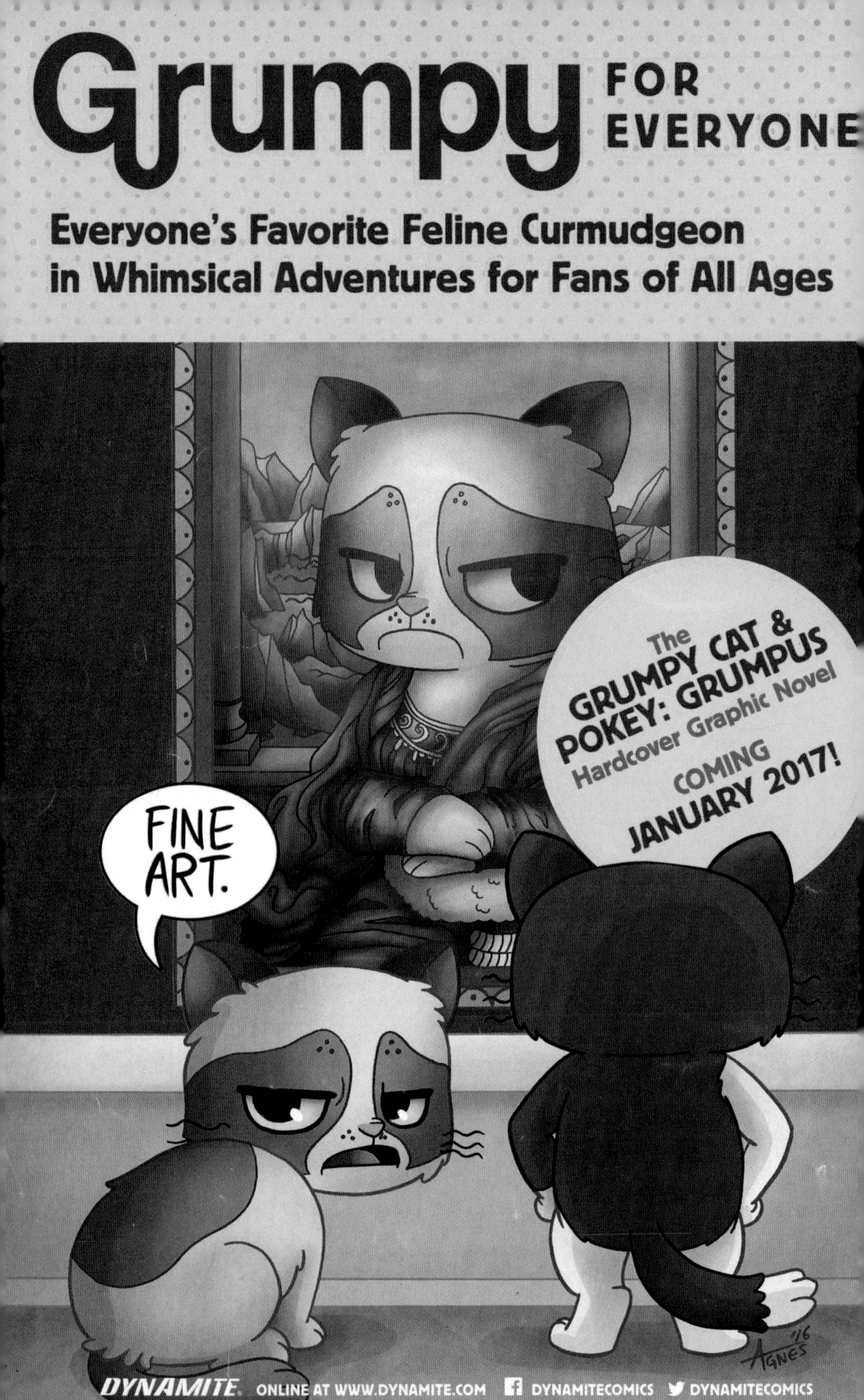

Grumpy FOR EVERYONE
Everyone's Favorite Feline Curmudgeon in Whimsical Adventures for Fans of All Ages
FINE ART.
The GRUMPY CAT & POKEY: GRUMPUS Hardcover Graphic Novel
COMING JANUARY 2017!
AGNES '16
DYNAMITE. ONLINE AT WWW.DYNAMITE.COM
DYNAMITECOMICS
DYNAMITECOMICS
Join discussion at GRUMPYCATS.com. Grumpy Cat and related Artwork © and ™ Grumpy Cat Limited www.GrumpyCats.com; Used under license.
Dynamite, Dynamite Entertainment, and its logo are ® & © 2016 Dynamite. All rights reserved. All art pending licensor approval.

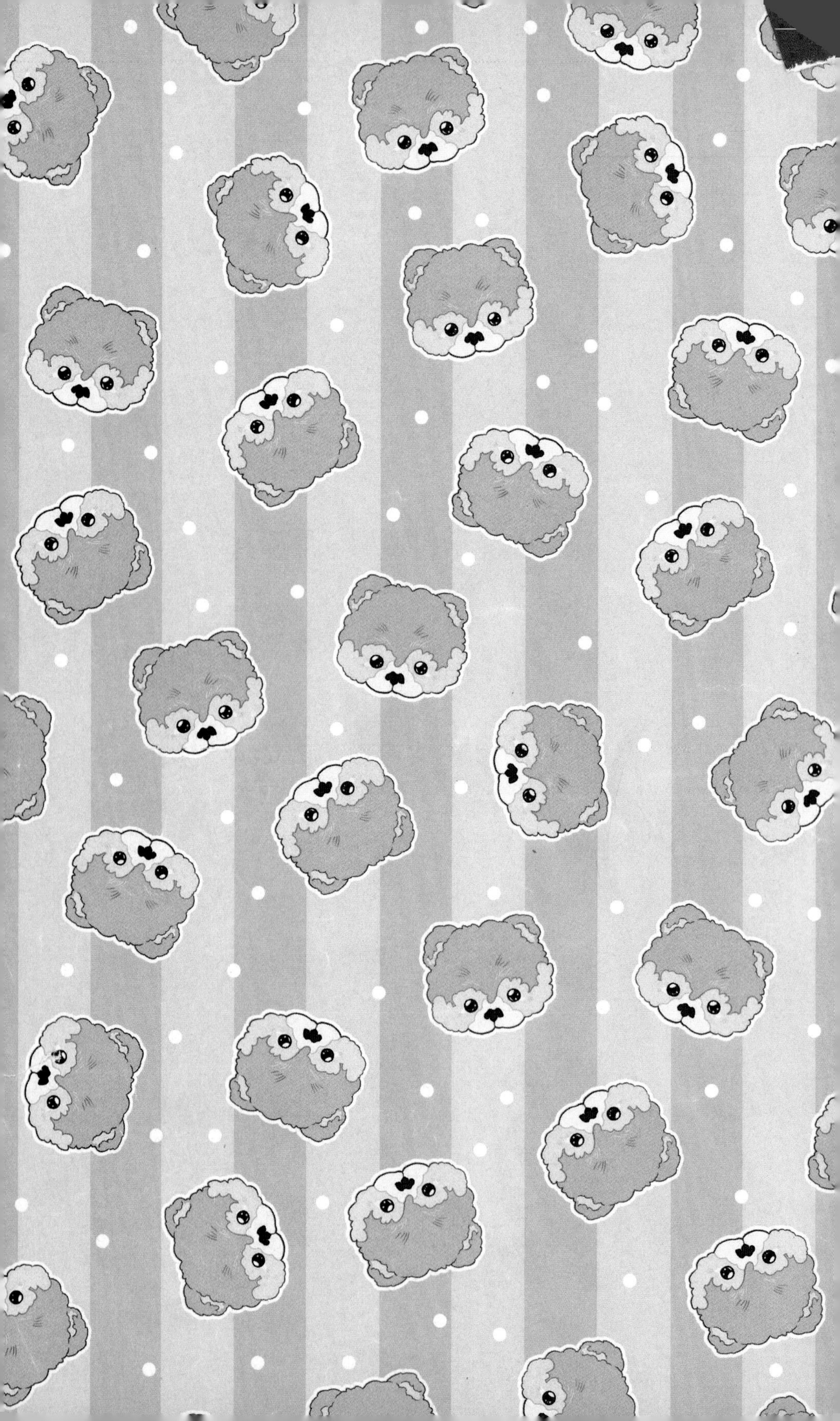